TAMING THE SAVAGE
MONSOON

Kathy Hopper
Oct 2005

TAMING THE SAVAGE
MONSOON

KATHY HOPPER AND MARTHA TEAS
WITH
JOYCE SMITH AND MARGARET GREEN

COVER ART BY ANNE MAGRATTEN

10-Digit ISBN 1-59113-786-1
13-Digit ISBN 978-1-59113-786-3

Printed in the United States of America.

The characters and events in this book are fictitious. Any similarity to real persons, living or dead, is coincidental and not intended by the author.

Kathleen Hopper
kkhopper@adelphia.net
2005

DEDICATION

Our dear friend, colleague, and co-author Martha Jane Teas was killed on August 19, 2003 in the bombing of the United Nations Headquarters in Baghdad. In Martha's memory, all royalties from *Taming the Savage Monsoon* will be donated to the Martha Teas Memorial Fund, which supports child amputees in Banteay Meanchey Province, Cambodia. We love you, Martha.

Kathy, Joyce, and Margaret

NOTE TO THE READER

The United Nations Transitional Authority in Cambodia operated in the early 1990s with a mandate that addressed human rights, free elections, military arrangements, civil administration, maintenance of law and order, repatriation and resettlement of Cambodian refugees and displaced persons, and rehabilitation of essential Cambodian infrastructure. *Taming the Savage Monsoon* is set in the years that followed UNTAC's departure from Cambodia. However, the story is in its entirety and down to its last word a work of fiction. Although many Cambodian places described in these pages do exist, as do King Sihanouk and Queen Monique, all other names, characters, and incidents are the product of the authors' imaginations and are used fictitiously. Any resemblance to actual events (past, present, or future) or persons (dead, living, or not yet born) is entirely coincidental.

TAMING THE SAVAGE
MONSOON

CHAPTER ONE
SATURDAY, MAY 15

L indsay March surveyed the heavens for the third time in as many minutes. The rain-swollen thunderheads that had hovered in a far corner of the horizon for most of the afternoon were now looming directly above the temple spirals of Phnom Penh, and Lindsay was still downriver, half a mile away. She leaned closer to speak into the ear of her Cambodian assistant. "Looks like I'm not going to make it back in time, Bopha," she shouted above the bone-rattling roar of the boat's uncertain engine. "Those clouds are going to burst any minute."

Until now, the Mekong River field trip with students from the Royal Agricultural College had been uneventful. But Murphy's Law was a practicing religion in Cambodia. Even if the *Luv Boat II* made it back—an unlikely prospect, judging from the increasingly frequent fits, starts, and lurches of the motor—Lindsay still had to get home in time to shower and dress for the reception.

She nudged Bopha again, pointing to the smudges decorating her worn blue T- shirt. "Maybe I should show up at my first royal reception in this?" she said. Bopha laughed. King Sihanouk's royal soirees were not casual affairs, especially this one. Tonight would be Lindsay's first appearance as the Public Information Officer for UNOIC, the United Nations Organization In Cambodia. As she glanced at her watch again, the *Luv Boat II's* engine roared to a deafening crescendo, then coughed its way through a final death rattle, followed by total silence.

Lindsay sighed and reached for the two-way radio that connected her to UNOIC headquarters. "Kimson, do you read me, over." Getting a clear response after a moment of sharp static, she pressed the send button again. "Lindsay March here, Kimson. Listen, I'm still out on the river." As nervous giggles sounded from the pilot and his son at the back of the boat, she added, "The boat is dead in the water, and we're still about a kilometer down the Mekong. Can you have a car waiting for me at the dock, please? Over." Kimson agreed, which was heartening, although it wouldn't get her to the palace any sooner.

As Lindsay slipped the radio back onto her belt, Bopha pointed excitedly downriver, where a plume of spray announced the rapid approach of a speedboat. "I think is Mr Nicky, Lindsay. He can help you!" And of course, it had to be Nick. While other vessels plying the Mekong were crafted of aging wood or rusted metal, Nick Graham's *Bonnie Lies* was fire-engine-red fiberglass. It stood out like a clown at a business conference.

Before Bopha had finished her sentence, Lindsay was hanging off the rear of the boat, flapping her *krema* in the air. "Goin' my way, darlin'?" Nick drawled, as the *Bonnie Lies* settled into the water beside the lifeless *Luv Boat II*. Lindsay was scrambling down from the larger boat when the first bolt of lightning struck the far bank. A deafening clap of thunder followed, bringing the rain flowing toward them like a liquid curtain.

In theory, Nick Graham monitored UNOIC's radio communications as part of his air conditioning repair service. In practice, though, his eavesdropping fed a pure and simple love of gossip. Combing his fingers through his untrammeled red beard, he shouted, "Don't you worry, sweet thing, I'll get you to the palace in time." As he nosed the boat back into the current, he called back to Bopha, who waved to them from the prow, "And I'll send help down for the rest of you."

Lindsay ignored Nick's endearments. "You've just saved me from apologizing to the king in my awful French," she said. "You are a lifesaver."

"Going to the bash, are you?"

She nodded. Of course Nick would know about the reception, although it wasn't likely he'd been invited. The reception was, after all, an elite affair, with a guest list dominated by heads of agencies, ambassadors of generous donor countries, and the upper crust of Cambodian society. With David Bullford, UNOIC's Country Coordinator and Lindsay's boss, out of town, Lindsay was taking her first turn as Officer-In-Charge. Fulfilling the agency's social obligations was part of that responsibility.

"Have you heard the latest from the palace?" Nicky's eyes sparkled with the glint of gossip, and he didn't wait for Lindsay's reply before adding, "Old Sihanouk's called in a new advisor!"

"On what?"

He paused, looking at her with glee and, she suspected, more than a little Glenfiddich. "No one knows. But he's from Colombia."

"Columbia. Good school," she remarked absently, holding up a hand to keep the now torrential rain out of her eyes.

"Country, darlin', country. They say he's filthy rich, and sinfully good looking." Nick revved the motor to full speed, sharpening the needles of rain on her bare skin. In a lighter tone, he added, "Maybe he'll have what you're lookin' for, darlin'."

"An umbrella?" Lindsay asked, her expression bland.

"You don't fool me," he chided. "Don't you worry, you'll be getting a chance to find out all about him tonight."

"Yeah, right. If I get there."

"And why shouldn't you?" he asked, his hazel eyes challenging.

"I'll probably be in traction, recovering from whiplash. You're about to collide with the dock."

Nick jerked the wheel and cut the motor with less than a foot to spare. A Land Cruiser with the UNOIC decal on its hood perched at the top of the bank, while the blue-uniformed driver, a thin man with graying hair and a sparse goatee, waited on the dock beneath a dripping umbrella. After stepping from the boat and onto the rotting wood of the pier, Lindsay leaned back to kiss Nick's cheek. "Thanks, Nicky. I'd promise to tell you all about the reception, but you'll probably know more about it than I will."

Nick looked at her wryly. "It's a treat to be seen as a rescuer for a change, darlin'," he muttered, reversing back into the current as Lindsay raced up the stairs beside her driver.

As the Land Cruiser splashed through the flooded streets of Phnom Penh, Lindsay glanced at her watch and calculated the remaining time. Could she get ready fast enough? A shower, formal dress, make-up—and her hair! Well, she'd do her best. If the royals didn't like it, too bad.

When the Land Cruiser pulled through the gates into Lindsay's compound, both of the elderly caretakers, husband and wife, were waiting, wringing their hands with concern that she would be late for her first royal audience. "Don't worry please, Auntie, I'll be ready *tout de suite*," she assured them as she ran up the stairs to her room.

And she was. After a quick shower, Lindsay used two ivory plastic combs to transform her shoulder length hair into an elegant French twist of burnished gold. The gown was a long ivory sheath, a mandarin style that clung lightly to the curves of her hips and breasts. The creamy silk contrasted subtly with her tanned skin, now rosy from the afternoon sun. The slit on one side of the tight gown eased maneuverability—and enhanced the allure of its wearer.

Climbing back into the waiting Land Cruiser, Lindsay heaved a relieved sigh. The rain had stopped, and her debut as UNOIC's first Public Information Officer, and her first official encounter with the upper echelons of Cambodian political society, would not be shadowed by a late arrival after all.

Hobnobbing with high society was nothing new for Lindsay. Throughout her childhood and early teens, she had attended hundreds of such events, organized by her father, a cultural officer with the US diplomatic corps. Although she hadn't anticipated that receptions would be included in her new job description, at least she knew the ropes.

As the Land Cruiser sloshed back through the flooded streets toward the palace, Lindsay recalled the briefing her boss had given her before his departure. "Be on the lookout for a big funding request, Lindsay," David had said. "Rumor has it the King wants us to support some scheme involving a royal nature preserve up in the northeast. Whatever you do, don't let anyone get the idea that you're even thinking about making promises," he had warned her.

David's concern was warranted. In Asia, a nature preserve could mean any number of things, from a true wilderness area, to a trashy Disneyland, to a laughable cover for yet another ill-conceived scam to exploit the country's resources. And even if the proposed project seemed above-board and economically viable, was it appropriate for UNOIC to fund it? In the brief two months Lindsay had been with UNOIC, she'd seen a confusing variety of funding requests directed at UNOIC's impressive coffers, which were a legacy of UNTAC largesse.

After the signing of Cambodia's peace agreement in 1993, the United Nations Transitional Authority in Cambodia—UNTAC—had been created to maintain the peace, monitor the elections, and nurture a new democratic government. Once the elections were over, UNOIC had moved in, doing whatever it could to support the country's fragile stability. An unfortunate side effect of this humanitarian effort was that many Cambodians still thought of UNOIC as the embodiment of an *apsara*, the national symbol of a heavenly being sprinkling gold on the earth. So while UNOIC would definitely be interested in supporting a true environmental conservation project, there was no way to know yet whether this new proposal would be worthy of its consideration.

As they plowed through the knee-deep floodwaters, Lindsay studied the young girls sitting on the raised shoulders of the road, where they sold bread, ice, fruit, or rat poison beneath the shelter of tattered blue plastic tarps or thatch. Where the water deepened, half-submerged motorcycles surfed the waves from larger vehicles.

The driver eased through the flood at a snail's pace, but Lindsay resisted urging him to move faster. The shooting of an expat by an irate motorcyclist who'd gotten a face full of backwash from the motorist's passage had been one of the first cautionary tales she'd heard when she'd arrived in Cambodia.

Sighing, Lindsay wondered just how David expected her to accomplish her task: "Find out as much as you can," he'd said, "without letting them know we might be interested." Easier said then done. Finally, the Land Cruiser turned onto Mohavithei Samdach Sothearos, the broad boulevard fronting the Royal Palace of the Kingdom of Cambodia.

The slender angles of the rooflines and the tops of spiraling *chedis* rose from behind the yellow walls of the royal compound like the caps of giant garden gnomes. At the imposing entrance, the driver presented Lindsay's invitation to the heavily armed guards, while a few passing motorcyclists and *cyclo* taxi drivers stopped to stare. Seeing the guards nod their acceptance of the invitation, Lindsay climbed carefully from the Land Cruiser and followed the guard's pointed finger around the corner into a courtyard redolent with rain and the scent of jasmine.

Making her way along the puddled walkway, Lindsay rounded the final corner to face the royal pavilion, illuminated and entrancing, a jewel in the rainy night. She stood motionless, gazing at the exotic tapestry of officials and their consorts murmuring in an intriguing mix of languages. In the background, traditional Cambodian music, a complex rhythm of strings, chimes, and drums, sounded an archaic dissonance so rich she could taste it.

Standing there unnoticed, Lindsay indulged in fantasy: the King would guide her on a personal tour of the palace. The Queen would rave about her gown. "De la Renta? Chanel?" she would ask, not even trying to disguise the envy in her voice. A dozen courtiers (all devastatingly handsome) would beg her opinion on environmental protection and human rights issues. Afterward, the press would deify her as a forceful new voice on the Cambodian scene. "Yeah, right," she muttered. Lifting her chin and straightening to her full 5 feet 8 inches, she strode into the pavilion.

Inside, she scanned the guests for members of the royal family, remembering David's final words of advice: "Whatever you do, don't turn your back on the king."

And there he was. With his elegantly coiffed queen by his side, the diminutive majesty stood at the head of a red-carpeted staircase that led down into the pavilioned courtyard below. A uniformed guard appeared at her side and directed her onward, his gloved hand presenting their royal highnesses, King Sihanouk and Queen Monique. She paced her approach to show respect commensurate with her status as the UNOIC representative. The Queen extended her hand, barely touching Lindsay's palm, while the King gave his famous jovial laugh and clasped her hand tightly in both of his own. "So pleased to see you," he said, his voice every bit as high in pitch and as excitedly sincere as it sounded in his radio broadcasts. The appreciative gleam in the royal eye reminded Lindsay of Sihanouk's youthful renown as a royal playboy. He was using his charms like other people used silverware, but still, his attention was flattering.

Moving away from the royal couple, Lindsay was approached by a waiter bearing a tray of champagne glasses. His traditional Cambodian livery—a turquoise Nehru jacket over black silk *jawng kbun* pantaloons with brilliant white knee stockings—brought the reality that she was actually in the Cambodian Royal Palace flooding into her consciousness. Sipping champagne, she descended the staircase onto the ancient tiles of the royal reception hall.

Near the kaleidoscope of the hors d'oeuvres table, Lindsay spied the Pavarottiesque figure of Rex Branson, country director for the World Food Programme and one of the few fellow Americans in the room. Rex greeted her warmly in European fashion, planting a kiss on each side of her face, his monstrous handlebar moustache prickling against her skin and his impressive paunch pushing gently against her breasts. Rex was a Wyoming cowboy who'd left his cattle behind to work disasters in all parts of the globe. He'd made a point of offering her his support and his friendship from her first day on the job.

"So, Dave figured this party'd be too hot to handle," Rex suggested bluntly, after greeting her. Rex's outspoken approach was legendary.

"So...'Dave' had a conference in Manila," Lindsay retorted, smiling, "And this isn't exactly the OK Corral. But maybe you're right; just call me Lindsay the gunslinger. What sort of shoot-outs should I be ready for?"

"You've probably heard about the new boy in town? The King's brought in a special advisor to develop a royal conservation project, somewhere up in the northeast. Seems this guy managed to develop some pretty original approaches to protect a section of the Amazon basin a few years back. Not easy, that area. I worked there myself, way back when. The place is crawling with drug lords."

So Nicky had, as usual, been right on the money. "Interesting. But David will be making any decisions on UNOIC's role. That's way beyond my job description."

Rex laughed, his hand on his rodeo championship belt buckle. "Smart decision, Lindsay. Say, I heard you put together some good debate sessions on this proposed rice export rule. WFP can help on that, you know..."

Rex continued to talk shop while Lindsay studied the room discreetly. Her gaze was drawn to a tall male figure lounging in the far doorway behind Rex, half in shadow. The flickering light caught a graceful line of shoulder, the sensual stance enhanced by formal attire.

As Rex's voice reasserted itself—"That would be in your area, I think, wouldn't it?"—the man in the doorway turned, the light now falling full on his face. Lindsay ignored Rex's question, wanting to ask her own: *Who is that man beneath the stairs?* But before the words could reach her lips, recognition washed over her, and a sinking dread rose from the pit of her stomach.

It had been more than ten years before, the summer she spent in Bolivia with her father after her sophomore year at UC Berkeley. With her dad, she had watched a professional polo match in La Paz. It had been a windy day. Not easy to forget, that wind. Its gusts had sent her wide-brimmed Isadora Duncan straw hat spinning through the air like a competition Frisbee, straight into the face of the man now standing across the room from her. She'd watched, horrified, as the opposing team scored the winning goal, while the man lay on his back glaring at the hat.

Rex's voice reached through the memory, filled with concern. "Lindsay, are you all right?"

She took a deep breath, reaching to give his arm a squeeze. "I'm fine, Rex. My stomach...just give me a moment."

Rex's hand beneath her elbow was solicitous, his expression concerned. In Cambodia, a stomach cramp could be serious. Meanwhile, the memories continued to flow. "I am Maximiliano Vega y Ortega," he had said later, at the post-game party. "You are a menace. And your hat is a weapon of mass destruction." She had never forgotten how those words had rolled from his beautiful wide mouth as he sat across from her at luncheon, nor the passion that mouth had awoken in her later that afternoon. For her, it had been a romantic fantasy come true. But for him, it had been nothing more than payback for his humiliation by hat. She'd never seen him again—but she hadn't forgotten, and she hadn't forgiven.

Well, she'd been fantasizing about this evening, but no fantasies had prepared her for this ghost from her past. Max looked like he hadn't changed at all. In fact, he looked so much the same that she half expected to see a polo pony trotting along beside him. As he turned in her direction, she slid closer to Rex, shielding herself from Maximiliano's view.

As she continued to watch, Lindsay saw a delicately built Asian woman in traditional Khmer court dress step into the doorway next to Maximiliano, stretching her supple body up to whisper in his ear. She heard Rex's laughter before she processed his words. "Feeling better, Lindsay?" he asked. "I see you're admiring our beautiful new princess. That's Juliette Sovannalok. And you're right—she's a looker. They say she left the National Ballet of Paris to get Cambodia's Royal Ballet back on its feet. I'm not much for dancing shows, but Cambodian ballets are something else."

He was referring not to the Bolshoi dance style, but to the exotic court dance of Southeast Asia. Traditionally, court dancers in Cambodia had been royal courtesans, selected from the most beautiful women in the entire kingdom. While the old custom of *droit du seignor* no longer survived—at least officially—the beauty of the dancers testified to the legacy.

As Princess Sovannalok and Maximiliano disappeared behind a thick carved teak pillar, Lindsay murmured something and excused herself from Rex. Before she'd taken two steps she collided with a dark paisley tie. She looked up into intense eyes, heavily fringed with dark lashes. For a moment, she was stunned, swimming helplessly in a blue as bottomless as the Adriatic. She had to force herself to turn away. The man's hair was blue-black, with gray frosting his temples. His skin was pale and finely textured, and the slightest hint of a smile played beneath the bristles of his clipped moustache as he stepped back, saying, "You must be Lindsay March, the UNOIC's new PIO, and OIC for your CC tonight, *ne c'est pas?*" The voice, supple and golden with a heavy French accent, managed to convey the man's delight in meeting her—and at the same time his disdain for the United Nations.

"Good evening, Monsieur Acronym," she replied.

The man then leaned forward and rested his smooth cheek against hers, wafting the scents of a musky aftershave and Cuban tobacco. His breath was warm in her hair as he murmured, "Do you know, Lindsay March, that UNOIC has ruined Cambodia! Do you suppose that you are perhaps destined to save it?"

Lindsay pulled her head back. Who was this man? "I'm afraid you have me at a disadvantage, sir. I don't know who you are, or what makes you so arrogant, and I don't really care. What I would like to know is why you know my name," she demanded.

"Let us say, someone described you to me," he responded, a warm smile sculpting asymmetrical dimples in his cheeks.

She looked away, refusing to be drawn again into his insistent gaze. The man was devastating, and insulting. What a combination. Before she could follow that thought, his voice interrupted again.

"Señor Vega y Ortega!" he exclaimed, spinning away from her. Lindsay took a deep breath, turned, and found herself face to face with her South American nemesis.

Max leaned forward, his nose just inches from hers. "No hat tonight, Señorita March? *Qué lástima!*" Before she could demonstrate her self-possession with a witty reply, Max turned to the unknown Frenchman. "It seems we have something in common after all, Major," he said with a cryptic smile. "Who would have thought it possible?"

"So, you have already have met the formidable Mademoiselle March."

"Ah yes, I have indeed. And I've had first hand experience of just how formidable Señorita March can be. Do you know, she is the only woman in the world who has ever brought me to my knees?"

Lindsay felt a deep flush blooming in her face, those private moments during which he had indeed been on his knees still clear in her memory, even after all these years. But her voice was nonchalant. "Yes," she drawled. "I'm known for bringing people down to earth."

The Frenchman—Major, Max had called him—took a step back. "Is it true that you pretend to proceed with this hill tribe circus for tourists, Señor, this nature reserve?" he said. He was smiling, but there was a warning note in his voice, and she could see the tension throbbing in his jaw line.

"It's quite true. It is time for Cambodia to respond to the concerns of the rest of the world, and begin working toward their own future," Max replied, equally amiable. "Especially now that the country is at peace." Lindsay sensed this was not a new conversation for them. The warmth of their politesse belied the palpable tension in the air, and both men had subtly changed their posture, their chins pointing with increasing aggression.

"Cambodia may be at peace, but all that means is that the people have more opportunity to enjoy their poverty, not to mention the injustice and brutality of their leaders," the Major countered. "Why don't we just let those who are lucky enough to live out of the government's reach alone? Don't let yourself be used, *mon ami*. This is not the Amazon." There were no smiles now. Lindsay remained silent, recognizing that this conversation was intimately related to her own interest as an officer of UNOIC.

When the two men fell silent, Lindsay said, "Major Acronym, how could you object to a project that will preserve Cambodia's natural beauty and resources, and protect its people at the same time. How can this be a bad thing?"

The Frenchman just shook his head, and she bristled at the patronizing expression she read in those blue eyes. "I will be happy to explain," he said, cupping her elbow in a lithe hand and pivoting her to face the dais at the front of the room, "but not now."

He was right. A uniformed musician had begun beating a bronze gong, signaling an end to conversation, and she watched a sudden flurry near the dais.

"In honor of our esteemed guests and at the pleasure of His Royal Highness King Mohavaraman Norodom Sihanouk, Her Excellency Princess Sovannalok will now perform *Bopha Lokei*— the Flowers of the World dance."

The princess glided onto the platform, a lotus blossom extended in her upraised hands. She bowed low to the king, and with a quick movement of her hand tossed the blossom directly to Max, who stepped forward and caught it deftly. She looked at him, laughter in her eyes, but laughter faded as the princess began to dance.

Lindsay would always remember the performance that night. The princess made every Khmer performer she had ever seen look like a stumbling amateur. Juliette's sensuality flowed within the strictly prescribed movements of the dance like the glint of fish in a shallow pool. Slowly, her arms bent and straightened in harmony with the deep flexing of her back as if she were embracing an invisible lover. If anything, the ritualized performance made the implied wantonness more powerful, and more explicit.

Wondering if it were simply her imagination, Lindsay glanced discreetly at the faces surrounding the dais. Lascivious smiles played on the faces of the Khmer men, while the expatriates seemed caught in a web of rapturous embarrassment. The faces of the foreign wives in attendance had turned to stone. Following the closing steps of the dance, there was silence as the haunting notes died into the night air. The gong struck a single note, and the crowd broke into wild applause.

"Thank you so much, *mes amis,* for joining me here tonight. Before I bid you good-night, I would like to make a special proclamation." Lindsay realized with a start that Max was no longer at her side. He was now the focus of attention, the arm of the rotund little king reaching up to clasp his shoulder. "This afternoon the Council of Ministers determined to create Norodom Park! It will be a nature reserve that will cover large hectares of forest in our northeastern provinces," King Sihanouk announced. "This has been my dream for many, many years—to save Cambodia's wild life and wild places for my children, and for their children."

"To make my dream come true, I have invited Señor Vega Y Ortega to assist. We are fortunate that he has the experience of developing such a reserve in the Amazon basin. He will be my Special Advisor, handling all aspects of the planning, fund-raising, and development, including working closely with UNOIC to involve the international community in this project."

Lindsay saw Max looking her way as the King spoke, and realized, belatedly, that she could anticipate spending quite a lot of time with Maximiliano in the coming weeks, whether she liked it or not. She wasn't sure that the prospect was all that daunting. She also realized, with dismay, that she could be finding herself the center of attention at any moment. But surely, Max would not dare to make a public request for UNOIC support without first consulting with her!

"I am honored to contribute to such a high purpose, your highness," Max began, "and I can promise your majesty and all Cambodians that I will not leave this country until the northeast nature reserve is a reality. Our friends at UNOIC have so often asked Cambodia to protect the rain forests of the northeast, not always considering what the cost might be to the people now living on those lands. So I know, Ms March, that we can anticipate your whole-hearted support for the funding and development of Norodom Park."

The smile on Lindsay's face hid the frantic activity of her brain, as she quickly worded a response to Max's implied question. Her thoughts, however, were cut short by the voice of the King, signaling the end of the formal part of the evening. "Señor Vega y Ortega, you and the beautiful Ms March will have much opportunity for discussion, I am sure. For all of you, I hope you have enjoyed the party this evening, and I bid you good night." He raised his hands in a Cambodian salute, smiling with delight for a moment before turning to leave, Queen Monique on his arm.

Once again, Lindsay found Rex at her side. "That's old Max for you," he said with a shake of his graying head.

"You know him?" Lindsay queried.

"I do, Lindsay, I surely do. Brazil, 1990. But that's another story." And he guided her into the crowd that had begun moving slowly toward the palace gates and home.

CHAPTER TWO

MONDAY, MAY 17

B y seven Monday morning, Lindsay was staring at her computer screen. Her first task of the day was to become better informed on UN precedents for support of government-initiated environmental projects. *Who could help me with this?* she mused, one nail rhythmically tapping her front teeth.

And then, with a brisk "All right, then!" her fingers began to dance across the keyboard. *Stewart,* her message read, *Help! The government is trying to set up a nature preserve, or maybe a national park, in one of Cambodia's most remote provinces. I don't know whether it's a serious effort to conserve the environment or not; the northeast part of the country does have a wealth of timber and gemstones. I want to know about similar efforts in developing countries. Can you help me? And...how are you, anyway?*

As the words appeared on her screen, Lindsay pictured Stewart's snort as he read into her message all the things she wasn't quite sure she should say, email not being a particularly secure form of communication. Stewart would run his slender fingers through that brown mop, shake his head, and smile his slow smile.

Lindsay landed back in the present with a lurch of guilt when she heard Bopha's voice outside the door. She hadn't given her marooned fellow travelers another thought since Saturday afternoon, when she had abandoned them and the *Luv Boat II!* But delayed concern, surely, was better than none, she thought, dashing to the door.

"Omigosh, Bopha! I was afraid you might still be out there floating on the Mekong! How did the rest of the trip go? And how did you get back to town?" Lindsay pulled Bopha into her office and kicked the door closed behind them.

"My watch stopped in the rain," Bopha laughed, "but if I have to guess, I think we wait maybe another half an hour. Not so bad. And what about you, Lindsay, do you get there in time?" she added, giving Lindsay a dazzling smile.

Bopha's grin was a gift of infectious sunshine, although Lindsay often wondered what was really going on beneath that sunny exterior. "Did I. Did I get there in time," she corrected automatically. "And yes, I did. Oh, Bopha, it was fascinating. I have so many questions for you about the palace and the royal family, but first—listen to this. The King has imported a special advisor to develop a proposal for a nature reserve or national park or something in the northeast. They are asking for our full support...and that means that you and I may be seeing some pretty exotic country! Have you ever been up to the northeastern provinces?"

"Lindsay, can you explain please, what are nature reserves?"

Lindsay squelched her impatience. Every day, she was confronted with the need to explain things that were not within the realm of her assistant's experience or English vocabulary. It was understandable, of course—Bopha had spent most of her life in a refugee camp. But it slowed things down.

Over their two months of working together, Lindsay and Bopha had developed a system of mutual trust and understanding, leading to Bopha's willingness to ask the questions, and to Lindsay's patience in answering them. The upside of the extra time required for explanations was that formulating a response often helped Lindsay to better clarify an issue in her own mind.

"You're in luck, Bopha, because I was just checking a listing of resources at the Cambodia Research Center. Someone's put together a book that explains all about the history and purpose of natural parks in other countries, and the Research Center has a Khmer translation."

"I will ask the driver to pick us up a copy today, Lindsay," Bopha offered. Bopha's rapid development of initiative was gratifying.

"That's a great idea—and why don't you get me a copy, in English? I've got a lot to learn about this, too. But maybe you should go to Beung Jepung and pick up the books yourself...I saw a really good looking guy there at the last coordination meeting. You wouldn't know who I'm talking about, by any chance?"

The smile was replaced by Bopha's other standard expression, one of polite passivity. "Oh yes, I think so, Lindsay. But he must either be playboy or married. He is Khmer man."

"You're probably right, Bopha," Lindsay said, turning back to her computer. "But it wouldn't hurt to find out. Just try to be back before lunch."

She waited politely for Bopha's automatic laugh and her departure, but Bopha continued to hover. "Yes?" she asked, "did you need something else?"

"So sorry to bother, Lindsay, but please, you said you would like to talk about the people at the palace. And I, I would like to know. Did you see the King and the Queen?"

"It was like a fairy tale, Bopha." Lindsay sighed romantically. "I did see them, and the King kissed my hand. He's quite the cavalier. Oh, and guess what? The Princess Juliette danced a dance with your name in it! And the Queen was so elegant. Her gown was the finest silk I've ever seen—I wonder where she found it? And the food! And the jewels! You wouldn't believe one ruby ring I saw—it was at least six carats!"

Bopha smiled. "I must be good teacher, Lindsay." During their years in the refugee camp on the Thai-Cambodian border, Bopha and her brother, Narong, had survived through their black market trade in sapphires and rubies from the wild border mines of Pailin, and lately, Bopha had begun giving Lindsay hints on spotting and selecting quality gems..

"You are a good teacher, Bopha. It's no wonder you and your brother did well. How's he doing, now that he's settled in Lyons?"

"He is struggling, but I think he will succeed. But about the palace—were there any handsome men for you there?" Bopha's grin made it clear that she was getting back at Lindsay for her own teasing earlier.

"Well, since you ask...there were a couple of intriguing guys," Lindsay said, wondering whether to mention that one of those fellows was a ghost from her past life.

"Intriguing?" Bopha queried.

"Yes, it means... Oh, hell. There are some words that are just too hard to define," she groaned. "Let's look it up." Lindsay opened the thesaurus on her computer and typed in "intrigue."

"Let's see, we've got conspiracy, illicit love affair, conniving, cabal... Oh, dear. Maybe intriguing isn't quite the word I want after all. Let's just say they were both a little mysterious. And very handsome, both of them."

"Why mysterious?" Bopha asked.

"Well, first the South American. He's the King's new advisor for the park. I guess the mystery with him is that...well, I wasn't going to tell you, but the thing is, I've met him before, when I was a college student visiting my father in Bolivia. Only back then, he wasn't a royal advisor—he was a professional polo player!"

"Uh...sorry Lindsay, but I don't know about polo?"

Lindsay laughed, feeling like a puppy chasing its own tail. "Okay, polo. Polo is something like soccer, I guess, but played by men on horses. Anyway, this guy's name is Max, Maximiliano Vega y Ortega. And something bad happened back then that really embarrassed me. So I wasn't that happy about seeing him last night. In fact, I tried to avoid him as much as I could. But," she said, ruefully, "he is definitely handsome! He's dark and tall, and very well built; he's got wavy black hair, brown eyes like bottomless pools... you know what I mean. Or maybe not. Anyway, he's got the arrogance that goes along with looks like that."

"Lindsay, you are being silly. I know you would not do anything to get embarrassed. Always, you are so sure, and so careful to do the right thing."

"Me? Oh, if you could only see me on the inside," Lindsay snorted. "You wouldn't believe how much I worry about protocol and being culturally appropriate, especially now that I'm with UNOIC."

Bopha looked at her, her eyes narrowed with thought. "Lindsay, is there something you are not telling about this man? Did you love him?" She waited a moment for Lindsay's answer, continuing to study her face. Then she said, "Never mind, Lindsay. You are blushing, so I can know the answer. Tell me about the number two man."

Lindsay laughed. "What are you, Bopha, psychic?" She held up a hand. "No, don't ask me what it means! You can look it up later. Now, about the other guy. He's the one I really wonder about." She hesitated, considering her choice of words. "I guess I'd say, in this case, that intriguing means—he interests me, I found him attractive. He wasn't as handsome, at least not in such an obvious way. He's not really that tall, maybe just a little taller than me. He had dark hair, too, but his eyes were blue, like your brother's sapphires. And he behaved very mysteriously, too."

"You mean he does something improper, Lindsay?"

"I'm not really sure. Not improper, exactly. He walked up to me, said my name—without introducing himself, either—and whispered something in my ear."

"What was it?"

"That's the other intriguing part, I guess. He said, 'UNOIC has ruined Cambodia—and perhaps you are destined to save it!'" Lindsay lowered her voice to a husky whisper, trying to match the Major's tone. "Just like that!"

19

"Where was he from, Lindsay? Who does he working for?" The second question was an obvious one—among Cambodia's expatriate community, standard introductions included both name and organizational affiliation.

"He didn't say, Bopha, but his accent was French."

At this, Bopha's eyebrows raised. "Does the French man have a little moustache, Lindsay?" When Lindsay nodded, she said, "Maybe it is my friend André. He is French, and his moustache is very short and stickery. Someday I will introduce you to him. He is a good friend to me, and I want you to know him, too. You will like him, I think."

Lindsay studied Bopha's face and wondered just what Bopha meant when she called the Frenchman her friend. "I'd like that, Bopha," was all she said.

As she spoke, Bopha glanced at her watch. "Thank you for telling me about the palace, Lindsay. I must go to the Research Center now, to get the park book. But first, I would like to tell you one thing that I am remembering now because you have mentioned the South American man."

"Okay, Bopha, shoot."

"Shoot? Oh, you mean go ahead. Okay. This is a strange thing, because you have just explained about the two men. Just yesterday, my *ming* asked me to bring her to the fortuneteller at Wat Phnom."

A few months earlier, Lindsay would have been mystified by this sentence, but she had since learned to call her housekeeper *ming*—the Khmer word for an aunt who is younger than one's parents—and she had visited the temple—the *wat*—atop Phnom Penh's only mountain—a *phnom*. Wat Phnom. "You went to the fortuneteller, Bopha? And?"

"I did not have a plan to ask my fortune, Lindsay, but after the fortuneteller used the cards for *ming, ming* asked him to tell about her niece—me."

"So—did she mention that cute man that you'll be seeing out at the Cambodia Research Center?"

"No, she did not, Lindsay. She talk about my work, and my boss—about you. She say, I must warn my boss about the danger from a dark man. She say, my boss should beware danger in a far place, with a dark man."

Lindsay silently considered Bopha's words. True, she had knocked on the wooden railing out on the Mekong, but that didn't mean she was really superstitious. Still, Bopha would be offended if she didn't give her well-intentioned words serious consideration. "How much do you believe in this fortune teller, Bopha?" she said finally. "Because you have to admit, if I've got to watch out for dark-skinned men here in far-off Cambodia, I'm in real trouble!"

"*Ming* say this is the one best, true, fortuneteller, Lindsay. I know you want to laugh—I can see your eyes—but I think you must be careful, at least. I remembered because you mentioned the men—and one is a dark man!"

And with these final unsettling words, Bopha was out the door and off to the Research Center. Lindsay began sifting through her in-box, reviewing the stack of official memos that awaited her attention. She was just beginning an email update to her father in Fiji when her office phone rang.

"You have a call," the receptionist said gaily, hanging up without providing Lindsay with the identity of her caller. In pointless revenge, Lindsay delayed answering the call to make a note on her to-do list: *Schedule telephone etiquette training for receptionist,* she scrawled.

Punching the blinking light on the front of the phone, she said simply, "Lindsay March here."

"Señorita March!" a melodiously accented male voice said, "May I invite you and your hat to join me for lunch?"

Feeling her stomach lurch but determined to keep that knowledge to herself, Lindsay's response was cold. "I'm sorry. The receptionist did not give me your name?"

But there was a laugh in the voice that made it clear she hadn't fooled him a bit. "I am Maximiliano Vega y Ortega," he said, "the man who is known throughout his country as the only polo champion to suffer defeat by hat."

"And I can still recall the death screams of my poor hat as it was trampled by a herd of wild polo ponies on the Altiplano,"

Lindsay said with asperity. "Sadly, it did not recover, and will be unable to attend luncheon, now or ever."

Max must have cupped the phone, because his laughter was muffled. "Do you think flowers would be in order? Or am I perhaps too belated with my regrets? I am so hoping that this does not mean that without your hat you will be unable to lunch?"

Yes or no? Lindsay gave herself a mental kick. Why didn't I make this decision before he called, she wondered. "No-o-o. I think we must meet, even without the hat, since it seems we are destined to work together."

"*Sí, querida,* I think we must meet as soon as possible. Shall we say, tomorrow? Midday? At Déjà Vu."

A quick glance at her calendar showed tomorrow's lunchtime unscheduled. "I'm afraid not, Max," she said. "I could meet for an early lunch on Wednesday, though." *Oh no you don't, buster,* Lindsay thought. *You're not running my life that easily.*

"Of course, Lindsay. I will adjust my schedule. The important thing is that we meet soon. Because there are many things to discuss."

Personal things, or park things? she wanted to ask. Better to keep it focused on the professional. "You're right, Max," she said, returning to a more formal tone. "I need to learn more about your plans. It's not even clear to me whether you are planning a nature reserve or a national park—or how they might differ in your mind. And, of course, I haven't yet seen your formal proposal for UNOIC's participation."

"You will, Lindsay, very soon. For, as you know, the King is anxious to assure himself of UNOIC's full support for his plans. I hope your friendship with André Balfour will not influence your decision against Norodom Park."

"André Balfour?"

Max response was brusque. "You are surprised? You seemed to be very intimate with him at the reception!"

"That would hardly be your business, Max. However, I have to tell you that I have no idea who this André Balfour is!"

This time Max didn't bother to stifle his derision. "André Balfour, *mi amor*, is the French military attaché. Silly of me, I

22

suppose, to suspect you perhaps knew him quite well, just because he was embracing you and whispering in your ear."

That solved one mystery, anyway, although Lindsay was left wondering why the French military attaché would have made that odd comment about UNOIC. "I wonder why you find my conversation with this person so interesting, Max? Does he have some involvement in your park project?"

"Major André Balfour is considered one of the better informed foreigners about the northeast provinces and the hilltribe cultures," Max replied. "And he is also a devious intriguer who strongly opposes the development of a nature reserve in the Cambodian highlands for reasons of his own. But let's wait and discuss this over lunch. Ciao."

Lindsay hung up the phone and, for a moment, stared at it. What she was seeing, though, was not the telephone but the disillusioned tears of a young girl who thought that she had found the beginnings of an exotic first love, all those years ago. Max had hurt her deeply, and the scars had never wholly healed. Now that fate had brought him back into her life, what should she do with him? This time, he seemed to be interested in her—maybe revenge was in order?

Of course, he also needed her—well, he needed UNOIC, and for the moment, that meant he needed her. She could refuse to offer the agency's support just to get even, or create unnecessary obstacles, at the very least. She shook her head, dismayed by the turn her thoughts had taken. She'd been given, for the first time, the chance to really prove herself with UNOIC—of course she would not let her leftover emotions cloud her judgment about the park. She was an adult, no longer the adolescent she had been at the time of her encounter with Max. And perhaps he had done some growing up of his own. Maybe he was interested in her, and he was certainly still an intriguing man. *...and the thing to do*, she said aloud, *is to keep the doors open, do my job as best I can, and just see what happens.*

CHAPTER THREE
TUESDAY, MAY 18

T he morning sounds of a new day at the Boun Thong Orphanage roused Sam Jarrett from dreamless sleep. Three months had passed since he'd landed at Pochentong International Airport and been whisked through the chaotic traffic into a city in the throes of rapid reconstruction.

Stepping off the plane at Pochentong, Sam felt he'd come home. In part, it was the unmistakable sounds and smells of Southeast Asia—the rich scent of frangipani, the pungent smells of frying noodles and garlic, the underlying but ubiquitous smell of steaming urine, the tinkling of traditional music, the heavy cloak of humidity. But it was also the warmth of the brown faces, and the pain hidden in the dark eyes, pain that was still purulent so many years after the war.

Thinking of that first day as he stretched himself fully awake led Sam to memories of his first visit to Southeast Asia in 1973, when he fought with the Australian Army's Special Air Service in Vietnam's central highlands. Like many in his platoon, he'd been drawn into the desperate escapism of drugs, drink, and sex to blot out the nightmare of combat. But during his last month in-country, everything had changed. In Aluoi, a tiny mountain village in Thua Thien Hue province, he'd met a Buddhist monk who spoke English. This in itself was a rare find, but even more surprisingly, the monk was not consumed with hatred for the enemies of his country, and he had had a profound effect on Sam, triggering a lifelong commitment to the precepts and practice of Buddhism.

The Vietnam War sent Sam home to Australia with a burning desire to study, to learn, and to help those who had been harmed by the war. He'd studied hard and become a Buddhist monk. Through the monastery, he'd joined a group of Cambodian students, and together they'd conceived the idea of returning to Cambodia to develop a home for Cambodian orphans—an orphanage with a difference. In their orphanage, every child would be wanted, would be loved.

The chaos of the airport arrival hall was a shock, but the sea of Cambodians waving hand-lettered placards (UNICEF, Chinese-American Friendship Association, UNOIC), had parted to reveal the madly waving hands and grinning faces of his fellow collaborators.

He made his way through the melee, following the cries of "Sam, Sam Jarrett! Over here!" until he found himself bending to wrap his arms around the three of them. Peter Chiv, Annie Samnang, and Ouk Mathak were all in their early twenties. Each had arrived in Australia as a young child, their families seeking refuge from the horrors of the Khmer Rouge regime. Their Australian-accented English was indistinguishable from Sam's, slang and all, but they had all worked hard to maintain their literacy in Khmer, their native tongue.

Sam caught the eye of a tall Cambodian boy, scruffily dressed but clean and beaming, standing just behind Annie. The boy's traditional *sompeah*—hands held palm-to-palm before an inclined head—somehow made Sam know that coming here was what he was meant to do.

The boy, Rachannak, they'd called him, grabbed Sam's backpack and somehow got them effortlessly through customs and the crowds of Khmer men touting cheap guest houses, private taxis, and ecstasy at 'best price.'

"Our car is this way," Annie yelled in Sam's ear, pushing him out the door of the terminal and onto the melting ooze of the tarmac. They passed Mercedes sedans, new Hondas with shimmering metallic paint jobs, and towering Land Cruisers, finally ending up in the far corner of the parking lot at the trunk of a battered Soviet Lada, the boxy cars that had filled the city's streets until the elections brought more modern vehicles flooding into the country. Although he looked much too young, Rachannak was the driver—"and our first orphan!" Annie said, by way of introduction.

Inside the car, Peter, Annie, and Mathak were bubbling over with their adventures during the two weeks since their arrival in Phnom Penh. "We've found the perfect house for the orphanage—" Annie said, while at the same time Mathak was saying, more soberly, "Oh Sam, you've got to see these kids! There are so many, and they need love so much—" and Peter was directing Sam's attention out the window, where children picked trash from a steaming mountain of garbage beside the road.

Sam held up his hands, laughing. "You guys are something else—you've become old hands in just two weeks!" He laughed softly. "I'm afraid it might take me a little longer—especially if you all keep talking at once. How about I just soak it in for a day or two?"

Rachannak directed their little car down tree-lined boulevards, finally turning sharply to enter a narrow dirt side street, deeply rutted and strewn with rubbish. Successive turns took them down increasingly impassable streets until they could go no further. At last, they stopped in front of a large dilapidated building surrounded by corrugated aluminum siding and topped with barbed wire. "Psar Kap Koh," Annie called the neighborhood— Slaughterhouse Market.

And it was happening. Things were working out, they were making progress. The Boun Thong Orphanage was becoming a reality. Lying on his bed, Sam stretched again, this time with satisfaction, counting up the obstacles they'd confronted and surmounted.

First, there was the landlord, an Army colonel with a shrewish wife who'd taken their obscenely large advance on the rent and then "forgotten" to make the agreed-upon repairs to the house. A little detective work had made it easy to fix that.

"Say, *Lok*," Sam had said, putting the colonel off-guard by his use of the honorific. "You want your son to study in Australia, I hear? You know, the Australian Ambassador will be here for the blessing ceremony next week. I'll bet he'd help you get the visa when he sees the good work you're doing for the orphans...." The next day, water and electricity were running and the painters were busily applying the first coat of bright blue paint to the exterior walls. The children had pitched in, helping to scrub out the debris and the dirt, and, already, brightly colored curtains fashioned of hand woven *kremas*—the traditional Cambodian cotton scarves—hung at each window.

Then there were the kids. Peter, Annie, and Mathak had spent hours hanging out on the streets, talking to street kids about their lives and their dreams. Some of the kids had homes and were working to supplement family incomes, and some found the independent life of the street to their liking. But others—lots of them—were hungry for stability and love. And all of them were just plain hungry.

"We want to work with you," Sam said politely, during his meeting with Mr Seng Ouern of the Ministry of Social Action. "But I will never be able to do my best for these kids without your support."

"Unfortunately, Mr Jarrett, it is expensive to obtain the necessary permits..."

"We know how hard it is, *Lok*," Sam began soothingly. But he was not about to pay bribes for the privilege of helping orphans, and his tone hardened as he added, "I understand the Prime

Minister and his wife have taken in some orphans themselves. Maybe I should ask them about the permit process?"

Another obstacle obliterated. Mr Seng Ouern had shown up the next day with the required permits and agreements, duly signed and stamped with red seals. And Annie was making headway in developing a database, the first step toward a permanency plan for each child. "But Sam," Annie had said yesterday, holding a sheaf of papers out for Sam's inspection, a frown on her face. "Look at these."

Sam had laughed. To him, the curlicues of the Khmer script resembled nothing so much as the muddy tracks of a beetle trailing across the cheap paper. "You know I can't read Khmer, Annie. Tell me."

"We've got intake forms filled in for almost fifty kids. And according to these papers—and to the kids, because I've asked them—almost 80% of the girls' forms say Ratanakiri! It just doesn't make sense."

Sam's questions had made everyone laugh: "Who's Ratanakiri?" he'd asked innocently. "And why do they all have the same name?" He'd blushed at the answer. "Not 'who,' Sam. It's a province—the province in the far northeastern corner of Cambodia," Mathak had explained. "It's isolated, and most of the people there are from the hilltribes—Cambodia's ethnic minorities."

Sam was intrigued. "Why would so many kids from a place like that end up in our orphanage, way down here in Phnom Penh?" he'd wondered. But none of them had the answers, so they'd set the question aside and kept on with their renovations.

Linking up with the other agencies working with orphans should have been Sam's easiest task, but it was proving to be an unending pain in the neck. *Who would have thought,* Sam pondered, sluicing cold water over his body to rinse away the sweat of the night, *that there'd be an orphan agency pecking order—and that Boun Thong would be somewhere down in the basement?*

He sighed as he considered his task for the day—more networking. Attendance at the monthly meetings of the NGOs involved with orphans and street children was essential to the success of Boun Thong—and today was the day. Not just the day for the meeting, but the day when Sam hoped to find out the truth about Ratanakiri. A close review of Annie's records had shown that all the children citing Ratanakiri as their birthplace were older girls, between eight and thirteen, and most had been found wandering on the streets of Phnom Penh. It didn't seem right, and Sam was anxious to find out whether any other agencies could explain this disproportion.

***

But it hadn't gone well. Sam's questions, he felt, had been clear and well worded. But the answers! The woman from Cambodian Children United had stood in the meeting and glared, her thin frame angled toward him with hostility. "Mr Jarrett, how long did you say you'd been in Cambodia?" And she'd laughed! "You newcomers, thinking there's a conspiracy behind every palm tree. Ratanakiri is one of Cambodia's poorest provinces. Should we be surprised that parents die and leave their children behind as orphans? Or that some parents make their children into social orphans, trying to find a better life for them? My organization has been assigned to work with children in the northeast, we have an office there, and we certainly haven't seen anything unusual that would require your attention."

"I don't claim to understand, and I'm not making any accusations," Sam objected politely. "I'm trying to learn, to understand. I thought this group could help me with that." He sat down, shaking his head. What were these people thinking, protecting their organizational turf while children went hungry? Working together, sharing information—it could only benefit the children.

After the meeting, two representatives of larger organizations made a point of pulling Sam aside. "Rene was a little hard on you in there," they'd commiserated. "But she's right about the poverty up north. It's appalling. In fact," added the representative of Rescue Children Now, "I could let you know next time we have a staff person heading up there. The best way is always just to go see for yourself."

"That'd be great, and I really appreciate your offer," Sam said, thinking maybe some of the group weren't so bad after all. But then the older man continued.

"But keep this in mind. The kids are survivors—and they'll say and do what they need to do to survive. If you guys are paying special attention to orphans from Ratanakiri, you can bet that they'll all be saying they're from Ratanakiri." He laid an arm across Sam's shoulders. "They're just like us, Sam. They need to let Jesus into their lives."

Sam bit his tongue, thanked them both, and walked out the gate, passing the waiting cars and drivers of the expatriates still lingering inside the compound. He was hailing a passing *cyclo* when he felt a hand on his arm.

It was Ong Krith, the director of a Cambodian NGO working to support local adoptions for orphans in Kompong Speu province. Sam had met him briefly outside the Ministry of Social Action the previous week. "*Lok* Sam, I just wonder...do you know *nhiek srey* Olga?"

"Who's Olga?" Sam queried, puzzled by the question.

Krith's smile was embarrassed, covered with polite fingers in the Cambodian custom. "Olga Herrin. Miss Olga lives here, and she is helping many many Cambodian orphans."

"Was she here at the meeting today?"

"No. I think maybe she does not get along with the other foreigners. Perhaps, they do not agree with her methods."

"Methods?" Sam asked, imagining night raids on street children and adoptions that slid through the Cambodian bureaucracy with minimal paperwork, lubricated with sizeable bribes to government officials.

"Well, you see..." Again the laugh. "Olga goes out at night, you see, to the brothels. She knows a lot of people in those places. And she helps those women take care of their babies, when they need her." Krith stepped away from Sam as April, the healthy, scrubbed-looking director of one of the orphanages, approached. "I must go now," he said, turning away and moving rapidly up the street.

Sam turned to the American woman. "Do you know someone called Olga?" he asked, hoping to get an address or phone number.

April's lips tightened into a line of disapproval. "I certainly do not! I've heard of her, though. She doesn't participate in the group—she's very stand-offish. Although she's certainly been invited. I'm so glad you understand, Sam, how crucial it is that we all work together. Besides, there've been some questions about what that woman is really up to. She's on her own, not with an agency. I think you and Boun Thong will do a lot better if you keep away from her. Why do you want to know?" Sam could almost hear her implied sniff of disapproval.

"I just heard her name mentioned, and got curious," he said, then changed the subject, asking April to help him get a copy of the orphan group's membership list.

What to do? Pander to the mainstream organizations by avoiding a black sheep? Or take a chance. For the next two days, Sam deliberated. He appreciated April's skepticism, knowing that Cambodia attracted a wide variety of misfits for an even wider variety of reasons—wariness was in order. Still, what could it hurt to make contact?

Discreet questions led to Sam's arrival, a few days later, at a large wooden house in Steung Meanchey on Phnom Penh's western outskirts. The house was surrounded by squatter huts—there were no Land Cruisers lining these narrow streets. Inside a sparsely furnished room, a young Cambodian girl directed Sam to cushions along the wall and asked him to wait. He was studying the Sanskrit blessings printed along the rough wooden ceiling beams when a tall woman strode purposefully into the room. "I am Olga," she said, the lilting cadence of just those three words revealing her Scandinavian background. Fixing him with a confrontational glare, she demanded, "Who are you, and what do you want?"

Sam struggled to his feet, amused by how small she'd made his 6 feet 4 inches feel. It wasn't every day that a guy had a T-shirt and sarong-clad Valkyrie towering above him. Olga's aggression made it clear that polite formalities had been left outside. Olga, Sam realized, wouldn't hesitate to tell him to go to hell if she didn't like what he had to say.

"I'm Sam Jarrett," he began, speaking slowly. "I'm new in Cambodia. I've been working to get the Boun Thong Orphanage up and running. Ong Krith suggested I talk to you about some questions that have been coming up with the kids."

Sam's decision to come directly to the point was rewarded by a spark of interest in Olga's light blue eyes. "Go on," she said tersely.

So Sam described the fight to get the orphanage in order, the fight to get permits from the Ministry, his puzzlement over the Ratanakiri connection—and his even greater puzzlement by the lack of camaraderie and support from the other children's agencies. "They laughed at me, told me to take it slow, said I should forget about trying to understand how things work here and just feed the kids. Bring them to Jesus, yet." Sam's expression was rueful, but determined. "But that's not why I'm here. Food, yes, but love and respect and teaching kids how to make a contribution—that's what I want Boun Thong to be. But to do it right, I need to know why the kids are here, how they ended up on the streets. Which brings me back to the Ratanakiri question." As he described the disproportionate number of girls from Ratanakiri and their ages, Sam caught the quick flash of anger in Olga's eyes.

"I can see you know what I'm talking about," he said softly, finding himself warming to Olga. She nodded slowly, still not speaking.

"What it boils down to," Sam finished, "is this. I'm the new kid here. And I'm the first to admit that I don't understand—anything. So I'm probably imagining things, but if I can't get anyone to explain things to me, I'll keep on thinking the worst." He looked directly into Olga's eyes and said, "Can you help me to understand?"

By now, Olga was sitting beside him on the floor, the tension in her body revealed by her large hands, clenched tightly as she hugged her knees to her chest. Abruptly she jumped to her feet, lit a cigarette, and paced across the room. Her mind was racing with questions of her own. *Finally! Someone else whose eyes were open, who dared—or was naïve enough—to voice his questions. But could she trust him?* There were high stakes—the lives of children, and the ability to continue to help them. Could she—should she—trust this Sam Jarrett?

Sam, still motionless on the cushions, watched the outer tracks of the wheels turning in Olga's brain as expressions flickered across her face. As she turned, finally, to face him, he said. "Olga, look at me. I am a real person, a true person. I'm not that smart, I don't have money, I don't have connections. But I have honor."

His words were well-timed, and they reinforced Olga's gut feeling. Looking deep into his soft gray eyes, she made a decision.

"You've made an interesting observation, Mr Jarrett," she said. "What will you do if I tell you that your Rataniri connection is all in your imagination, nothing more and nothing less?"

Sam shrugged. "Well, I'll go back to my orphanage. I'll do the best I can for the kids. And I'll keep asking questions. Because it's not my imagination. And one of these days these Ratanakiri kids are going to trust me enough to tell me their stories. And when that happens, I'll know what to do next."

"Fair enough," Olga said, the sketchiest of smiles playing around her lips. "And what will you do if I tell you you're right? That something is very wrong, and you're right to be concerned."

Sam looked up, his eyes narrowing. "It's true then? Something is going on—but do you know what it is?" He stared at her for a moment, then an abashed grin appeared on his face. "I don't know what to do now. I never dreamed you'd say there was something to all of this!"

"You don't want to do that, Sam," Olga replied, laughing. "Jumping into things without looking ahead is dangerous in Cambodia. The problem is, I'm not sure what's going on, although I have many theories. The only thing I'm sure of is…no matter which theory is right, they all spell bad news for the children."

Sam returned Olga's gaze. "I'm beginning to realize that," he said, "And I know I have to do something. Maybe we can work together, find out what's wrong—and maybe we can fix it."

A feeling of relief swept over Olga as she saw the resolute look on Sam Jarrett's face. *At last,* she thought, *I have an ally.*

CHAPTER FOUR
WEDNESDAY, MAY 19, PART I

T hrough the fronds of a glossy potted palm, Lindsay admired Max's carefree confidence as he climbed the cement steps to the colonial villa that housed Déjà Vu Restaurant. Max had selected the elegant setting, she felt sure, not only for its delicious food and surprisingly extensive selection of acceptable wines. She could almost hear him reasoning to himself: "The intimate surroundings of Déjà Vu, her embarrassment over the hat debacle—topped off with my Latin charm, *seguro* will induce Lindsay to officially commit UNOIC to my project." *But Max is in for a surprise*, she thought—never suspecting that the surprise was to be her own.

The original proprietors of Déjà Vu, a trio of young and enthusiastic French twentysomethings, had fallen victim to the chaotic lawlessness of the country the previous year, when they'd been abducted and murdered by a band of renegade Khmer Rouge. Although the restaurant remained open, a pall of gloom had hung over the villa, sending most old Cambodia hands to more light-hearted establishments.

Recent months, however, had brought some serious remodeling that was helping to exorcise the ghosts. The new owners had repainted the yellow exterior walls a pale blue and divided the restaurant into two distinct dining areas. Downstairs, where Lindsay waited, a carved and polished bar gleamed with mirrors and brass, and small bistro tables clustered beside large open windows. In the gardens, lush with banana and mango trees, a gazebo housed additional tables.

Those looking for more invigorating entertainment climbed the winding staircase to the eclectic café on the second floor, where curved stone benches were decorated with oversized silk cushions in bright greens, blues, and golds, and a steady pulse of soft jazz filled the air. Finding this marvelous mix of relaxed hip in Cambodia bordered on the miraculous.

Lindsay watched Max as he reached the door and searched the room. *If only he's changed*, she thought, her eyes lingering on the dark waves of his hair as they shifted, tousled by the lazy revolutions of the teak ceiling fans. But Max caught her eye and began moving through the room toward her, and the thought remained unfinished.

"Déjà Vu. Fitting name, no?" said Max, taking Lindsay's hand and pressing it briefly to his lips before easing into the seat across from her.

His lips were warm, hotter even than the heat of the day, but Lindsay kept her welcoming words cool. "Max," she said, "how does Colombia's most eligible polo player come to be a Special Advisor to the King of Cambodia?" As she spoke, she realized that she'd totally failed to recognize Max's most obvious reason for choosing to meet at the Déjà Vu. Her guess at his imaginary logic had been way off target.

"Oh, I still play polo, Lindsay," he said, his teeth gleaming a warning that he was about to say something wicked. "But between games I've gotten comfortable around a few universities, a few governments, and a few nature reserves. How about you?" He looked around ostentatiously, first beneath the table, then at the ceiling, finally lifting the tablecloth to inspect her lap. Maintaining his innocent expression, he said, "Your hat was not able to come?"

Lindsay blushed. "I think you have punished me beyond all proportion for that incident. Let's just put it behind us, shall we?"

"Actually, you know, it took me a long time to forgive you. That was an important game—and I'd planned to impress the daughter of the Governor General by my skill on horseback. I succeeded with the Governor's daughter, of course, but still—"

"You're terrible!" She paused, then looked directly into his eyes. "What you should be worried about is whether I have succeeded in forgiving you."

Max's lips were still curved into a smile, but this time his dark eyes were serious, and the touch of his hand on her arm was the gentle touch of a friend. "Lindsay, you're right. I think we must talk, just a little, about our past, before we can put it behind us."

Lindsay felt instant butterflies batting against the lining of her stomach. Max had paused, but it was impossible to let the silence continue. "Max," she said, "It was a long time ago. You hurt me, it's true. But I'm not the kid I was then, and I think you've probably grown up some yourself. I'd like us to just move forward and do the work we're both paid to do."

"Look at me, Lindsay," Max said, his smile parting his dark lips to reveal the moist pink inner flesh. Her breath catching, Lindsay looked away, biting her own lips to maintain her composure. But Max's hand was reaching for her. Catching the tip of her chin with two fingers, he turned her face back to meet his now serious eyes.

"Yes, I was young, true. And you were younger. But I've never forgotten you, and never forgiven myself for being too stupid to know what I was doing. You were something special, Lindsay, *una tesora*, and I squashed you like a mosquito."

"Max," Lindsay began, but Max shushed her with a broad finger across her lips. "No, I want to finish. I'm truly sorry for what I did to you. You need to hear me say it, and I've needed to say these words for more than ten years."

Lindsay shuddered away the memories of humiliation and heartbreak—and the last of her doubts about Max's sincerity. "All right already, Max," she laughed. "I forgive you—and from now on, can we just pretend that we met here in Cambodia, and forget what happened back in that other life?"

"*Absolutamente,*" Max said. "Here's to getting to know each other, from the beginning. Because there are more important things than the past." Max's voice was deep and cultured. Although a slight Latin accent was apparent, his diction and grammar were impeccable, if sometimes overly formal.

"*Es verdad,*" she agreed, picking up her menu. "Food and drink chief among them." The hovering waiter approached, politely taking Lindsay's order for gazpacho and fresh orange juice.

"And for you, monsieur?" he said, turning to Max.

"I'll start with a garden salad," Max said, "and then please bring plain white rice with steamed vegetables. And two iced lemon juices as well."

As the waiter moved away, Max responded to Lindsay's look of questioning surprise. "Yes, it's true. I've even astonished myself. I never planned to become a vegetarian, but after working with so many endangered species when I was on the Brazilian project, I just couldn't look myself—or a dead animal—in the eye anymore, at least not as a potential meal. I find I'm quite content with good vegetarian food."

Lindsay's curiosity was piqued. "Even here in Cambodia?" she asked. "I've heard some vegetarians complain about not being able to find enough protein."

"What? How could they say that?" Max said, serious for once. "There's tofu, plenty of other soy foods—sprouted or fermented. I haven't had any problem at all."

"And you said you'd been here how long?" Lindsay began, determined to find a weak spot in Max's self-assurance.

"Just two weeks, *querida,* so laugh if you like. But I've been a vegetarian for six years now, and believe me, those years have not been spent in places rife with gourmet vegetarian restaurants. How about you, Lindsay, do you enjoy the Phnom Penh restaurant scene?"

Lindsay's response, to her dismay as she remembered the conversation later that afternoon, included an explanation of how distant her home behind the tile factory was from the expatriate restaurants, how difficult it could be to get back and forth—and exactly how to find the house.

As the waiter reappeared, placing the cold tomato and cucumber soup in front of Lindsay and a plate of artistically blended greens in front of Max, Lindsay felt a stab of apprehension. Surely Max knew she didn't have the authority to commit UNOIC's support for the park? Or, as Officer-In-Charge during David Bullford's absence, was it her responsibility to make such a commitment? She knew, instinctively, that Max was about to broach this subject, and she rushed to forestall him. "So, Max, do you stay in touch with the rest of your polo team?" she asked.

"Oh, one or two of the ponies," he said, grinning. "But Lindsay, we are not here to talk about our mutual past. Or whether we should have had more of one. It's time to get down to business."

"How ominous," Lindsay said, keeping her tone light. "But carry on if you must. I'm all ears."

Max, it turned out, could not eat, even vegetarian food, and talk at the same time. He laid down his fork, rubbed a hand across his forehead as if polishing his words, and began, his voice low-pitched and pulsing with sincerity. It may have been a pre-packaged spiel, but he had it down pat.

"Lindsay, as you so correctly pointed out, I haven't been here that long. But there are a few things I am convinced of. The first is that this country needs help, needs to save itself—from itself! If Cambodia doesn't act fast to set aside natural reserves, parks, conservancies—whatever you want to call them—its botanical, biological, mineral, and every other kind of natural wealth will just disappear. Not because it'll be used up, either—it'll be stolen. I've never worked in a place where there were so many people with the money to give bribes, and so many with the willingness or the desperation to take them."

Lindsay looked out the window, focusing on the crimson plumage of the parrot perched in the rattan cage swinging from the verandah. She knew what he was talking about. But how could this man expect her to focus on the damn park if he kept looking into her eyes like that? Max had now stopped speaking, apparently waiting for her to turn back to face him. "Keep talking, Max, I'm listening," Lindsay said flatly.

And he did. "Another thing I know," Max said firmly, "is that this can be done. It can be done, done right, done successfully. I've made it happen before, in a political environment that was just as murky as Cambodia's.

"The third thing I know—and Lindsay, this is where you come in—is that, even with the full support of the King, the park cannot be developed without UNOIC. The King is just as aware of this as I am, and he will not proceed until he is assured that your position will be one of support that includes funds and technical assistance, not only your good offices." Max laid his hands flat on either side of his untouched salad. "So. What do you think? Can we work together on this?"

Although sincerity and commitment had echoed throughout his speech, Lindsay felt that Max's words had been overly idealistic, even naïve. "Max, what you've just said sounds like the *au jus*," she said. "But where's the beef?"

Max had just begun to season his plate of vegetables—fresh carrots with sprouts and cabbage—and Lindsay watched his face for a response. But Max was lost in his efforts to sway her decision.

"Lindsay, please. There's plenty of time for us to get into the details, to plan our approach and map out our strategies. Before that happens, though, I have to know that we're on the same team."

"You're right, of course, Max. I'm perfectly aware that there are many issues and details that can only be addressed by the experts. But my qualms are more basic. Have you even been to the northeast? Where is this reserve to be located, precisely? What is the area being used for now—and who lives there? How will the conversion to a nature reserve affect the local people and their economy?" Max had again stopped eating, and was leaning back in his chair looking at her with surprise. Yesterday's hours on the internet, and the time spent reviewing the documents Stewart had sent, had been invested to good purpose. She was on a roll. "What is a park, anyway? I mean, a park to you may be a place where *everything* is protected. But what is it to the King?

"And the biggest, most basic question of all—who stands to profit from this enterprise? What kind of motivations are behind this proposal? Who supports it, and why? For example, what could a park mean for the General Quartet?" Lindsay's question referred to the four army generals who were widely believed to be the real powers behind the Cambodian throne.

"Lindsay, you—" Max began, but she cut him off, afraid she would lose her train of thought.

"Look, Max, maybe Sihanouk thinks a park is a giant Disneyland. Remember, he did come up with that revolutionary notion that the entire country could be declared an international monument or something. Or maybe those generals think a park would be the perfect cover for logging the country bald. I don't know! But I do know it's naïve not to realize that every person in this country has their own agenda, and that every one of them is looking out first and foremost for their own main chance!"

"Lindsay, Lindsay, *cálmate!*" Max said soothingly, and Lindsay realized she'd been speaking too loud and too fast. "You're right. It's clear you have some ideas and some local knowledge that are going to be a big help to me. All I'm asking for now is something general, in writing, that commits UNOIC's support in principle to the idea of a reserve area for the purpose of conserving Cambodia's natural resources in the northeast. There is no need for something complicated." Max paused, considering whether his next words would offend Lindsay, and produce an effect the opposite of his intentions, or whether he might win her over by giving her the chance to circumvent UNOIC's infamous bureaucracy. He decided to give it a try and appeal to her spontaneity. "We don't need one of those interminable expert missions that take six months to conduct studies—six months spent lazing around the pool at the Hotel Cambodiana—and then submit ambiguous and lengthy reports that lack conclusions and are never read, anyway!"

But Max had misjudged Lindsay. She was, after all, trying hard to justify the trust David had placed in her by naming her Officer-In-Charge. "I think this project is a good example of how important expert missions can be," she said, "and speaking of putting things in writing, Max, I can't do anything until I see something substantive from your side. Like a written proposal that specifies exactly what you plan to do and exactly what you are asking from UNOIC to make it happen."

Max blew a dismissive puff of air through pursed lips. "Spoken like a true acolyte of bureaucracy, Lindsay."

Lindsay was nettled. "Look, Max, I may not be a career diplomat, but even I know that no international agency is going to even comment on, much less commit to, a proposal that isn't written, isn't detailed, doesn't even exist outside of an announcement at a party, for God's sake! Even if it is the King's very own brainstorm."

Max, too, was no longer calm. "Lindsay, don't you get it? I can't go ahead—hell, the King won't *let* me go ahead—without your support. All I'm asking is that we come to a preliminary agreement on the vision, what we aspire to and hope to achieve. That's what UNOIC is for, and what it does best! I've got to have your commitment from the beginning. And that means now."

"Look, Max, I'm sorry if I sound overly cautious." Lindsay recognized the genuine sincerity in Max's voice and wanted to respond in kind. "Personally, I do care about conservation, a lot. I've worked on environmental and ecological projects myself, and I know how important they are. But there are a lot of important questions that need to be answered, and this is not a decision for a junior officer who is just a temporary OIC. I'm sorry."

"You and I are going to work on answering those questions, Lindsay, and I know we can do it if we work together," Max said, his dark eyes riveted on Lindsay's hazel ones as he again reached across the table and gripped her hand. "And I can't tell you what it means to me that you are making at least a personal commitment to this project."

Lindsay gently extricated her hand, not letting her reluctance to do so, or the effect his touch was having on her, show in her face. This is dangerous, she thought, her instincts rising in defense as a quote from somewhere sprang to her mind. Was it the romance of possible danger that attracted her to Max? Or the danger of a possible romance? She knew that Max wanted something from her, but she wasn't sure what it was that he wanted—or how far he would go to get it.

"I didn't say that," she objected. "I said I believe in conservation, not that I'm personally committed to this project. But anyway, Max," she temporized, "at least we've made a start. Tell you what. I'll start putting together some initial points that we'll need clarification on before there can be any discussion of UNOIC support. In the meantime, you can start working up a more formal proposal. By then, my boss should be back from Manila."

Max leaned back, tipping his chair onto its back legs, his intensity vanished. He pulled out his wallet, dug out a card, and placed it squarely on the table in front of her. "Send your parameters to me at the palace," he said, the sultry smile back on his face. "Coffee? Princess Juliette tells me it's the best in town. Or do you need to get back to your office work?"

But Lindsay was still thinking about Norodom Park. "You know, Max, David may not even assign me to work on this. Even if he does support the idea. And I can't discuss it knowledgeably with him, anyway, when I haven't even been to the northeast."

"I haven't let that stop me, have I, *querida*? But you're right— we must go, both of us. Shall I arrange a trip for us next week? We can use the King's Cessna, I am sure."

"I don't know, Max. Maybe we should just wait and let David deal with it."

"Lindsay, don't you know what a great opportunity this is? And not just for your UN career. Have you ever seen a virgin rain forest?" Lindsay was shaking her head, so he continued, his voice passionate with his appreciation for the natural beauty. "The trees tower miles above your head, while down below you walk in a world of green light, like swimming in a mountain lake. Everything's bigger than life—the leaves, the flowers, the smells. I tell you, seeing a rainforest for the first time is like falling in love. You remember that, I suppose? Besides," he added, his voice falling almost to a whisper, "it could give us a second chance."

"Planning a trip, are we?" interrupted a voice, and a dark head turned to face them from the table just around the corner. "Perhaps you will also invite the French military attaché?"

Max's back was to André, but his impatient expression made it clear that he recognized the voice. "This is a private conversation, Major," he said stiffly, anger flooding his face as he stood to his feet.

Although Max was several inches taller than the Frenchman, who rose to his feet as well when Lindsay stepped over to stand beside his table, the Major was not discomfited. Not in the least. "You must remember, *mon ami*, that, in Cambodia, private conversations should never be conducted in public places. But I ask your pardon. May I present my friend, Madame Solange Dumaurier? Solange, I present to you Mademoiselle Lindsay March, the UNOIC Public Information Officer, and Señor Maximiliano Vega y Ortega, Special Advisor to the King for the conservation project." As the trio shook hands, André added, "Perhaps we may all lunch together one day, for friendship sake." His smile was pleasant, but his eyes were not friendly at all.

Lindsay was surprised by a sudden surge of jealousy. "A pleasure to meet you again, Major," she said quickly. "And now we must be going. For UNOIC, the lunch hour is over, I'm afraid."

As they rounded the stucco wall outside the restaurant, Max took Lindsay's arm. "Lindsay, I know you won't take kindly to this, but please listen, just for a moment."

"Of course I'll listen, Max. I'll even take your advice, if it's any good."

"Major Balfour is not what he seems, Lindsay. I know he's charming, but he opposes the park and the King's efforts to preserve the environment. Balfour even attempted to dissuade the King from appointing me—he told him I was a worthless playboy, or some such lie. As if the King would consider that an insult! Anyway, I'm sure he has reasons for opposing the park—and I'm just as sure that those reasons have nothing to do with what's best for Cambodia."

Lindsay gave Max's arm a squeeze. "I'm not that naïve, Max, no matter how I may look," she assured him. "Believe me, I don't take *anyone* at face value." Her narrowed eyes made it clear that she was including Max himself in that policy. "By the way," she added as Max climbed into the car where his palace-liveried driver waited, "the northeast is a pretty big area. Where exactly does the King propose to site the park, and which province will it be in?"

"In Ratanakiri, Lindsay," Max said, waving from the window as his car sped away down the tree-lined street.

CHAPTER FIVE
WEDNESDAY, MAY 19, PART II

O n the way back to her office after lunch, Lindsay couldn't keep the thoughts and memories of Max from chasing around in her head. She wasn't at all sure she could trust Max as a colleague, but being around him made her feel alive. And hadn't his arrogance mellowed at least a little in the hour they had spent together? He'd even pressed her into exercising her rusty Spanish on their way out to the street, a curiously intimate exchange that made her laugh aloud.

The office felt frigid after the sultry heat outside. Dampness from the sweat that had trickled down her back felt cold, and she shivered. "Hello, Lindsay. You got a lot of messages. You want them now?" Bopha said when Lindsay walked past her desk.

"Sure, thanks." She leaned against the edge of Bopha's desk, taking the small pile and checking the names. Her messages were

45

more interesting these days, with David off in Manila. Two embassies, a journalist, an under secretary of state. Ordinarily, David delegated the more boring tasks to her—check on who was sponsoring land mine awareness, or review a request for a seminar on polio immunization—but he talked to the major players himself. During his short absence, she had garnered a much broader understanding of UNOIC's work, and she'd met a cast of bigger players than those in supporting roles with whom she normally dealt.

But her mind had wandered back to Max. "Bopha, I read through our budget documents this morning. Did you realize that we have funds already approved for a conservation project?" Lindsay said.

"I didn't really know, until you explained what park is to me," she answered. "But I remember from Bunna." Bunna was David's secretary, on vacation during David's absence. "You know, sometimes we talk, because Bunna needs help on her English, and asks me to help at what her problem is."

Contemplating Bopha helping Bunna with English was interesting. "I know that the money was from last year, when UNTAC wanted to protect the forests. But they never use it." Bopha said.

The office door opened slightly. "Bopha?" a male voice said softly.

Bopha leaned over to see who was there. "*Om!*" she squealed, laughing. "*Ot juep yu hauy nah!*"

Lindsay turned to see André Balfour—again. As Bopha jumped up to greet her guest, she said, "Lindsay, it is André, my friend I was told you about. I have not seen him for so long."

"Uncle André is it?" Lindsay said, *om* being part of her limited Khmer vocabulary. She remembered Bopha's description of the Frenchman as her "good friend," and studied the two of them for clues to the nature of their friendship. Was Bopha looking at all embarrassed?

André just laughed. "Not really," he said. "But you know how complicated Cambodian relations are."

"I can't say that I do, really. But how can we help you? Did you have some indigestion perhaps?" Lindsay said. "We may have some antacid..."

"Oh no, I had a wonderful meal. You know we French, we eat anything. I wanted to ask Bopha if she could leave a little early today." He seemed totally at ease.

"Considering her adventure on the river this weekend, I think she deserves an early afternoon at the very least. You heard about the boat already, perhaps? You seem to be keeping up with everything."

"*Mais no!*" André said, then pointed his finger at Bopha. "Have you been riding in boats without telling me?" She giggled in response.

"I'll just slip into my office. You two go ahead, and have a great time." Lindsay moved into her own office, resisting the urge to slam the door behind her. Inside, she grinned sheepishly, and applauded herself for recognizing the complete irrationality of her response for what it was.

"Thank you, Lindsay!" Bopha called from the outer office. And Lindsay found herself feeling, for the second time that day, a rush of jealousy on seeing André Balfour with another woman. *What an idiot*, she told herself, as she began the long and arduous process of returning phone calls. Her pleasure over lunch had flown right out the window. *Nothing is as it seems in Cambodia*, she reminded herself. Even the French military attaché could have a liaison with a Cambodian woman without reproach, evidently. But Bopha was bound to be hurt, and that made Lindsay angry.

Her thoughts were interrupted by a brusque "Hello," as her first phone call was answered.

"Is this UNICEF?" she asked.

"Yes, it is!" the voice said, sounding delighted that she'd guessed correctly.

"Could I please speak to Roger Honold?" Lindsay said.

"Who is calling please?"

"Lindsay, from the UNOIC Public Information Office."

"How do you spell that, please?"

"L. I. N. D."

"T?"

"No, *d* as in darling-sweet-heart," Lindsay said. The receptionist laughed. Part of the fun of speaking on the phone in Phnom Penh was coming up with replacements for the military's stodgy Alpha-Bravo-Charlie phonetic alphabet.

Getting through four phone calls took over an hour. By that time, Lindsay's good mood was restored, although her curiosity remained piqued. How did André Balfour know her assistant anyway, she wondered. They seemed to be pretty close—could she trust Bopha not to share UNOIC information with him? And why didn't Bopha ever call *her* by a familial term, which implied a certain intimacy between people? And, given André Balfour's strong feelings about the project, wasn't it a little strange that Bopha didn't understand what a park was? Maybe they didn't spend their time together talking? Lindsay groaned, disgusted at the turn her thoughts had taken, and returned to the pile of papers waiting in her in-box.

***

Highway 1, in spite of recent widening, remained a maelstrom of traffic: dust-covered taxis returning from the Vietnamese border jostled *remarque* drivers balancing precarious loads in their motorcycle-powered flat carts, their merchandise ranging from stacks of wooden planks to squealing pigs to whole villages. The tinny horns of heavily overloaded trucks shrieked interminably as they plowed their way through the smaller vehicles; the more sonorous tones of late model sedans with red license plates and darkened windows demanded precedence for high-ranking government officials, their demands enforced by armed bodyguards riding abreast on Honda motorcycles. And this was only a Wednesday. Weekends were worse.

The rice fields glowed with the last light of the setting sun, which lent a bizarre serenity to the chaos of the road. Bopha watched André drive, her face troubled. Every now and then the traffic lightened enough for him to glance over at her.

"What?" he finally said.

"I am just wondering, *Om.*"

"Wondering what?"

"Why before you never let me tell Lindsay about you."

He sighed. After a few moments, he said, "It is not her business. She doesn't need to know about me."

"But she is my boss. And my friend."

"That's good."

"I think you would like her," Bopha said.

"Fine. But my business and her business don't mix. I don't want there to be any connection. And I don't want to put you in the middle of something that could be a problem for you."

Bopha shook her head, but said nothing. Compared to refugee flights, the Khmer Rouge murder of her family members, and her cross-border smuggling endeavors, this situation hardly seemed a problem.

André considered his words. "Not that you would have any trouble, but I just want there not to be any... complications."

"Is this about your work, *Om,* what you are trying to do in Cambodia?" Bopha said.

"Yes. But please, *kmuey*, don't ask me any more about it. I beg you."

Because André had addressed her as his niece, Bopha bowed her head in acquiescence, turning to watch the deepening color of the evening sky. Within moments they had arrived at their destination, Hotel L'Imprevu.

Her first visit here, Bopha had been completely abashed. The place was a well-known weekend getaway, and foreigners flocked to the restaurant, rented the air-conditioned bungalows, and brought their children to enjoy the rarity of a swimming pool filled with clean water. But on weekdays, L'Imprevu was quiet, the guests tending to be those who sought discretion, most often western men bringing local girlfriends.

Neither André nor Bopha lingered at the restaurant or poolside patio. Bopha disappeared into the dressing room, getting into the most concealing swimsuit she had been able to find in the market and tucking her thick hair into a beflowered lavender swimming cap. Then, donning the goggles that André had brought her from

France, she returned to the pool. By the time she reached it, André was already in the water.

"*Alors*, my little fish. First, you are going to work on treading water today."

She nodded shortly, and moved into the deep end, her movements still clumsy, despite now having had more than five swimming lessons. She had longed to swim her entire life, but until André, had never thought it possible. In Cambodia, if you didn't learn to swim as a toddler, you never learned.

André had been patient and careful never to touch her, which she deeply appreciated. She trusted him completely. In Bopha's mind, André was a benevolent deity right up there with Jesus and the Buddha.

"Don't splash your face so much!" André was telling her. "Do it like this." He demonstrated, and Bopha slowed her arm motions, keeping afloat.

"I heard from Narong yesterday," André said, ducking another splattering of water. Bopha's brother, who now lived with his wife and son in France, had been André's interpreter three years before. André had rewarded his service by helping him get a scholarship to the university in Lyons. "He got put on the day shift. He seems happier."

"I heard too. He says now he can see his family again." Bopha said.

"So, how do you like working with Lindsay, Bopha?"

"A lot," she said, concentrating on her strokes.

"Did she tell you about King Sihanouk's announcement at the reception?"

Bopha nodded.

"Well, what did she think about it?"

"She is not sure. She is trying to understand it more."

"How is she doing that?"

"I thought you didn't want me to get into a problem," Bopha said, scowling and turning away to cling to the side of the pool.

André swam to her side, keeping a polite distance. "You're right, *kmuey*. I'm just curious. She is very young for her post, you know."

Bopha wasn't sure she about this, but did not reply.

"Do you know the man she went to lunch with?" André asked.

" No. I think his name is Mack. *Om*, what is wrong?"

André hesitated, then said, "*Kmuey*, Lindsay must not trust that man. His name is Max, by the way. She doesn't understand what she is getting into."

Bopha was reminded of the fortuneteller and shivered.

"How can I tell her that, *Om*?"

"Maybe you shouldn't tell her; just watch out for her. If anything happens, you must let me know."

"But how will I know what thing to tell you, *Om*?"

"Just anything to do with that man, or the park."

"If you really think it will be good for Lindsay," Bopha said uncertainly.

"It is very important, *cheri*," he said, and she wondered at his seriousness. *Om* André was hardly ever serious. "And I hope it will never involve Lindsay at all."

They swam for a few more minutes, then climbed from the water and toweled off. Bopha returned from the dressing room in a loose t-shirt and flowered sarong for the next part of their ritual—a mango smoothie, specialty of the house.

As they sipped the creamy shakes, Bopha wondered how to break through André's preoccupation. She decided to talk more about Lindsay. "Lindsay is special, *Om*." She hesitated, and sensing his attentiveness, continued. "Sometimes I think she lives in another world, where everything is all right, and all the people are good." She told André about her visit to the fortuneteller. She swallowed and promised solemnly, "I will help to protect her."

André's smile was tender. "I think you are a good friend to Lindsay, *kmuey*. She is lucky to have you."

As they chatted over the remains of their shakes, one of the L'Imprevu staff came hesitantly to their table, holding a sheet of folded paper gingerly between a thumb and forefinger. He handed it to André. "*Pour vous, monsieur*. They said they tried to reach you by your phone, but no answer. Pardon to molest you, *monsieur*." André looked upset as he read the note, and Bopha grew even more concerned.

"Bad news, I'm afraid," André said, crumpling the note with tense fingers. "It seems I have some unexpected business in the city tonight. We must return to Phnom Penh immediately."

CHAPTER SIX
SATURDAY, MAY 22

Muffled laughter echoed the gentle lapping of the Mekong against the sides of the floating casino, a recycled cruise liner anchored offshore just downriver from the Royal Palace. The evening air wafted a gentle breeze perfumed with the night-blooming jasmine that flowered beside the river where couples walked hand-in-hand, their heads bent together for whispered intimacies. Above the river, the sky shimmered with the light of a million stars. Down below, the twinkling lights from the ship's upper decks reflected on the dark surface of the smoothly flowing river. Altogether, it was a dark and entirely romantic setting.

Inside the casino, things were not so pretty. No longer muffled, laughter brayed from the throats of drunken gamblers. Loudest of all were the four men seated in the corner of the casino's exclusive VIP salon.

The room was a decorator's nightmare—purple velvet swags at the windows, or where the windows would have been if they hadn't been covered. To protect the privacy of casino guests, all but six inches at the top of each window had been swathed with matching velvet. Another pragmatic move on the part of the casino management was the carpeting, a dark flowered pattern in low, indoor/outdoor pile. Easy to clean after the nightly spills and heavings of drunken players. The chairs, upholstered in emerald brocade, were spindly and inadequate to support the girth of some guests, or the gymnastics of others. The salon's ceiling was upholstered, too, in the same velvet brocade as the chairs, and crystal and gold chandeliers lighted the tables. Near the entrance, where a black marble bar stretched across the end of the room, a waiter was polishing the already shiny surface, carefully keeping his eyes averted from the gaming tables.

In the furthest corner, isolated from other guests, a lone table stood on a slightly elevated dais. A nearly empty bottle of Hennessey VSOP perched like a centerpiece on the intricately carved Chinese table. At the table, surrounded by a blue haze of cigarette smoke, sat four men. Although all four of the flushed faces smiled, and all four men joined in the bursts of ribald laughter, a discerning observer would have had no difficulty identifying the leader of this, the General Quartet.

Three of the men could have been brothers—the same brilliantined black hair, the same solid paunches sheathed in Hawaiian flowered shirts in varying garish hues, heavy gold neck chains dangling images of the Buddha, tiger's teeth, and other good luck charms. And the same aura of deference toward the fourth man, a man with a very different air about him indeed.

General Som Sak, his back facing the corner of the room, measured his fellow generals through narrowed eyes. His spare body, nattily dressed in khaki slacks and short-sleeved black broadcloth button-down shirt, coiled insolently in the velvet padding of the chair. The overhead lights outlined his close-clipped gray hair and accentuated the cruel angles of his face. His only movement was in the slender fingers that steadily caressed the stone of the ring on his right hand.

The waiter approached the table with a deferential stoop. "Generals?" he inquired softly, gesturing at the bottle. The three shiny black heads turned in response, each man's expression and hand motions managing to convey annoyance at the interruption while signaling that yes, more cognac was certainly in order. Throughout this exchange, Som Sak stared at the ceiling, his thin lips compressed. Clutching the now empty bottle, the waiter scuttled off like a soldier returning from enemy lines.

"General, how did our French friend like your little gift?" inquired General Thy Beng, the shortest and roundest of the four men. Thy Beng's condescension toward the waiter had softened magically into an oozing obsequiousness. His predilection for diamond rings was reflected in the glitters that shot across the ceiling as he motioned vaguely to the outer room, where fifty of Phnom Penh's most beautiful women sat in folding chairs, numbered placards hanging from cords strung around their necks, waited to be selected as a gentleman's companion for the evening.

"Ah yes, our good friend André ... an interesting man. I'm not sure how much of a *man*, however," mused General Sak, contemplating his glass as he swirled its amber contents dangerously close to the rim. A sardonic smile flitted across his face, and he spoke in a hoarse, uninflected monotone, his voice barely above a whisper. "I sent another two gifts from Madam Nhu to his villa just last night, to thank him for his...future assistance. But it seems he had no use for them."

Som Sak's companions greeted this opportunity to demonstrate their allegiance with alacrity. One of the trio, General Rith Ken, posited some graphically described anatomical explanations for the Frenchman's lack of interest, while General Thy Beng suggested that perhaps the Frenchman preferred boys, setting off another round of snickers and snorts.

General Som Sak, however, merely raised one graying eyebrow. "No," he whispered. "After he refused the first girl, I sent twin boys. He sent them away, too."

While Som Sak was speaking, General Boon Chu began to fidget, eager to speak but not daring to interrupt his commander. He continued to squirm while Som Sak took a long swig from his glass, then, unable to restrain himself any longer, he burst out, "I imagine he prefers the sharp-nose women. You recall his approach to that UNOIC woman at the palace reception? Or...maybe he is going after a *khun ying*, like the South American," he added. His use of the title, reserved for female members of the Cambodian nobility, was meant to remind his table mates of Max's friendship with Princess Sovannalok.

Without replying, or even acknowledging Boon Chu's theory, General Som Sak snapped his fingers and turned his face back to the ceiling. When the waiter approached the table, he whispered tersely, not deigning to look at the frightened man, "Tell the security guards that General Sak is expecting a French visitor, a Monsieur André Balfour. Inform me when he arrives, but do not allow him into this room until I give the order. Delay him, let him become a little impatient. Do you understand?"

The waiter bowed and backed away from the General without speaking, his eyes glued to the huge ruby glinting on the fourth finger of Som Sak's slender hand. Flawless and blood red, it measured at least 20 carats. What such a stone could mean to his family—they would live like kings! Glancing up from the mesmerizing stone, he caught Som Sak's eye and turned in terror, scurrying away to do the General's bidding.

A blast of raucous laughter followed the waiter across the room, out the windows, and through the soft night air to the ears of Major André Balfour, who was crossing the causeway that led to the floating casino. The causeway, constructed to entice those foolish enough to expect the goddess of luck to be waiting for them inside the casino doors, was decorated with intricately carved native hardwoods and inlaid balustrades and lighted by palm torches held aloft by young men in traditional court dress.

Stopping between two of the torchbearers to light a small cigar, André leaned for a moment against the sturdy railing and listened to the raucous merriment wafting down from the casino's upper deck. Upstream, a flotilla of four tiny Vietnamese houseboats had anchored for the night. André watched the dim light of their oil lamps and listened to the voices echoing across the water as he reached back to massage the tense muscles of his shoulders and neck, willing himself to relax and breathing deeply to sharpen his wits for the coming confrontation. Without further pause, he flexed his shoulders, wheeled sharply, and continued toward the ship. The causeway ended in a series of broad steps leading to a carved dragon curling on itself to form the entry to the casino.

Striding into the dragon's maw, his heels clicking on the glossy polished wood floor, André stepped into the elevator, which rose smoothly to the casino's fifth floor. As the door slid open, he shuddered. Swallowing to disguise his disdain for the decor, André looked up to find a diminutive security guard blocking his way. "Please sir, you must deposit money before play."

A look of annoyance flashed briefly across André's face. "Please tell General Som Sak that Major André Balfour has arrived," he said.

"No money, no enter," said the security guard. His voice was flat and bored, but his eyes were alert. The attempts of westerners to play tourist in the high-rolling VIP salon were becoming tiresome.

André was not impressed. "I am here as General Som Sak's guest," he repeated, his steely gaze fixed on the guard's face. "I presume you would not want to upset the General by delaying my arrival."

While the security guard blocked André's path, the nervous waiter rushed to inform the General. "Give him a few minutes. Then bring him to me," said General Som Sak negligently.

So it was with some surprise that General Sak looked up at that moment to see André approaching the table. The General turned angrily to berate the waiter, only to see the tail of his jacket disappearing through the door to the kitchen.

"*Bon soir, mes generals,*" André greeted the General Quartet, shaking hands with each of the four men with studied formality. "*Mon Dieu,* surely the management here must learn that Asian antiques and European modern cannot be mixed, at least not with success," he said. "But you are not playing? I came anticipating some good winnings tonight. I find I have a need for extra cash.

Perhaps you, General Som Sak, can help, *ne c'est pas?*" André joined the men in friendly laughter at his joke, but the laughter did not soften the metallic blue of his eyes.

"We were waiting for you, my friend. We, ah, did not expect you quite so soon. But before we begin, you must join us for a drink." Continuing his toadying to Som Sak, Boon Chu's too-loud voice echoed off the walls as he shifted away to make room for the chair the waiter carried to the table and placed beside Som Sak.

The conversation continued with polite exchanges about health and family until André tired of formalities. Clearing his throat, he turned to the General. "That was quite a gift you sent, yesterday, *mon general*. Exceptionally beautiful. All in all, very tempting."

Identical smirks decorated the faces of the three sycophants as André continued. "However, as before, I must request that you send no more such gifts, male or female. As I have explained to you, such gifts could threaten my cover as the French military attaché. There are many with agendas of their own who would wish to damage my reputation to have me removed from the embassy.

General Boon Chu winked at Som Sak, reaching over to clap André on the shoulder. "Are you sure that is the only reason, my friend? Or could it be that you don't want to upset a certain sharp-nose lady, eh?" he guffawed. "The pretty little UNOIC girl you were so friendly with at the reception, perhaps? Have you tasted her— *ooomph*."

Som Sak had discreetly knocked Boon Chu's elbow, preventing him from completing his sentence. Recovering his drink as it teetered on the edge of the table, Boon Chu fell silent, and his eyes watched Som Sak warily. The moment passed, and all four faces shifted back to André.

"To business, *mon generals*." André said, sitting back to watch the eyes of his tablemates narrow as they straightened in their chairs and leaned closer to the table. Although there were no occupied tables near them, he lowered his voice before continuing. "I think it is safe to say that the opening of the nature reserve is now imminent, judging from the response to His Majesty's speech at the royal reception. It would appear that our efforts to prevent this were unsuccessful. Although," here he stopped and smiled at each face around the table, "we certainly did our best, and no one should be blamed for this failure." The nervous laughter of the sub-generals was full of relief.

"I'm afraid that the tourists and bureaucrats that will soon be overrunning the northeast will make it very difficult to keep our operations under cover, perhaps to continue them at all," André said obliquely. "But all this really means is that we must find a way to profit from the new situation at even greater levels." For over a year, André had worked diligently to build trust with these men, to establish his credibility as a greedy renegade diplomat untouched by morality wherever there was money to be made.

"You are right, my friend," said General Rith Ken. "The arrival of that South American piece of pig shit is an unfortunate complication. I cannot understand why the King is so taken with him. He has saved some insignificantly tiny speck of the Amazon jungle. So what? But, if we argue too vehemently against saving the forest, the King is sure to become suspicious."

"*Merde*," André interjected. "How did the bastard get so much influence with the King in such a short time? Who is he?"

André's question brought the conversation to a momentary halt, then General Som Sak spoke. "We will know soon," he said laconically. "A… friend of mine is getting close to him, gaining his confidence. Then we will know what the South American's real agenda is. Or whether he is that rare and even more dangerous of creatures, a genuine environmentalist."

The light of the chandeliers glinted on the oiled hair of the three underlings as they nodded their agreement. As André sipped his cognac, the generals began to chat amongst themselves in Khmer. André managed a look of boredom, disguising his fluency in their language. It was a simple strategy, but it worked, allowing him to glean information that would otherwise have been unavailable to him.

His eyes on his drink, he listened closely as the generals continued their conjecturing. Was Maximiliano a genuine conservationist? they wondered aloud. Or was he, perhaps, fronting for a Colombian drug baron eager to compete with them for the growing Asian market. Here, the South American could avoid the obstacles put in place in his own country by the imperialistic Americans. How would his involvement damage the beautiful simplicity of their operation—bringing tribal women and children to Phnom Penh and exporting the best of them on to Thailand, where they were exchanged for high quality and high potency drugs. Most of the drugs were then sold to overseas buyers, although some methamphetamines were reserved for sale to loggers and miners in Cambodia's northeast. Not only did this create a guaranteed market, it also completed the circuit, as the villagers, craving the drugs, were eager to sell sisters and daughters to feed their addictions.

Would the park, the generals wondered, increase the visibility of the tribal people to the point that it would interfere with their access to this unlimited wealth? André's discipline was tested to its limit when he heard the hoarse whisper of General Som Sak. "Here is the key to our success. The South American does not yet know it—perhaps the King also does not know it—but the King's plans will call for relocating all tribal peoples in the entire province inside the boundaries of the park. The King will like the idea of creating an anthropological as well as an ecological preserve. In practice, it will give us a much greater selection, and much easier access."

When their conversation had begun to wander, André summoned the waiter—a different one, this time—to order more cognac. Turning back to the table, he recommenced the conversation in French.

"So, what shall we do? How will we secure our operations?" he asked, ignoring the sub-generals and looking directly at General Som Sak.

General Som Sak smiled thinly. Before speaking, he reached into a front pocket for a pair of wire-rimmed glasses. Slipping them on, he said, "We must think not of 'how' but of 'whom.' As a military man, you will appreciate the ingenuity of my contingency plan. If we cannot stop the park, we will control it. I will ensure that an appropriate director is selected for the nature reserve."

"And have you made that selection, *mon general*?" André smiled, playing straight man for the General.

Som Sak tilted his chair onto its back legs and lifted his face to the ceiling, replying to André's question without looking in his direction. "Is it not a fortunate coincidence that a certain young man has just received an advanced degree in Tropical Forestry from the Java Institute of Environmental Sciences? And is it not fortunate that the young man returned to his homeland from his studies just two weeks ago? And is it not certainly appropriate to the mood of the country for a well-qualified Khmer to assume this position, rather than resorting to the humiliation of appointing yet another *barang*?

"And," Som Sak continued, bringing his chair to the floor with a sharp thud and laying his hands flat on the table top, his fingers outspread. Som Sak's whisper was loud in the silence of the room as he finished, his voice still expressionless, "Is it not indeed fortuitous that the young man in question is the nephew, the adopted son, in fact, of the General Som Sak!"

André's smile was forced. "Fortunate indeed, if it can be arranged..." André hesitated, anticipating the general's reply.

"It has been arranged," the general was announcing, when he was interrupted by a flurry of activity. Turning to face the door, André saw Juliette Sovannalok sail into the room, one arm resting on the expensive sleeve of Maximiliano Vega y Ortega's tailor-made silk jacket, the other fastened tightly to the elbow of one of the minor princes that abounded in the upper reaches of Khmer society. A small entourage floated in their wake, as the casino's general manager, bent almost double to show his respect, ushered them into the room.

The five men seated at the corner table rose instantly to their feet, the generals saluting smartly. A member of the Princess' party jogged her elbow, alerting her to the greeting coming from the darkened corner of the room. Her glance slid over them without interest, but her eyes lit up when she spied André standing in their midst.

"Ah *mon ami*, André!" she cried, advancing and kissing him airily on both cheeks. "You did not tell me you would be playing this evening! Why did you not invite me? You know you must not keep secrets from me," she cried. Juliette's eyes were glittering, but it was not the glitter of coquetry. Max, standing beside her, winced at the huskiness of her voice. Juliette's approach to men was that of a savage collecting scalps.

Before André could reply, Juliette continued. "General Sak, of course, I know," she said, focusing her smile on his face, "but who are your companions?"

"My dear Princess, I am shocked that you, the most beautiful woman in Phnom Penh, do not know these important gentlemen, all generals in His Majesty's Royal Armed Forces."

Juliette responded brightly, "Oh, but you are right, *mon ami*. It is despicable that I do not know the valiant heroes of our motherland. I blame this on you, André. You are after all the French military attaché, and certainly I am a French citizen. You should keep me informed. You will make it up to me!" she commanded, looking directly into André's eyes. Without waiting for his response, she turned to face the generals, still standing around the table. "May I have the honor of your acquaintance?"

General Som Sak stepped back, observing the reaction of his underlings. The evening's consumption of Hennessy, in combination with the gentle movement of the ship, left the three sub-generals swaying from side to side like a macabre chorus line. But when they seemed unable to tear their eyes from her deeply plunging neckline, unable even to provide self-introductions, Juliette laughed. "Perhaps some other time, gentlemen, when you are feeling more talkative," she said, turning abruptly to face her entourage. "And now for a little baccarat. I feel lucky tonight!"

"I, too, must soon take my leave," André said quickly, as the generals resumed their seats. "However, let me give you something to consider. I have heard that the palace, through the South American, will arrange a tour for UNOIC as a first step in winning their support for the park. The members of that first tour will play a major role in determining how the project proceeds. I suggest you consider who should accompany them."

"My nephew will go," Som Sak said quickly. "It should remain just a small group, this first visit. The South American, the UNOIC woman, and my nephew." He stopped, his narrow lips curving in dangerous amusement at the words he spoke next. "It will be a congenial group. My nephew has a certain...affinity for beautiful women."

"As you wish, *mon general*," André replied. "I suggest you make the arrangements quickly. According to my sources, the visit will take place in the coming week."

CHAPTER SEVEN
MONDAY, MAY 24

Yes, Udo, I *know* that policies are important. I *know* they're the very foundation of the United Nations, but here's the deal—I need the password so that I can *follow* the policies. And it's perfectly within the policy guidelines, because I am OIC. Even though I'm only a lowly Public Information Officer most of the time, I'm also Officer-In-Charge at the moment. There's no one here to authorize this but me! You can help me, can't you?" Lindsay was on the phone with New York, trying to convince them that she really was entitled to the password that would allow her to access environmental management information on UN websites. "Yes, of course, I'll hold," she continued, her voice dripping with unaccustomed sweetness.

Bopha's face peering around the door was a welcome interruption. Lindsay rolled her eyes, signaling to Bopha her annoyance with the party on the other end of the phone, then watched, intrigued, as Bopha entered the room carrying a rough wooden packing crate.

"What in the world is in there?" she whispered to Bopha, as the box rocked precariously on the corner of her desk.

"I don't know, Lindsay. A man brought it for you. He didn't leave messages."

While the bureaucrat at the other end of line droned on, Lindsay peered curiously through the slats into the crate. A deep droning was coming from the box, and luminous eyes shone in its shadows. "It's a cat, Bopha," Lindsay said, after completing her call. "Help me get it open?"

Although the animal shrank from the bright fluorescent lights, it continued to purr. Almost twice the size of a house cat, the creature retained the rounded features of a kitten. Its muted markings and magnificent tail were a grayish brown, and a lighter colored patch marked its chest. Two well-defined stripes ran from the cat's eyes up over the crown of its head. Enthralled, Lindsay reached out to stroke the cat, drawing her hand back with a jerk at Bopha's scream.

"Yee-e-e-e! *chmar prei!*" Bopha shrieked, causing the cat to cower into the corner where it crouched, hissing.

"Bopha!" Lindsay said. "You're scaring it." She put her hand back into the box and scratched the dark lines between the cat's ears, soothing and calming its fear.

"Lindsay, *chmar prei* is wild cat! It can hurt you," Bopha said, stepping backing from the box.

"Maybe this one is tame, though. It's certainly affectionate." As the cat moved against her stroking fingers, Lindsay noticed an envelope lying at the bottom of the box. "Who did you say brought it?" she asked. "Was it a foreign man?"

"No, a messenger. Maybe from the palace, I think."

Reaching slowly into the box with her other hand, Lindsay eased the envelope out from under the cat's hindquarters. It was a plain white envelope with her name hand-printed on the front. There was no return address. Setting it to one side, she continued to pet the animal, wondering why she wasn't more worried about bites and rabies and ticks and other practicalities. But the thought slipped from her mind as the cat butted its head against her hand, demanding her attention.

Although its fur was the like the fluff of a dandelion, the pressure against her fingers was insistent. Lindsay increased her gentle tickling, and the animal's response hummed like a swarm of bees. She glanced up, realizing that Bopha was still expecting her to emerge with a bloody stump. "This animal is amazing, Bopha. I haven't got a clue what it is, but it's beautiful. Don't you want to see?"

But Bopha had seen enough, and Lindsay remembered that Cambodians could be extremely practical about animals. Animals were for eating, performing tasks, or selling. "What is *chmar prei*, anyway, Bopha?" she asked

"It's mean forest cat. They're wild. They live in the jungle."

"Yes, but what do people *do* with them?"

"They use them for medicine."

"What kind of medicine?"

"Chinese medicine," Bopha answered briefly.

Lindsay sighed. Another game of Twenty Questions. Whenever the subject was embarrassing, complicated, or the least controversial, information had to be dragged out, one bit at a time. Once she had learned to recognize this particular conversational dance, she'd been amused at the spice it added to misleadingly simple communications between Khmer and foreigners.

"Okay. Do they have to kill it for the medicine? Is it in its bones or something? Or is just having one around medicine?"

"I don't know, Lindsay. It is Chinese."

"But I know," a now-familiar voice drawled from the office doorway.

"Major Balfour. What a surprise. Going swimming again?" Lindsay said stiffly.

"No, sorry. Maybe next time. Why, you need swimming lessons, too?"

So that's what they were up to. Lindsay had tried to ask Bopha about their relationship, teasing her a bit, but had run into a brick wall, learning only that they'd been swimming at L'Imprevu. Before she could reply, André entered the room. "May I see?" he asked, approaching Lindsay's desk. She moved aside, and he studied the animal in silence for a moment or two, then put his hand into the box. The purring intensified immediately, diminishing when he stepped away. "Ah, yes. Of course. There's really no doubt," he said.

Lindsay stared at him with distaste. "Come, Major, what is that supposed to mean?" She gestured at the cat, which was now standing on its hind legs, peering over the edge of the box.

"Merely a figure of speech, Ms March."

While Lindsay could tolerate playing Twenty Questions with Cambodians, she wasn't about to put up with it from a fellow westerner. "You just said, 'Ah, yes, of course, no doubt,'" she mimicked. "Just tell me what you meant. Then maybe I can get back to work."

André ignored her hostility, gathering his thoughts as if the subject were complex. Then he nodded. "You can see that this is not a domestic cat. My guess is that it's a fishing cat, the *prionailurus viverrinus*. They used to be quite common all across Southeast Asia, but these days they're pretty rare. They're hunted for selling to Chinese traders. Sometimes it's for their fur, but the main interest is their bones. The medicine restores potency. For men. You understand? That's right, isn't it, *kmuey?*" he asked, turning to Bopha, who nodded but remained silent.

"But it seems tame," Lindsay said, picking the cat up and cuddling it to her chest. "It must have been a pet. Why would someone send it to me if they planned to sell it for medicine?" Remembering the envelope, she set the cat down and reached across her desk to pick it up.

As she tore open the flap, André said, "Why, indeed? I quite agree. This gift is a very special one, with a special meaning, just for you."

Lindsay temper flared. "Oh, cut it out, Major! Why am I cursed with people who speak in riddles?"

At her words, Bopha turned and left the room. But André was unaffected. "Ms March, look at this cat. You can't help but notice how affectionate she is? Well...watch this." He took the animal from the box, cradling it in his arms and rubbing its neck. The cat stretched languorously, raising her rear against his hand, her purr transforming into a throaty meow of desire. "This girl's in heat," he said. "If she weren't, you wouldn't find her nearly so friendly."

As he returned the cat to the box, he added nonchalantly, "Now what I'm wondering is, who would give you such a unique gift as a fishing cat in heat?" But he sounded like he already knew what she had just discovered. She looked down again at the note in her hand. "A bit of the forest for you, Lindsay. *Besos*, Max," it said.

André was still petting the cat. Would he never leave? "Well, I still think she's beautiful," Lindsay said honestly.

"She is beautiful, *certainemente*. But she belongs in the forest," he said, handing the cat into Lindsay's outstretched arms.

"I know that, André," she said, finding to her surprise that this discussion had somehow placed them on first name terms. "But we don't know her story, do we? Maybe she was injured, and she would have died if someone hadn't rescued her. Or maybe Max found her for sale in a market or something."

"Ah yes, it would be from Max, wouldn't it? Who else would make such a gesture?"

Lindsay felt that his words somehow sullied her, and said with exasperation, "Look, what is it you're implying here? If you've got something to say, maybe you should just tell me what it is so we can stop this ridiculous dancing."

"*Oui*, maybe I should," he said, his voice challenging.

"How about now?"

"Why not?"

"Maybe you would like some coffee to go with it?" she asked him, her voice anything but inviting.

"No, thank you. Although it's hard to resist such a gracious offer," he replied in the same tone.

André made himself comfortable in one of the rattan chairs in the corner of Lindsay's office while Lindsay put the cat back in the box, placing it on the floor beside the chairs. Bopha came in and sat down quietly on the couch, making room for Lindsay to sit beside her.

When they were settled, André leaned forward, elbows on his knees. "His Majesty, King Sihanouk, is in his seventies now," he began. "He's not in very good health. He's seen a lot, and is wise enough to no longer pursue personal ambition. I very much respect this man.

"But, because he is old, he feels pressure and he is afraid, afraid that when he dies, Cambodia will fall apart. He understands that there are many ways in which Cambodia might destroy herself when he is gone. One of these ways is logging. Sihanouk understands only too well that the men involved with the logging trade would be happy to destroy every tree if there were gain in it for them. So, instead of playing chess with them, several small moves, contemplated over a long period of time—he has chosen to play something that I fear is closer to Russian roulette."

Lindsay's exasperation had dissipated, leaving behind a sharp interest in André's words. This was what she needed, to learn the historical and political background behind the park proposal. Bopha, too, was raptly attentive.

"So for the king, it is not stupidity to propose this nature reserve. It is simply the blindness of desperation. Is it wise? Most certainly not. Will it stop the rape of Cambodia's rain forest? He believes it will. And perhaps he is right—it could stop the logging, if by some miracle Cambodia's powerful were to suddenly lose their penchant for corruption. He cannot trust anyone to carry on his rule. After all, he saw the Americans install Lon Nol, and he himself lived with the Khmer Rouge.

"Unfortunately, the vultures surrounding the king are using his fears for the future to feather their own nests. Do you understand, perhaps, a little better why I cannot support the nature reserve? Quite the contrary to protecting the forest, I believe the reserve will give Cambodia's kleptocracy *carte blanche* to continue looting the forests not just of logs but of resources of every kind."

Bopha was nodding her head in time with his statements, like a Moonie at church.

"Oh, yes," Lindsay said, nodding as well. "It's clear to me what you're saying. But I think you are relying pretty heavily on subjective reasoning. I could just as well use your greed and corruption argument to support the establishment of the nature reserve."

Instead of being annoyed, André smiled. "Lindsay," he said, "you really want to believe that everything, all things, will always be all right, don't you?" he said.

"Yes! If judging things at face value is a crime, I'm afraid I'm guilty. But I choose to trust first. If I'm proven wrong, I admit it," she said.

"That is an admirable quality. But in this situation, it's just idiotic," he said. "Because unfortunately, there is more at stake than just the nature reserve. It is more about ecological systems than environmental protection."

"And that means...?" Lindsay demanded. But her tone showed her interest, so André told her.

"Southeast Asia is experiencing an unprecedented degree of human trafficking," he said softly. "The Cambodian government, in partnership with other countries in this region, is working hard to establish an Anti-Transnational Crime Center to deal with this, because they are finding more and more cases in which young women, teenage girls, and even younger children are lured from their homes and villages by any bait that works. They are trapped in sexual bondage, forced labor, or forcibly incapacitated and sent out to beg. Sometimes they are injected with drugs that make them look and feel sick, so they'll make more pitiful beggars. And some of them are forced to have sex with men who have AIDS.

"These women and children are exchanged for money or swapped directly for drugs and traded in an underground network. Most of them never escape. My fear is that the proposed park will end up being nothing more than a cover for even more trafficking, never mind that it will also permit the powerful to continue extracting the other natural resources from the region without governmental control."

"What do you mean, Major? If it's a government park, wouldn't the government control what happens in it?"

"In that best of all possible worlds where you seem to live, Lindsay, yes, it would. But the man who's been named to direct the park is not known to be particularly honorable, to say the least, and he has direct connections with the military. Believe me, this is much bigger than just irresponsible logging and endangered species like your fishing cat. The potential for profit makes the stakes high, and with high stakes, the danger goes up. My advice is, don't involve yourself. For your own protection, you should let your boss handle this situation when he returns."

But his argument couldn't have been less likely to win Lindsay's support. *Oh, right, it's a boy's game,* she thought, gazing at André silently. He must have read her mind.

"This goes far beyond egos, Lindsay. And the game is being played by people who have very little respect for human life."

"Perhaps we must agree to differ on this issue. I'll think about what you've said, but until I see more evidence to convince me otherwise, I'll be recommending to David that UNOIC support a proper park. Thanks for sharing your theories, really. It helps me to put things into perspective." Lindsay's tone was dismissive, and she stood to her feet to emphasize the finality of her message.

André shrugged as he rose from the chair. "You are welcome, Lindsay. I wish you were hearing as well as listening, and trusting me as easily as you trust others you are willing to take at face value. One day, perhaps."

Bopha escorted André out the door, returning a few minutes later. During her absence, Lindsay re-read the first paragraph of Max's note. "The King has put his private plane at my disposal to visit the park site for a day trip. Day after tomorrow. Can you make it?"

Lindsay scrambled through the scraps of paper in her top drawer, searching for Max's card. After she dialed, she laughed at herself, realizing she'd been so eager to learn about the trip that she hadn't even checked her diary to confirm the date. As she waited for the call to go through, she thought about David. Although she'd only been with UNOIC for a few months, she understood that David liked the limelight—when it reflected well on him. But would he want the publicity of this trip—or would he send her anyway, in case it got messy? The phone was still ringing when she came up with the perfect justification for taking the trip herself. If she didn't accept the invitation of the King's Special Advisor, the government could accuse UNOIC of stalling, of refusing to cooperate in their efforts to practice responsible environmentalism. "It's even true!" she said aloud.

"*Por supuesto*," Max said, "I should hope everything you say is true."

Lindsay smiled, but said only, "Max. I got your note."

"My note? Only that?"

"And the cat! She's lovely, Max," Lindsay said, not mentioning the cat's condition. If Max were making a point, he'd have to contend with intentional obtuseness on her part.

But Max was busy explaining. "She was found in the forest at the reserve site some months back, Lindsay, and her mother was dead. Since then, she and her littermates have been cared for up there by some villagers, but they were ready to sell her to the traders, and that would have been the end of her. One of the staff brought her back to me, and I thought of you. If you can't take care of her, there are people in town who run a wildlife shelter."

"That may be wise, Max. I loved seeing her and having her here...but would you set that up for me?"

"*Con gusto, mi amor.*"

Paging through her diary, Lindsay saw with relief that there was only one routine appointment for the day Max had planned the trip. "About that field trip," she said. "I can go, as long as you're sure we can make it up there and back the same day?"

"No problem," Max replied. "Trust me."

"You are very sure of the park, aren't you?" she said. "Doesn't it seem a bit risky, though? The country is barely at peace, everything's still in chaos—do you have any doubts about the government's real motivation at all?" Her question had more to do with gauging his reaction than expressing her own view, but that wasn't the way Max read it.

"You want out?" he asked calmly.

"No, Max, it's not that. I just want to make sure that I'm looking at this from all possible angles, that's all."

"Once again, spoken like a true bureaucrat, Lindsay. Like the rest of them, you cannot make a decision or a commitment without committees and studies and experts and reports. So you aren't alone—you just aren't with me."

The impact of his words startled Lindsay. Normally, she would have been amused or annoyed at his personalization of the discussion. But this time, she found herself wanting to respond to his challenge. An instinctive awareness of impending intimacy flooded her, and she shook it off with effort. "I'm with you so far, Max. But only until I find a reason to take another route."

He laughed. They arranged the logistics for the trip in short order and said goodbye. Lindsay scooped up the cat again and cradled it in her arms, extending a finger for it to play with. "Are you some kind of trick?" she asked the animal soberly.

The cat blinked its eyes, yawned, and revved its motor up another notch.

CHAPTER EIGHT

TUESDAY, MAY 25, PART I

Olga sat motionless in the canvas sling chair, her eyes closed. The deep verandah of the wooden house was secluded in the waning gloom of early morning, but readily admitted the sounds of chanting from the nearby pagoda, Wat Sambor Meas. Catching a stronger than usual whiff of *prahok*, the pounded paste of fish left to ferment underground until its aroma brought tears to the eye, Olga coughed her way back from her daydreaming. *Prahok* was too strong a taste for her own liking, but since her neighbors in the thatched huts in the compound below enjoyed it with every meal, there was no way of escaping the caustic fumes.

Olga had spent the night in that chair, not an unusual occurrence. Although she'd picked up the pieces of her life and didn't waste time dwelling on 'what ifs,' somehow along the way she'd forgotten how to sleep. Especially at night, when the demons slunk closer to her bed. More often than not, Olga's sleep quota was met through afternoon siestas.

She stood, glanced up at the gilt-edged clouds that still shrouded the early morning sun, and began her morning stretching routine. *Only way to keep the old body young*, she muttered to herself, *and the best time to do it is when I'm half asleep.*

***

While Olga stretched herself awake, Sam was being awakened less gently. "Wake up, Sam, you must come quickly." In one smooth movement, Sam pushed the pink nylon mosquito net to one side and rolled to his feet, landing in a crouch with his big hands in a defensive karate position, his eyes wide and wary.

"Please, hurry," Peter repeated, averting his eyes and thinking that it was lucky he'd come to call Sam rather than sending Annie. Sam was stark naked and erect with early morning vigor. Peter kept his eyes on the open window.

Sam followed Peter's gaze. "What is it, Peter?" he asked. As he spoke, he wound a sarong around his midriff and the two men moved to the window. A bright blue *cyclo* stood just outside the rusted gate of the orphanage. Its driver was bending over the seat, fretting over a small figure huddled in the passenger seat.

"You're right—somebody's in trouble." The last words were shouted over Sam's shoulder as he scrambled down the steps and out the door.

In the street, Peter gingerly pulled the straw mat to one side. "*Lok, lok, juey pong!*" The urgency in the *cyclo* driver's voice was surprisingly well-contained, and he was speaking in a hoarse whisper. "*Knyom klaj geh jap! Yok wia dtao knong, pliam, knyom ot nou ban dteh!*" Sam, not yet conversant in Khmer, continued to examine the figure huddled on the *cyclo* seat. It was human, a girl, a small child he guessed, by the size.

As the *cyclo* driver made room for Sam to get a closer look, Peter whispered a translation of the driver's words: "He says we should

75

get her inside fast, Sam. He's afraid of the police if he's caught bringing her here."

Sam lifted the scarf and saw that, despite her diminutive form, the girl was not really a child. Her face was bruised, and blood stains soaked her tattered shirt and sarong. Her feet were bare and callused, with dirt engrained in the cracks on the bottoms of the soles. The nails had been freshly polished with bright pink lacquer.

"Help me," Sam said simply. Together, he and Peter lifted the girl from the seat. The weight of her body had barely cleared the cracked vinyl cushion before the driver leapt onto his seat and pedaled away, his brakes squealing in the quiet dawn.

"*Lok! Mok winh!*" Sam yelled in broken Khmer.

"Sam, no," Peter cautioned. "There's no use calling him back. He doesn't know anything—probably he just found her on the street. He doesn't want to be involved, that's for sure."

As they moved inside the gates, the girl cradled in Sam's arms, Peter took care to slide the gate's bolt home behind them. "But he could be a witness," Sam protested, "or at least tell us what happened."

But Peter was shaking his head. "This kind of accident, there are no witnesses, Sam."

"Are you sure the driver didn't say anything else, Peter? He must have known something." But Peter was still shaking his head.

Inside the orphanage, Sam placed the girl gently on the cushions of the rattan couch. As Peter continued to explain the dangers the *cyclo* driver—and in fact, they themselves—could face if they became involved, the girl moaned and muttered a few words in a clicking language that was clearly not Khmer. "She's not Cambodian," Sam said wonderingly.

The small dark eyes fluttered open briefly, closed, then opened again, staying open as the girl took a deep breath. As she returned to consciousness and became aware of the two men looking down on her, her eyes widened in terror. A thin high-pitched wailing shivered from her throat, and her body began to quiver uncontrollably.

"Get Annie and *Om*," Sam said softly. Not wanting to make things worse for the girl, he stepped away, but continued his examination from a distance. The bruising beginning to show on the girl's neck and arms, and the stains, thick and dark on the skirt of her sarong, left Sam with the certainty that the girl had been brutally raped.

Annie and the housekeeper rushed into the room moments later, gasping when they saw the girl looking up from the couch with the despairing eyes of a rabbit watching a hawk circling in the sky above it. Their voices soothing, speaking the soft reassurances that women know so well in every language, they knelt beside the couch. "Peter, bring me a basin of warm water and some clean cloths," Annie said softly. "And Sam, you've got to get help." As she spoke, Annie kept her eyes fixed on the girl's, rubbing her arms with a soothing rhythmic stroking that seemed to calm her.

"But Annie," Sam said, "Peter says we shouldn't call the police. But she needs more than just warm water! Shouldn't we get her to Calmette?" Calmette, the city's largest hospital, seemed, even as he spoke, to be an unlikely solution. The girl was indeed in need of medical treatment, but she needed it to be accompanied by the kindness and understanding that she was already getting from *Om* and Annie.

"No police, Sam. Don't you know anyone from those meetings you go to that you'd trust to help us?"

And suddenly, Sam remembered Olga. He hadn't seen her since their meeting the week before, but he was certain that she would know what to do. But would she come?

Hell, he thought, as Olga's phone rang for the eighth time. The worst Olga could do was say no. But she couldn't even do that if she didn't answer her damned phone.

When she finally answered, Olga's "Hello!" was exasperated, not, as Sam thought, because he'd awakened her, but because she was still dripping from the shower. "Who is this?" she demanded.

Sam explained as briefly and clearly as he could, while Olga listened in silence. "It's Sam Jarrett. I'm calling from our orphanage in Toul Tompong. A few minutes ago a *cyclo* driver banged on my gate and delivered a bloody parcel that I am just not equipped to deal with." The sound of the girl's wailing could be heard in the background as he continued. "We're ready to help, but we don't know what to do. And she isn't letting Peter or me get anywhere near her. Can you help?"

Olga broke in on him. "Have you called anyone? The police?" To Sam's emphatic denial, she said, "Good. I'll pick up a doctor I know on the way. She's dealt with this sort of thing before." And the connection was cut.

A wave of relief washed over Sam, and he began to attend to details that would make the girl—Meng, Annie had called her—more comfortable. The commotion had awakened the rest of the children, and they were crowded around the door of the room, eyes wide and mouths clamped shut. Sam shepherded them gently out the back of the house, turning them over to Mathak to get started on breakfast. When he returned to the front room, he was carrying an armful of kapok pillows and three brightly colored blankets. "I've got Valium, too," he said to Annie, holding up a small amber vial, "but Olga said she'd be here with a doctor in minutes. I'd rather we wait and see what she thinks before we give her any medicine."

Olga's stentorian voice, when he finally heard it in the courtyard below, brought a smile of relief to Sam's worried face. By that time he'd brewed a carafe of strong coffee and started a pot of *bobor* cooking. He'd quickly adopted this traditional Khmer response to fatigue or illness or misfortune, a thin rice gruel he'd been offered upon his arrival, "to help you get strong again, after your flight," he'd been told.

At the sound of footsteps on the stairs, Sam stopped his pacing, and waited while Olga and a tall, thin Khmer woman clutching a bulging olive drab canvas duffle bag approached. Olga made no introductions and limited her greeting to a terse, "Where is the girl, Sam?"

Sam gestured toward the open door of the living room, and followed Olga as she and the doctor moved into the room. Olga's confidence and empathy were obvious, and her matter-of-fact approach to the injured girl was perfect. With no hesitation, as if she'd been put on earth for just this purpose, Olga knelt beside the couch and wrapped the girl in her arms, rocking her as a mother comforts a crying baby. After a few moments in Olga's arms, the girl's whimpers collapsed into heaving sighs.

While Olga comforted Meng, the doctor moved a small wooden table from the side of the room to the foot of the couch. With a flip of her wrist, she opened a clean cloth and spread it over the top of the table, then proceeded to select items from the depths of her bag and place them in precise positions on the cloth. To Sam's surprise, the woman hummed softly as she prepared her instruments. He was further puzzled to recognize the tune—*No One Shall Sleep* from Puccini's Turandot—as the moving solo that brought Sydney Schanberg close to madness in *The Killing Fields*.

Seeing Sam's glazed stare, Olga said, "Some coffee for us, Sam? I will take mine white. Kek takes hers black and sweet."

"It's already brewed, Olga," Sam said. "And I've got a pot of *bobor* cooking, too."

Smiling at Sam's eagerness to be of help, Olga laughed. "That is a good boy, Sam. Do not bring it in, though—keep it hot until we come out."

Sam closed the door softly behind him and walked to the kitchen. *What a woman*, he thought, amazed by Olga's competence and compassion, and flooded with gratitude that she'd come when he'd called.

Nearly thirty minutes passed before Olga emerged from the room. Kek, the doctor, remained inside with the girl. Olga's face looked even more worried now than it had a half hour earlier. "How bad is it?" Sam blurted, "I mean, I know she's been raped. But is she going to be okay?"

Olga nodded slowly. "Well, she survived. That is a good start. There do not seem to be any serious internal injuries, and she does not have any broken bones. She has lost a lot of blood, and there is some tearing. There is always tearing, when this happens. But tears heal more quickly than the emotional scars. I hope the bastard does not have AIDS, because with all those tears she would be infected for sure. Kek will give her many antibiotics anyway, to keep her from getting any other infections."

Sam's face suffused with emotion. "But she's so young! What kind of man would brutalize a child like that?"

But Olga didn't answer, her mind elsewhere. When she spoke, her voice was soft, but the inflection was hard. "It has been one year," she said. "And now it is starting again."

Sam couldn't believe his ears. "What are you talking about? You mean this has happened before? What are you saying?"

But Olga's eyes were closed, and again she ignored his question. After a moment's, her eyes opened and she looked directly at Sam, her gaze suspicious. "Why did you call me?" she demanded roughly.

Sam was taken aback by this shift in Olga's attitude, and his response was defensive. "I know it sounds stupid, but I couldn't think of anyone else. Maybe I was inspired, I don't know. A sort of inspired panic. My Khmer friends didn't know what to do, especially since the girl doesn't seem to speak much Khmer. And I sure as hell didn't have a clue how to help her."

"You know, Sam, your friends are more clever than you think." Olga said. "They know a lot more about the darkness of Phnom Penh than you—and they know that the way to survive is to stay away from trouble. Being Khmer, they are vulnerable, and they have a lot to weigh before they decide to get involved. They want to protect you, too, I am sure."

Sam accepted her words in silence, his face preoccupied. He got up to stir the *bobor,* then returned to the small table where they sat sipping their coffee. Sam broke the silence a few minutes later. "Olga, I may have called you because I didn't know what else to do. But I know I called exactly the right person. How were you able to find a doctor so quickly? Who are you, Olga?"

Putting the intent of Sam's question aside, Olga held out her hand. "Sam Jarrett, I am Olga Herrin. And you—you were very sensible not to call the police, and not to take little Meng to the hospital," she offered, her face opening like a flower with a growing smile.

But Sam wasn't about to be diverted. "Tell me what's going on, Olga," he demanded, softening his tone by putting a gentle hand on her shoulder.

Again she fixed him with a direct gaze, the light color of her eyes guarding her thoughts. "Sam, I—it is not my story to tell. How can I know that you will not share information that could bring trouble to people whose lives have already fallen apart? Maybe later...."

Sam persisted. "How much later? Do I have to wait for more of these kids to get brutalized? Or killed?"

Olga eyes widened at the anger in Sam's voice. She looked at him speculatively, then made a quick decision. "All right. But we cannot talk here."

She got up and tapped softly before opening the door into the living room. Kek was sitting quietly beside the couch, where Meng slept curled on her side, a delicate hand cupping one cheek. The blankets were smoothed over her, and Kek held the other small hand in her own. "We are going out for noodles, Kek," Olga whispered, handing her the mug of steaming black coffee. The doctor nodded and waved them on their way.

They walked through the early morning traffic, dodging the motorcycle taxis, ducking beneath dangling electric lines, and ending up in a tiny noodle shop two streets away. An elderly Chinese couple greeted Olga with the enthusiasm of parents greeting a long lost daughter. After ordering iced coffees and *ktiov gok*, dry noodle soup, Sam glanced around the shop. "Are you sure it's okay to talk here?" he asked. "I don't even know why I'm asking—couldn't we have talked at the orphanage?"

Olga laughed. "This is one of the few places I am sure of, Sam. You saw the owners come out to greet us? I rescued their daughter over a year ago. As for the orphanage, well, I do not know. And I do not talk in places I am not sure about. Now sit still and listen. I am about to tell you more than you ever wanted to know about sex, lies, and Cambodia."

Olga paused to gather her thoughts, then very succinctly explained what she had seen herself, heard from others, or deduced about the serial rapist-killer, who was once again stalking the street children of Phnom Penh.

Sam listened to the details, horrorstruck, until he could stand it no longer. He stood abruptly, knocking over their small table. Oblivious to Olga's worried question and the shocked faces of the proprietors, he strode from the restaurant.

CHAPTER NINE
TUESDAY, MAY 25, PART II

I t cost a dollar, but the entry fee more than paid for the tranquility found in the grounds of the Silver Pagoda. Sam needed, badly needed, a quiet place to think. The riverfront, with its early morning crowds and aggressively insistent beggars, was impossible. The orphanage was even worse, with the constant clamoring of the children and demands of his colleagues. And Olga! Her disclosures were what had driven him here.

As Sam passed through the heavy wrought iron gates that fronted Samdach Sothearos Boulevard, he could see the Silver Pagoda glinting through the foliage, deep in the grounds of the palace compound. The local attraction was deserted as usual, offering him the silence and sanctuary he craved. The solitude soothed him, a balm easing the knifing pain of Olga's words. After the obligatory walk through the pagoda itself—interesting, but not spectacular—he turned to pace the covered walkways that sheltered the peeling murals lining the temple walls. The images of war and struggle drawn from the ancient Hindu Ramayana epic echoed Sam's own inner turmoil.

How can people be so evil? he demanded from the shrubs that bordered the walkway, as if imagining the author of all perversities lurking in their shadows. Olga's revelations had disturbed him more deeply than he would have imagined possible. With all he had faced during the war, why hadn't he learned, by now, to cope with the ugliness of human nature? *I've gone soft*, he muttered, sitting down on a stone bench in the painted corridor beside the carcass of an ancient refrigerator. A tiny lizard chirped mockingly from the ceiling, and he found himself envying it the simplicity of its existence.

Olga had told him about someone, a someone still unnamed but known to be highly placed among Cambodia's elite. Someone protected by the powerful, Olga said, because of his highly valued services. And what were those services? "The procurement of virgins, children just entering puberty, for wealthy Khmer men who are no longer so young themselves." Virgins, she'd explained, had long been considered a fashionable cure for impotence, a much more pleasurable cure than the drugs prescribed by western medicine. Olga swore that many Khmer held an even more bizarre belief, that sex with virgins could strengthen promiscuous men in a way that would protect them from AIDS infection, even when they were exposed to the virus through other women.

Sam had scoffed at this. It wasn't just implausible, it was ridiculous. After all, many of the country's leaders had been educated overseas. How could they retain such superstitions? But Olga merely shook her head. It seemed the legacy of tradition was stronger than a western education.

"Wait, Sam—it is worse than this," Olga had said. "This man is a monster, and I do not exaggerate. What you saw tonight was a unique mistake. This child is one of the few victims to survive his brutality."

"How many have there been?" Sam had asked grimly, needing to hear the worst.

"Two dozen that we have seen. There may be many more. But we do not know enough to bring this to the authorities. We must investigate without making things worse," Olga said. "And I know we cannot do this without official support. What I do not know is how to get that support without alerting whoever is supporting this devil."

After his abrupt departure, Sam had walked the tawdry streets of the city for over an hour. The walk had distracted him, and now the serenity of the gardens amidst the *chedis* of long-dead Khmer kings had nourished his thoughts. In the distance he could hear the chanting of monks at prayer. He sat motionless beneath a banyan tree, letting the prayers flow into his mind.

Eventually, he rose and began to stroll again through the grounds, admiring the topiary and lush tropical blooms—heliconias, gingers, hibiscus. Spotting a small shrine nestled in a miniature bamboo copse, he turned to admire it—and froze. Deep within the shade of the trees, two forms, their bodies silhouetted against the sunlit wall of the compound, caught his attention.

He turned back to avoid what was clearly a private conversation, but could hear behind him a strident female voice. Although he could not understand the Khmer words, the tone was unmistakably imperious. When the pair moved away from the shrine, he stepped to one side. Realizing that he might as well be invisible for all the notice they paid him, he studied their faces as they passed. The woman continued to speak, her tone commanding in spite of her tiny stature.

The man, his dress and bearing more western than Khmer, nodded subserviently to each of the woman's commands, but he did not speak. Sam's eyes were drawn to the man's face, which bordered on beauty in its features but was marred by a large dark mole just above his upper lip, and by its expression. Suppressed rage? Greed? Who'd have thought the two emotions could wear such similar expressions. The couple brushed past Sam, still ignoring his presence, and disappeared through a guarded gate into the inner compound of the palace.

The encounter had lasted only seconds and Sam continued his stroll, mulling over the day's events. By the time the path brought him back to the pagoda, he'd reached a decision. First, to see Olga and repair the breach he must have created by his abrupt departure. With Olga's help or without it, he wouldn't let this go. He couldn't.

Striding rapidly from the grounds, he caught a motorcycle taxi to Olga's wooden house, hoping she had returned to her home after he'd left her at the restaurant. As he climbed the narrow stairs, he glimpsed Olga waiting on the veranda above him. He paused on the top step, then felt relief wash over him as he saw her smile. "You took less time than I did," she offered.

"You didn't have such a friend to help you, perhaps," he suggested, tentatively. She nodded gravely. "That is right. I did not." As Sam bent to remove his shoes, Olga stood and pumped a mug of coffee from the thermos on the table beside her.

"Did you see the Phnom Penh Piper?" Olga remarked casually, watching Sam over her shoulder. "This week's edition?"

"No. Why?" Sam asked, surprised at the *non sequitur.*

"See for yourself," she said, passing him the crisp white pages with one hand and the steaming coffee with the other. "Page five."

After a few moments of reading, Sam dropped the newspaper and sighed. "Pretty virulent," he said.

Olga nodded in agreement. "It makes me wonder. I mean the concentration on logging. Is the reporter just naïve? Or do they not know that the forests are only one of the protection issues in the northeast?"

"I know that UNOIC is not all it claims to be, but still..." Sam hesitated, fully aware of his ignorance about the large international organizations. "I really don't know anything about bureaucracies—thank God!—but I wonder why they wouldn't choose a more seasoned veteran for a job like this. Wouldn't you think, Olga?"

"I do not know, Sam. But if this Public Information Officer is truly as inexperienced and naïve as this article makes her sound, it may work in our favor. I have never met her, but it may be that this Lindsay March is a good person who is way out of her depth. If we get to her first," Olga said, watching Sam's expression change as he followed her intent, "we may get a human reaction, rather than a political one. And," Olga added, pointing again to the pages of the newspaper, now scattered around Sam's feet, "did you notice that it also says she is in charge of the office during the UNOIC Country Coordinator's absence? Maybe we could make her understand that she must take some action!"

"You really want me in on this?" Sam asked, pleasure evident in his voice.

"We are a team, ja?" Olga smiled gently. To Sam's adamant nod, she said, "Then we must get to work."

CHAPTER TEN

WEDNESDAY, MAY 26, PART I

The early morning sun, like a tangerine beach ball suspended in mid-throw, cast long shadows on the vivid green fields of rice seedlings that bordered Pochentong Boulevard, the blue of the sky reflected in their flood and heightening the rich red loam of the dikes that separated the paddies.

Lindsay savored the crisp bright colors as she rode to the military airfield just west of Pochentong International Airport. At dawn, traffic was still light and they soon reached the aging quonset huts surrounded by cracked cement and Russian helicopters. On the far side, a newly painted hangar stood aloof from its neighbors, and the nose of a plane was sticking out from the cavernous interior.

"This must be it," Lindsay said to the driver, a safe guess since it was the only plane on the field, except for the decrepit fighter jets lined up at the far end of the airstrip. She directed the driver to park near the building and, after checking her radio and spare battery with the UNOIC radio control room, climbed down from the Land Cruiser and strolled over to the plane. Reaching it, she realized that it wasn't deserted after all—there were two men sleeping, one under each wing, their bodies sprawled in the uninhibited postures of the unconscious. She coughed loudly, but got no response. Concerned, Lindsay moved closer. "Are you all right?" she called out.

The men sat up, snorting, and looked up at her with bleary eyes. Mumbling in Khmer, they stretched—just like my fishing cat, she thought—and scrambled to their feet. "Good morning!" she said. But they looked at her without speaking. *Unfriendly, definitely hungover, but not dangerous*, she concluded, turning as she heard the sound of an approaching vehicle.

A black Mercedes, its windows darkened, braked to a stop next to the UNOIC vehicle. A wiry young Khmer man with a crew cut jumped out of the shotgun seat, turned neatly, and opened the door directly behind him.

A second Khmer man, this one with blow-dried and heavily moussed hair, his eyes hidden behind the latest fashion in shades, eased himself from the car. He looked to be in his late twenties, and was wearing tailored silk pants, navy blue, and a blindingly white linen shirt. A dark mole protruded just above his upper lip. *Oh God*, Lindsay moaned to herself, *look at him! God, I should have known this would be one of those tea-with-the-local-officials trips.* She considered her choice of khakis and t-shirt, calculating how long it would take to rush back to the used clothes market for a skirt and blouse. On the far side of the car she watched as Max's tall form emerged. To her relief, he was wearing a faded Greenpeace t-shirt, ragged denim shorts, and lightweight hiking boots. Comfort ruling out over style.

Max moved purposively in her direction, kissing her soundly on both cheeks. She caught the scent of Ivory soap like a rare perfume, gone before she had time to savor it. "Have you been waiting long?" he asked.

"Nope, just got here," she said.

The nattily dressed Khmer joined them. "Weather looks good this morning," he announced. "We can take off immediately." He directed his eyes expectantly toward Lindsay.

"Hoktha, please meet Ms Lindsay March. Lindsay, this is Mr Som Hoktha. He's just been made director of Norodom Park Nature Reserve—our host for the trip."

Not 'is expected to be appointed' or 'acting director,' Lindsay noted curiously, but 'is the new director.' How had the King appointed a director so quickly? Max had not been here long enough to recruit, much less to check credentials and get his selection approved by the king. And the king had only announced his intention a week and a half ago. There was something out of synch about that—or maybe this was a good place to use the word intriguing.

"I hope I don't have to call you Ms March," Hoktha said, sounding both flirtatious and arrogant.

"Not unless as I have to call you Mr Som," Lindsay laughed back, leaning slightly toward him in a deliberate return flirt. He seemed like the kind of man who needed a role, and she would rather he play a ladies' man than the typical Khmer male role of dictator.

Her instincts were right. Hoktha laughed back, flashing a set of brilliant white teeth. The ice had been broken, and his response revealed how excessively good looking he really was. Max looked subtly pleased too, as if she had passed a test, as if they were performing to some script known only to him. He went back to the car, and Lindsay watched his muscles flexing beneath his shirt as he bent to retrieve a worn daypack.

Hoktha, delving into his own sporty black leather pack, pulled out a cell phone. After speed dialing, he spoke rapidly in Khmer, his accent not quite right. This, together with such muted tailoring and the styled hair, cued her that this Hoktha was an expatriate Khmer. It was an encouraging sign. As a rule, native sons of the Heng Samrin regime were as eager for the future as anyone, but were apt to suffer skewed perspectives. They had learned what they knew of the outside world through B movies and eastern European educations. While quaint and certainly colorful characters, local Cambodians could easily become lost in the confusing layers of needs and issues associated with international development. This wasn't necessarily a weakness, but in developing the conceptual framework of the nature reserve, it could have been problematic.

"You're American, aren't you, Linseed? I'm French. Dual citizenship," Hoktha said.

"Your English is excellent. I was guessing Canadian," she replied, hoping he would consider it a compliment. Apparently he did, his smile gleaming again beneath the opaque glasses. *Easy to please*, she thought, and decided not to correct his mispronunciation of her name. All she would have to do to keep him happy would be to keep feeding him compliments, like fish to a seal.

The two hungover sleepers, it turned out, were their pilot and mechanic. They disappeared into the hangar and began preparing the plane for take off while Hoktha and Max murmured together in a businesslike fashion. Lindsay had quickly grown used to being the odd woman out in the mostly male world of international aid work. Like many of her female colleagues, she made conscious decisions about when to intrude, when to insist, when to be coy, when to play the dumb blond. And she could do them all with equal grace—it was pure pragmatism at work. Today, she elected to stand silently to one side. She would have plenty of opportunity to find out more about Hoktha and the role he would be playing as director of the reserve during the trip.

A few minutes later, the plane—"a 1982 Cessna Conquest II," Max had enthused, as if he'd built it himself—emerged from the hangar and taxied out onto the tarmac. One of the men dropped the collapsible stairs to the ground and they boarded, Hoktha climbing up first, then Lindsay, then Max following close behind.

Inside, a couch in soft gray leather and two matching captain's chairs faced a small refreshment center. Lindsay took a seat on the far side of the couch, leaving the captain's chairs to the two men. As they waited for takeoff, Max pulled a topo map from the front pocket of his daypack. He seemed a little embarrassed. "I admit it—

I have a weakness for geography," he confessed, shaking the map open. He traced one finger up the Mekong River, then moved east and circled a patch of ground in the upper right corner of the map—the province of Ratanakiri.

Lindsay leaned toward him to pore over the section he'd circled. The terrain appeared similar to the rest of Cambodia's northeastern provinces—spatters of hills, long valleys, and winding rivers. No roads intersected on the section, although two dashed lines indicated oxcart trails traversing the area. No villages were marked either, although this didn't necessarily mean there weren't any. The map was a leftover from the 1960s.

Lindsay liked maps, too. They were a quick short cut to understanding a country. On any map of Cambodia, even today, the most obvious features were the large empty spaces. These forested areas had only recently been reconciled to the government after 20 years under Khmer Rouge control. Although the maps still showed them as nothing but emptiness, Lindsay knew those blank green spaces could be sheltering secret settlements, tribal villages, illegal cross-border paths, and logging roads, all hidden under the canopy of the mysterious rain forest.

"Was the park site a Khmer Rouge stronghold before?" she asked, looking inquiringly toward Hoktha.

His reply was immediate, and annoyed. "No, absolutely not. This is a safe area. You think I would put a park in a Khmer Rouge zone?" With his words, his entire demeanor changed, from the flirtatious man of the world to a bundle of nerves.

Max stepped in without hesitation. "I was wondering the same thing, Hoktha. I know it's government land now, but up until last year, weren't the KR in control of all the forest zones?"

Hoktha calmed down, becoming pedantic. "Never in this zone, my friend. Except for the very early years when the Khmer Rouge were still working with the Viet Cong. A lot of local people got recruited as arms carriers, though, and were carried off with the army. They're still out there in the northwest provinces somewhere."

Hoktha turned to Lindsay, his tone almost conciliatory. "They have the funniest language, Linseed. Lots of *clicks* and *clucks*. You'll like it."

Accepting this as Hoktha's idea of a peace offering, Lindsay revised her assessment of his character and pondered again how to manage him. If his anger were French, she could keep charming him. If his anger were Asian, on the other hand, it was a bad sign. No matter what she did, he would feel he had the right to stay angry with her. She would keep her mind and eyes open to make sure that didn't happen, she decided, glancing at Max to gauge his reading of the exchange.

There are times in an adventure, minor or otherwise, when an odd link is established. When it happens, it can feel like telepathy, or sometimes, more like magic. As Max's eyes met hers, they entered that space, and their gaze locked long enough for them both to recognize it. Several long seconds passed, then Max's expression changed, and he turned to engage Hoktha's attention again. Was it just to massage the Khmer man's ego—or was he feeling a need to rescue her?

"How many hill tribes are there up at the site?" Max was asking. "I've heard different counts, but yours is the official opinion from here on out."

"What, you mean the *Khmer Loeu*? Well, there are over a dozen different minorities in the province, probably five or six in the park area. The largest group is the Kui—they're the ones with the funny language. Then there are some Lun, maybe 5,000 or so. There are some thousand Prov along the Lao border, then there are bits of Kachak, Phnong, Stieng, Kraveth. But the most interesting group in the reserve itself is the Tamin."

"The Tamin? That's a name I haven't heard before," Lindsay said. She'd studied the tribal descriptions in the latest UNESCO report on ethnic minorities in Cambodia, but the Tamin hadn't been listed.

"You wouldn't have," Hoktha replied, his tone supercilious. "They came from Laos about 200 years ago, according to French ethnographers who've studied this area. Now there are only three villages of them left. They used to be real forest people, but they got settled into rice farming like everyone else during the Pol Pot regime. It pretty much destroyed their old culture. Now they're just a bunch of beggars, waiting to die."

Lindsay was shocked. This was a hot topic—lost tribal groups were global treasures. What, maybe fewer than 1,000 of them left in the world? She wondered fleetingly if André was aware of these Tamin, if that could be why he was so set against the park. "I knew there were tribal groups in the area, Hoktha, but this is the first I've heard of a group that's dying out," Lindsay said. "It could make a big difference in winning the support of UNOIC. I mean, if the reserve is going to help preserve a dying culture, that would change everything."

"Culture?" Hoktha snorted. "They have no culture! They're nothing but drunks and bad rice farmers." Then his expression changed, becoming cunning as he hurried to add, "But you're right, of course. We must help them as much as we can."

Max stepped in, his voice loud in the plane's small interior and more than a little pompous. "We dealt with the same thing in the Amazon basin. Only there were eight groups, not just one, and half of them were at war with the other half. One of our biggest risks was landing in the crossfire of poison dart fights. This should be easy to manage, compared with that. But Lindsay, if these people's culture has already been destroyed, they won't stay in the forest. They'll probably all be begging in Phnom Penh within five years."

"That's pretty harsh," she remarked softly.

"Yes, that's why I prefer working with animals," he said.

As the plane taxied out onto the runway, the engine noise drowned out further conversation. Buckling up and leaning her head back into the soft leather cushion, Lindsay closed her eyes, retreating into herself as she always did on flights. Within minutes, she was asleep. About forty minutes later the subtle change in altitude and turbulence woke her, and she opened her eyes to find Hoktha still asleep. Max held a book open on his lap, but his eyes were fixed on her. Deliberately, Lindsay lowered her sunglasses to meet his gaze, and again, their eyes held. Simultaneously, they broke the connection and turned to peer down at the ground gliding smoothly beneath the plane, the intense green of the Southeast

Asian rain forest canopy. They floated over thinning forest, then barren looking scrub before seeing the lighter green of cultivated fields.

The town of Banlung, provincial capital of Ratanakiri Province, lay ahead on the horizon, its metal roofs sparkling like Christmas tinsel in the morning sunlight. Lindsay felt her pulse quicken with anticipation as the small plane swooped down toward the town. The airfield was paved with compressed red laterite, and three cows grazed on the field, forcing their pilot to circle the field twice while a farmer herded the animals off the landing strip.

Minutes after a routine landing, they were breathing the thick air of the northeast, rich and loamy with vegetation, carried to them on a fresh breeze. She wanted nothing more than to head directly for the forest, but had resigned herself to the inevitable need to first endure the formalities. Although they weren't in business dress, local officials were used to seeing *barang* dressed in hiking clothes, given the nature of their work in the field. It made provincial work a lot more comfortable.

An unmarked silver Land Cruiser pulled up in a storm of dust, its windows opaque. Hoktha gestured Lindsay to the front. "Sit up front, Linseed," he insisted. "You'll have a better view of the road."

Thanking him, she climbed in expecting to see another paramilitary crewcut. Instead, the driver was a wizened gnome, scrawny as an underfed chicken. She said hello, and the apparition grinned back, revealing a mouth remarkable for its missing teeth.

"How do you like Kal? Best driver in Banlung," Hoktha said smugly, observing Lindsay's reaction. "He has eight wives. Say's his tattoos make him irresistible to women."

"I'll try to control myself," she said dryly.

They sped away from the airstrip on the road that led to town, but instead of slowing down, the driver proceeded straight through the tumbledown shacks and passed the market plaza. "Wait a minute," Lindsay said, turning. "Shouldn't we be stopping at the governor's office?"

"Why? He's an imbecile." Hoktha said dismissively.

"Lindsay has a point, Hoktha," Max said. "This is our first official trip up here, and who are we? You, the new director of the

94

reserve; Lindsay, a UNOIC official; and me, the King's very own Special Advisor. We'd better stop. We'll be needing the governor's support as things develop. It's a good chance for a little relationship-building."

Lindsay considered that they were being a little hard on the governor, although he might be undereducated in comparison with their own elite standards. Hoktha sighed in resignation and directed the driver to turn off on a side road. Behind them, huge clouds of red dust from the ubiquitous laterite billowed, hanging in the air before dissipating slowly in the breeze. How did they manage during dry season? she wondered, then laughed as she realized that there were probably simply not enough cars up here to worry about.

The governor's mansion was a large wooden house, built on stilts in the traditional Cambodian style. Inside, a male secretary sat in a room lined with shuttered windows behind a sky blue wooden desk. He looked young enough to be still in high school, and probably was. It wasn't easy to find educated people to work in a backwater like Ratanakiri. After learning the identity of the visitors, he rushed into an inner room, looking back over his shoulder several times on his way through the door. In moments he was back, inviting them to enter with palsied wavings of his hands

He bowed them into the darkness of a large interior room, lit only by blinking Christmas lights strung through sets of tiny antlers mounted on the walls and topped with perky pink satin shades. *Like party hats*, Lindsay thought. As her eyes grew accustomed to the dimness, Lindsay gasped at the display of tropical hard woods. Not just the massive desk, but the over-sized salon set (four chairs and a coffee table), two gigantic armoires against the back wall, bookcases, the floors, the walls. Even the ceiling. It felt obscene to even be there, considering that the three of them were tasked with preserving a forest filled with these very woods.

As she suppressed a shudder, a rotund little man approached from behind the desk, spouting French greetings. "*Bonjour, bonjour, mes amis*," he cried, his arms outstretched in greeting. "I am Chea Ros, Governor of Ratanakiri." He wore a gray silk lounge suit and diamond rings on each pudgy finger. His hair was black, glossy and gleaming in an elegant pompadour. His words bubbled from a mouth bursting with rounded yellow teeth, and loose rubbery lips. His hand felt rubbery too, as he grabbed Lindsay's and squeezed her fingers moistly.

The governor was so happy to see them! His delight at receiving visitors seemed to bubble over as he grabbed Max's hand, then Hoktha's, bowing over the latter's obsequiously. In fact, the man's demeanor bordered on hysterical. Hoktha greeted him in French, laconically, and the man replied with fluent ease. Lindsay recognized the type. Probably an administrator from one of the border refugee camps, most likely Site B, the Royalist FUNCINPEC party's territory, since he spoke French.

Hoktha must have explained that she was from the UNOIC. "Our good friends, *oui, oui, tres, tres chers*," he panted happily.

Max was circling the room, his arms folded. But when the governor offered them tea, calling to the young man outside the door to bring it, he declined firmly, explaining that they had a long trip ahead and must get started. Where were they going? the governor wanted to know. "As I said," Hoktha replied shortly, then turned to introduce Max. "This is the King's Special Advisor, uncle. He will be helping on the park as well. We are inspecting the nature reserve the king has just proposed. I myself am the newly appointed director, and Mademoiselle Linseed March is assessing the possibility of lending our project the support of the UNOIC."

"*Samdech Ao*? The King proposed this himself?" The governor seemed genuinely puzzled, revealing for the first time an intelligence in his expression, which had until then remained carefully blank.

"Yes, the King. He announced it himself at his birthday reception just last week. *En face du toute le monde.*" Hoktha spoke slowly, as if the man were a stupid child.

"But is this on Phnom Sitha?" the governor asked, still bewildered.

"Yes, yes," Hoktha said impatiently. "And we are heading there now."

Lindsay stood, flexing her shoulders. "We so much appreciate your warm welcome," she said, exercising her limited French. "If we are not too late on our return, we would be happy to brief you on our visit."

The governor acknowledged her words without seeming to have heard them, more preoccupied with trying to grab her hand again. He continued to babble his appreciation and delight at their visit as they left him in the comfort of his dark wooden chamber.

They stepped back out into the sunlight. "Now can we go?" Hoktha asked Lindsay in a voice heavy with sarcasm.

"*Certainemente!*" she replied, teasing him in French.

CHAPTER ELEVEN
WEDNESDAY, MAY 26, PART II

Down in the compound, Kal was waiting, squatting beside the car. Dark smoke spiraled from the tiny pipe he held loosely between his lips. He stared unabashedly at them as they approached. Not deigning to glance at the driver, Hoktha directed him peremptorily in Khmer, then climbed into the rear seat on the passenger side.

He's so grotesquely ugly he's cute, Lindsay thought, surprised at herself. He was also refreshingly gallant—the first driver who, when faced with the choice of opening the door for a man or woman, actually chose the woman. Lindsay thanked him with a smile. Living in Asia did strange things to conventional value systems— she found herself hoping he really was the fulfillment of every fantasy for those eight wives.

Leaving the governor's house, they continued along Banlung's main street. It could have been the screen set for a spaghetti western. It wasn't just the dusty roads, but the whole feel of the place—the warping wooden structures with their zinc roofs, constructed so quickly that windows were simply rectangles sawn out of the planks after construction; the rifles slung on the backs of the men in the street; the horse-drawn wagons. In the front of each shop, rickety wooden folding tables held ancient brass scales prominently arranged beside small glass display boxes.

"Are they selling gold?" Lindsay asked, turning to address her question to Hoktha.

"The name Ratanakiri does mean Gem Mountain, you know, Linseed. Mostly, they mine zircons here. Have you seen them? Fresh from the ground, they're red, like garnets, or amber colored, but when they're heated they turn light blue. They're a favorite with the girls." Leaning forward to speak into her ear, he added, "You can get some real bargains here. We'll stop on the way out and I'll buy you one, to match your eyes."

Lindsay didn't care much for light blue stones, but responded politely, pleased to be back in the man's good graces. Turning to check the back seat, she saw Max staring out his window, his arms loosely crossed and his expression fixed in the distance. Hoktha, on the other hand appeared to be growing more restless; he had pulled a coin from his pocket and was rubbing it rapidly between his thumb and index finger.

He began speaking to the driver in Khmer, at first only phrases punctuated by long pauses, but soon becoming a monologue. The driver increased their speed, and occasionally nodded his head in ritual assent. Hoktha's tirade continued as they passed groves of newly planted bananas, rice fields, and rubber plantations with coconut shells wired to the tree trunks to collect the dripping latex. Then, the beginnings of the true forest. The road wound gradually upward, and they entered denser tree cover. With a jerk and sudden spurt of speed, the driver pulled the Land Cruiser onto the shoulder of the one-lane road, narrowly avoiding collision with a new-looking truck carrying massive uncut logs.

Although this near miss silenced Hoktha for a moment, he resumed his jabbering almost immediately. Lindsay was curious. What on earth could he have to talk about at such length, and to the driver he'd treated with disdain just moments before? His voice, becoming louder and more strident, was getting on her nerves.

"I wonder how many logging trucks come down this road a day?" she said, not really caring, but hoping to put an end to Hoktha's diatribe.

Max looked up from his dreams with vague interest, as Hoktha replied authoritatively, "In the dry season, as many as 40 a day."

"My god, that seems an awful lot! How many cubic meters would that be?"

Hoktha shrugged, but Max finally spoke. "One truck carries about 80 cubic meters. They do overload sometimes, but not usually with these new trucks. They're too valuable to abuse.

"How expensive are they?"

"Oh, maybe $200,000? I'm not sure what kind of transport costs are involved in getting them here."

Hoktha chimed in, sounding like he was reading from a script. "Once the reserve is established, we will put a stop to uncontrolled logging in my park, and we can also cut off the loggers' access to the road. They will have to move on, somewhere else."

Lindsay wondered uneasily if Hoktha's use of the word "uncontrolled" was intentional. Did he mean that, in the future, logging would continue, but that he would control it? What was the point? It all seemed so futile.

Max was reading her mind again. "It's still the good fight, Lindsay," he said, giving her shoulder a discreet squeeze. Lindsay turned to catch his eye, happy to see him coming back to life. His words acted like a catalyst, putting an end to Hoktha's monologue. Max reached into his pack to dig out another map, this one an enlargement of a portion of the original, laminated in plastic.

"*Pues*, we are getting close to the turn off, yes?" There was no track in the vicinity, but Max seemed able to interpret the terrain around him. She had always been impressed with such skills, figuring they signified a rare sort of intelligence.

Hoktha was impressed, too—and suspicious. "Yes. But how did you know? You said you hadn't been here before!" Lindsay tensed at the suppressed hostility in Hoktha's voice.

"No, you showed me earlier, on the map, remember?"

Hoktha apparently considered this a bit of voodoo, but Max stared back at him confidently. The car reeked of machismo, but eventually Hoktha backed down. "I probably care too damn much about this place," he said airily, sounding very western again. "It's like having a beautiful mistress that you don't want to share."

Max acknowledged the metaphor with a knowing smile, then changed the subject. "You know, there are over 400 different orchids growing in just the section of the Amazon I preserved, and they have separate names for each one in the tribal languages. How many orchids are named in Khmer, Hoktha? Maybe we can each name one for ourselves, hey, Lindsay?" he said, looking at her enigmatically. "How about *orchidiae lindsidium*?"

"I'm sure the tribes up here have named them already, Max. We have at least as many orchids as the Amazon," Hoktha said, apparently offended by Max's joking. "Here's the turnoff. This is where the fun starts."

The driver seemed to know the way. Immediately after making the turn, he pulled off the road next to a break in the trees where an oxcart trail began and jumped out to adjust the hubs of the front wheels. Returning to his seat, he shifted the Land Cruiser into four-wheel drive. While the door was upon, the tropical heat filled the cabin, squelching the air-conditioned cold like a wool blanket. With the heat came a faint rushing sound. Lindsay looked around with anticipation. At last, they were in the forest.

As soon as they turned onto the trail and were moving, the light deepened, becoming greener. The wheels no longer crackled in the gravel. And the feeling inside the car, that was the main difference. Hoktha was leaning forward eagerly, peering around the driver for a better view of the road. Max was keyed up, too, and his face was watchful. It's as if this place is making us more ourselves, and less what our roles demand, she thought. This disturbing idea heightened her excitement, and a *frisson* tingled up her spine.

Already the trees were beckoning, making her long to be walking among them. From inside the controlled climate of the Land Cruiser, it was easy to ignore the heat and the insects that were a reality of the forest. She remembered the haunting rush of wind? or water? that she'd heard when the door had stood open those few moments. It was like a soothing fragment of music, or a childhood memory.

Musing on the source of the sound, it took a moment for Lindsay to realize that they had finally achieved silence in the car. She congratulated herself for having distracted Hoktha from his speech, whatever it had been, and resolved not to ask him about the sound. It was better not to know than to sully the quiet.

The road was still climbing slowly, although the thickness of the trees limited their perspective. There was little undergrowth. The massive tree trunks rose straight into the air, unadorned with branches until they blossomed, at great heights, into the thick growth of the forest canopy. She could see orchids sprouting amid the thick jungle vines that twined up the massive trunks of the trees. Unwilling to break the silence, she glanced back at Max to find, once again, that uncanny connection. Leaning forward, he peered out her window, pointing to one particularly beautiful specimen. But he, too, did not speak.

It was a shock to spot the first sign of human habitation, a deserted hut tilting at an angle beside a soaring durian tree. It was roofed with fronds that reached almost to the ground. Max saw it too, and turned to Hoktha. "Is this the first village?" he asked quietly.

"Did you see a house? Yes, we must be there," Hoktha said, instructing the driver to slow down.

As they rounded a bend in the road, they saw a cluster of huts, built in the same style as the first one, with the area around them beaten down into bare red circles of earth. As the Land Cruiser slowed to a crawl in the middle of the clearing, Hoktha ordered the driver to stop the car.

As they stood in the deserted clearing, stretching away the stiffness of the ride, a dog began a slow, steady yipping. Lindsay was fascinated. She was accustomed to the sights of lowland Khmer villages, with their busy clearings, scummy ponds, oxcarts, and cultivated fields, but this was a completely different culture. While the houses seemed poorly maintained, there was ample evidence of market goods—the ubiquitous pink, blue, and yellow plastic bags used by market vendors hung haphazardly from the walls of the huts like party balloons, evidently for storing household goods.

Several of the houses had miniature huts beside or behind them. "See those?" Hoktha pointed, covering his mouth to stifle a giggle. "They're virgin huts. You're not going to believe some of the customs they've got here—best in the world. Each family builds private quarters for their teenage daughters to audition prospective mates! Can you believe it?"

Lindsay rolled her eyes at Hoktha's insensitivity, and they continued to wait in silence until a pair of men appeared from behind one of the huts. Flapping cloths dangled from thongs around their waists, covering their genitals. Their chests and shoulders were embellished with intricate tattoos, and both men wore their dark hair long, tied back with bits of plastic. Although they looked surprised to see the Land Cruiser, they moved toward the waiting group purposively, with no sign of fear or shyness.

Hoktha stepped forward to meet them, motioning over his shoulder for the driver to accompany him. They looked like creatures from different planets, with the driver a bridge between species—the features of his face were mirrored on the faces of the villagers.

Lindsay walked slowly toward them as did Max, his hands clasped loosely in front of him. Thinking that this might be a gesture of courtesy, Lindsay followed suit.

Hoktha's expression was the same one he'd tried using to charm Lindsay earlier that morning, although in this setting it looked decidedly bizarre. He was speaking fluently in Khmer, waiting impatiently for the driver to complete his translations, which were peppered with dentals, lots of hard 't' and 'k' sounds floating musically in a tonal language. The men listened respectfully, then the older of the two spoke. His expression was serene, but somehow she understood that he wasn't pleased with the message the driver had delivered.

Max's voice was low, his breath soft against her ear. "See how much he's talking? That usually means they're not happy with something and they're explaining why. If things are *simpatico*, they don't feel a need to talk." He shrugged. "At least that's how it was in the Amazon. Maybe it means something different here."

"How do you do that?" she whispered back.

"What?" he looked at her.

"You...seem to read my thoughts or something. It's very strange."

"Wait until it stops feeling strange. That's when things really get interesting," he said. She started to ask what he meant, but stopped. She would understand without asking. "Let's see if we can find out how serious this is," Max said, walked closer to the men for a better look.

Hoktha was pulling packets of red 500 riel notes from his pack, each stack of 100 notes equal to a little over ten dollars. He thrust a handful out to the driver who, strangely, ignored him, and stood looking pointedly off into the forest, his hands hanging at his sides. When Hoktha spoke sharply to him, however, the driver put out a hand to accept the packets. Reluctantly, he turned to the two tribesmen, speaking to them at length while Hoktha waited, grinning broadly. Finally, the younger of the two men took the money from the driver, but both men's faces remained impassive.

From behind a hut at the far end of the encampment, two more villagers appeared. An emaciated man, his skin strangely grayish in the green forest light, entered the clearing supported by a younger woman. An intricate tattoo, mimicking the vines they'd seen twining the trunks of the towering forest trees, encircled each of the woman's bare breasts, and there were gaping piercings in her earlobes. Lindsay thought at first that the man was ill, but the sharp odor of alcohol wafting from him as they approached made her revise her diagnosis.

The woman's birdlike voice was whiny and tremulous. The younger man responded to her complaints by tossing one of the packets of riel in her direction. It landed in the dust at her feet. She bent and picked it up, although her expression remained sharp and dissatisfied. The first two villagers seemed anxious to end the conversation, a message they delivered by ending eye contact with the driver and turning their backs on the four visitors. The driver shrugged and spoke softly around his pipe to Hoktha.

"What was that all about?" Lindsay asked Hoktha, when the driver had finished speaking.

"Oh, they're not too happy about having strangers here," he said dismissively. "They aren't really experienced in dealing with outsiders. But I try to help them out a little, introduce them to currency and things like that. They're going to have to learn, and it's better for them to learn from someone like me than someone else, like the loggers."

Getting back into the car, Lindsay felt deflated, and her cheeks burned with shame. "Those were the Tamin?" she asked incredulously.

"Yeah, now you see why we don't want to advertise them too much, eh?" Hoktha said.

Her shock turned to dismay. Where was the excitement she should be feeling on encountering an exotic, almost undiscovered tribe? She found herself agreeing with Max—maybe it was better to work with animals. And how did it happen that Hoktha knew so much about this place and about the Tamin, when his involvement was supposedly more recent than her own?

They drove ahead, perhaps sixty minutes further, in silence. This time the car came to a stop in an empty meadow that stretched down the slope in front of them in a shimmering mass of bright yellow sunflowers.

"This is it," Hoktha said.

While still disturbed by the encounter with the villagers, Lindsay's dismay faded as the majesty of their surroundings spoke to her. They stood on a small rise, and before them the sunflower meadow spread down and away, melting into the darker green of the endless forest. Birds drifted above the treetops, flashes of color shooting from their wings, and towering cumulous clouds reared up in the far horizon. The beauty was breathtaking.

"Well," Hoktha demanded, "is it perfect or what?"

"Oh yes," she breathed.

"This clearing will be a great place for a tourist lodge, parking, maybe some beer stalls. Later, we'll pave some of the roads to make it easy for visitors to see the whole park."

Max's scowl was immediate. "Rain forest reserves are a bit more complicated than a standard tourist resort, Hoktha. Too many tourists, and you'll be destroying the ecosystem we're trying to preserve."

"I've seen Khao Yai," Hoktha said, annoyed. "The Thais have built lodges all over the place."

"Yes, you're right. Unfortunately. But why do something like that, when you can do something unique, something better, instead?"

Hoktha shrugged and glanced at his watch. As if on cue, a group of men, dressed in black fatigues and carrying dull black AK-47s, emerged from the forest at the foot of the meadow.

Lindsay nudged Max and pointed. "Here comes trouble," she said quietly. "Those guys don't look like villagers to me. And I don't suppose they're park rangers, either, are they, Hoktha?"

But Hoktha was waving his arms and calling out to the men, who brandished their weapons in the air and began wading through the waist-deep sunflowers up the slope toward them. "What else would they be?" Hoktha responded, pride in his voice. "I brought them in from Samrong a few weeks ago to keep an eye on things in my park."

So the park wasn't a spur-of-the-moment brainstorm on the part of his majesty, Lindsay realized, finally. Nor was Hoktha's involvement as new as she'd been led to believe. Maybe the whole project had started out as some other venture entirely, and was being conveniently turned into a nature reserve to mollify the king? There were so many unanswered questions.

The men quickly moved up the hill, their boasting voices preceding them. There were eight of them, all wearing colorful *kremas* and sporting blue ribbons tied to their AK-47s. On their feet they wore simple rubber sandals. Their faces were almost feral, with sharp eyes and sullen expressions.

Hoktha welcomed them in effusive Khmer, and reaching again into his pack, pulled out cartons of 555 cigarettes along with more packets of riel. The men broke into grins, their faces suddenly reverting to the adolescents they were. They started chattering all at once, quarreling playfully over the cigarettes.

"These are my boys," Hoktha said proudly. "They'll do anything I tell them to do, no questions asked."

"Where do they stay?" Max asked.

"Oh, out there," Hoktha gestured vaguely. He turned to the boys and began joking with them, clapping one on the back, and giving a tug to the bulging crotch of another. They responded childishly, gathering around him like groupies.

Max turned to Lindsay. "I think we should take a walk. What do you say?" he said courteously.

"Absolutely," she said. Returning to the car to grab her daypack, into which she had packed a first aid kit, water, and some lunch, she added over her shoulder, "I can't think of anything I'd rather do than get out into this forest."

She stood by the car, watching Max pull Hoktha to one side to tell him which direction they were heading, and that they'd be back within an hour. Hoktha seemed pleased that he'd be alone with his boys. "Take your time," he called after them, as Max led the way into the trees at the top of the clearing.

At the tree line, he paused and pulled a compass from his pocket. "Sometimes those GPS units don't work in a forest. Too many blocks to the satellite, I guess. Besides, I like good old fashioned orienteering, don't you?"

"Never having used either, I wouldn't know," she said, smiling at his childlike enthusiasm.

Although the uphill slope was evident and there was no clear trail, the hike was not strenuous, and they quickly established a rhythm. Max set a steady pace, slowing down when he saw something interesting, and nodding his head to draw her attention to whatever caught his eye. All in all, she was content to have him play tour guide.

As they neared a damp low point that was caked with yellow leaves, Max stopped. Taking her hand, he tiptoed forward, his movement as slow and graceful as a stalking cat. At first she was puzzled, then startled, as the leaves rose into the air and she was suddenly immersed in saffron wings, butterflies fluttering against her face and arms. They stood motionless, letting the insects settle around and on them. The effect was startling, the featherlight brush of the gossamer wings exquisitely sensual. When the butterflies had moved on, Max laughed. It was a nice laugh, infectious, filled with *joie de vivre.*

He moved on and she followed him into the deepening shade of the central forest. Suddenly, Max stopped again. This time, he knelt next to some foliage, beckoning her to join him as he gently stroked the frond of a small fern-like plant. The leaves responded to his touch, folding inward in a curiously dramatic and graceful motion. Kneeling beside Max, Lindsay again smelled the soap of his morning shower, now mixed with the salty clean scent of his body. As they bent closer to the fern, their heads almost touching, Lindsay found her eyes drifting to Max's hands. They looked so rough, but so able. She felt a sudden welling of desire, imagining those hands on her body.

"Look at that orchid," Max said pointing into the tree trunk in front of them. "It's not a variety I recognize, but it's amazing. Maybe it's the *lindsidium?*" Following his pointing finger, she saw a cluster of pointy pink blossoms with red and white flecks suspended from the trunk of the tree. She hoped the greenish light disguised the flush on her cheeks as she watched his fingers, ever so gently, stroke the smooth velvet of the petals, probing just where they widened like the lips of a woman.

She felt his expectant eyes on her, waiting for her response. "Do they have a scent?"

"No, not these. Some do, though. The ones in Hawaii. I always thought those were a little brash. I prefer the more understated," he said, looking fondly at the flower, then back down at Lindsay. Leaning toward her, he put his face into the curve of her neck, inhaled lightly, and drew back. "You, on the other hand, smell just right," he said complacently, ignoring her gasp at his touch. "Now, if we were out here in the evening, I'll bet we'd smell some great blossoms—moon flowers, *dama de la noche,* for two. Olfactory senses increase at night, too."

Lindsay felt more than heard his voice, feeling that he was as much a part of this experience as the trees themselves. Somehow, while everything he said was new, his presence was familiar and comfortable. She wondered briefly if it were Max or just the setting, but put the thought from her mind without further examination. Although she had an overpowering desire to feel the warmth of his breath at her neck again.

"Did you have a particular destination in mind?" she asked, "Or are we just wandering?"

He looked at her again with that sense of pending interest. "You don't know?" he teased. "Guess you'll have to wait and be surprised."

"Oh, I'll be surprised, I promise," she laughed. "Even if I had a map, I'd have no idea where we are. I was just testing my ability to figure you out. You're not offering any road maps to yourself, you know."

"Am I a river, or a mountain?" he said, smiling enigmatically at her comment.

They walked on in silence, Lindsay realizing that she was hungry for the sound of Max's voice. It was a soothing voice, but stimulating. Resonant, with just enough foreign inflection to intrigue, a voice that hinted of subdued passion. Suddenly, she was dismayed by the thought that, in just a few hours, this would all be over.

Ahead of her, Max stopped abruptly and she walked into his back, using her hands to steady herself by gripping his shoulders momentarily. In the distance, she caught again that rushing sound, now deeper in pitch. "I think we're almost there," Max said. "Can you tell where the sound is coming from?"

A test? She listened carefully, moving her head to check for changes in volume. "That way," she guessed, pointing her finger to the right.

Max nodded, leading her up the steep embankment to their right. It was only a short climb, and at the top she laughed with delight. A waterfall cascaded down into a steep canyon, obscuring gigantic boulders that formed a series of pools beneath. Shade and sun moved in a flickering dance on the waters, while the shadowed areas tinted the waters a delicately cool green.

"You're a good sport for coming here with me, Lindsay," Max said, standing close beside her.

"It's pure pleasure, Max. Sporting is if there had been bugs."

He frowned. "Well, the malarial mosquitoes will be out before long, but we'll be gone before then. I've got military-grade repellent if we need it, but I'm sure we're safe for now.

Lindsay's sigh expressed her glory in the scene below them.

"It does look inviting doesn't it?" Max said. "Too bad we don't have time for a swim. Lindsay, just imagine this place, this temple of nature, littered with garbage from junk food picnics. Imagine snotty-nosed kids screaming. Imagine cigarette butts floating on the edges of the pools, used condoms among the rocks. It is criminal. It is worse than murder, what this place will become if I am not able to control Hoktha's greed."

"How could you possible control it, here in Cambodia? That's how people treat parks," she said. Again, she wondered about André. Was the scene Max was describing at the root of André's objections to the park? Had André ever seen this place? And why, for that matter did that man keep intruding into her thoughts? He was such an annoyance, even when he wasn't there.

"Through the King, Lindsay," Max was saying, responding to her question. "Hoktha's a jerk, but I want him to be our jerk. He'll have to listen to Sihanouk. Between the two of us, I'm hoping we can convince him to play his little power games in the city, going to receptions with important people, traveling to other countries on educational tours, giving interviews to the press. He'd love it, he might even be good at it. And you and I—the Special Advisor and the UNOIC Public Information Officer—can manage the reserve ourselves." His laughter rose above the crashing of the waterfall. Moving to the water's edge, he knelt down to test it with his fingers. Scooping water up in both hands, he splashed his face, soaking his hair and neck.

While Lindsay enjoyed the flattery of being included in Max's fantasy version of the future, she had no illusions about her involvement in the park management. "You, Max. You'll be the manager. But can I come visit, maybe have some VIP tours?"

He looked pleased. "Any time, *querida*. I am at your service." He shook his head, sending drops of water flying in a halo that caught the sun's rays in a rainbow that mirrored the shimmering in the waterfall below.

Lindsay swallowed. She badly needed to be distracted from the physicality of the man. "Max, look at the time," she said. It was late afternoon. The shadows were lengthening, and their return flight to Phnom Penh was scheduled to take off well before dark. Max nodded and returned to her side, leading the way back down the embankment.

At the foot of the hill, he turned and headed back roughly the way they had come, this time twice as fast, with no stopping for nature studies. In less than fifteen minutes, they had arrived at the head of the open meadow. It was deserted. Hoktha, the black-garbed boy soldiers, the Land Cruiser—all had disappeared without a trace.

CHAPTER TWELVE
WEDNESDAY, MAY 26, PART III

W hile Lindsay and Max waited beneath the forest canopy, gathering firewood and erecting a shelter against Hoktha's failure to return for them before nightfall, the chaotic pulse of Phnom Penh life pounded on.

At the UNOIC office, Bopha's growing unease mounted to concern, and then to out and out worry as darkness settled down with no sign of Lindsay's return. She tried to reach André, but a recording informed her that his mobile phone was out of range. Long after both expatriate and local staff had switched off their computers and mounted their motorcycles for home, she remained at her desk, waiting.

Earlier, Lindsay's driver had called in on his radio from the airport, giving a confusing report about the King's plane arriving, without Lindsay. It had, he said, refueled and then taken off again, after spending only two hours on the ground. Bopha had instructed the driver to ask around and get as much information as he could, and to stay at the airport until it closed.

Where could Lindsay be? If she were in trouble, how could Bopha possibly help her? And what was this strange relationship one had with foreigners? Most of the time, Bopha felt like a child, with the foreigners seeming to know so much more about the rest of the world and its strange ways. Other times, it seemed the foreigners were the children, unable to look after themselves.

But there was no purpose to this line of thinking. Acceptance, just accepting things the way they were, that was the key. Although Bopha was a good Buddhist, her practice was largely limited to the concept of acceptance. Because her early years had been lived during the Khmer Rouge regime, Bopha had missed out on the cultural lessons, including Buddhism, that would have filled a Khmer childhood in normal times. Although many of her memories, thankfully, were vague, she could remember the endless walk, her mother's disappearance, the work camps with other children. And she remembered hunger, hunger so strong that it entered her dreams for years after the Vietnamese had taken over her homeland.

But those days and dreams were gone, the country was quiet now, and she had a good job with UNOIC, earning enough to support her invalid father and two sisters. The years were passing quickly, and she was growing old, well beyond the usual age of marriage for a Cambodian woman. Not that she wanted to be enslaved in a relationship with a Khmer man. At 27, she had resigned herself to spinsterhood, but finding a friend in André had brought a new dimension into her life.

Narong had known André first. Then, when André had arranged for her brother's student visa, Narong had asked André to promise to take care of his sister while he was gone. And André had taken his promise seriously, checking in with Bopha at least once each week, and usually making sure she knew how to reach him when he was out of town. When they were together, André treated her with great respect. He had made her feel like a real person. In fact, he had been the opposite of most of the men she had ever met, who seemed to love talking about themselves and treated women as possessions. But neither André's words nor his behavior had suggested any interest beyond that which he proclaimed—he wanted to be her friend, a kindly uncle.

Bopha's friends at the French Embassy gossiped that André was a spy for the French government, and maybe it was true. Why else would he consort with such a man as General Som Sak? Or maybe…maybe he was not the man she thought he was, perhaps he was a man with a heart full of evil, like the General himself? But no. Throughout Bopha's life, time and again her survival had depended on her ability to judge people, and she knew in her heart that André was a good man.

Which left the question—should she tell André the truth about Som Sak's past? Her blood ran cold at the thought of the General. Although he was now a powerful member of the government, she knew what he had been. During the Khmer Rouge years, General Sak had been in control of the province to which her family had been sent, and he had been personally responsible for some of the most horrendous atrocities of those Khmer Rouge years. She must tell André, and she would, when they met for dinner again. But where was he now? She'd promised him that she would protect Lindsay, and she feared she had failed them both tonight.

She gave herself a shake and brought herself back to the present. Where was Lindsay? Better to deal with the here and now, especially when time could make the difference if Lindsay were in trouble. When Lindsay did arrive, she must tell her about the terrible letter in the English newspaper. But how could she do that? Lindsay would be so hurt, and so mortified at the public exposure of her innocence. She was trying so hard, so determined to do well in her new job.

Sheet lightening brightened the deepening gloom, followed by a low grumble of thunder. *A big storm*, Bopha thought. *The plane cannot land in this weather. It means they will not be returning tonight.* Slipping into a rain poncho, she locked the office and ran to the street, flagging a passing motorcycle taxi and directing it to the northern edge of the city.

***

Across the river at the Hu Fang restaurant, the General Quartet was enjoying the last of what had been an extended dinner. The plates on the table were scraped clean, and a litter of gleaming bones decorated the floor beneath their chairs. Just a kilometer beyond Spean Chrouy Changva, the Japanese Friendship Bridge, the Hu Fang Restaurant stood beside the river like a carnival queen among its shabbier neighbors. The green, pink, and orange bulbs threaded across every horizontal, vertical, and diagonal surface ensured that there would never be a dark and stormy night at the Hu Fang.

In an air-conditioned back room, the four generals sat slurping the last of their peppered pig's stomach soup, the house specialty, from over-sized bowls. Exuding the satiety that comes with a good meal, the generals leaned back in their chairs to set their stomachs at liberty and facilitate a better view of the young woman approaching their table.

Gliding gracefully from chair to chair, the woman set a cut glass tumbler before each man, pausing to pour measures of amber spirits from the bottle of Johnny Walker Red Label she'd brought from the Hu Fang's locked storehouse. The generals had been specific about this. They wanted none of the cheap Vietnamese counterfeit whiskeys that were paraded on the shelves behind the bar.

The young woman was dressed in a floor-length velvet gown; the jade green color emphasized the creaminess of her exposed shoulders. Her hair was drawn up in an Edwardian arrangement with tendrils curling symmetrically to tickle her neck. A beauty queen banner crossed her tiny bosom, emblazoned with the words *Rémy Martin*.

A flurry of lesser girls appeared momentarily in the doorway, their faces curious, but sullen with envy. Unlike the Rémy Martin queen, these girls wore miniskirts in varying hues, and color-coordinated baseball caps. On the caps were logos for Fosters, San Miguel, and Victoria Bitter beers. No one knew these girls' names; they were called simply the blue-red-green girls. Whispering conspiratorially, they moved down the corridor, pulling the curtain across the doorway of the room as they left.

The tremor of the Rémy Martin girl's hand betrayed her fear. It was slight, but it was enough to catch the generals' attention, like sharks smelling blood. General Som Sak smirked as Boon Chu patted her ass, pinching the tender flesh with a cruel twist of his nail. Vanna, the Rémy Martin girl, gasped, splashing whiskey onto Boon Chu's lap. *"Mehta apeidtao, lok tom!"* she apologized, moving away from his fingers, which were still pincering in the air.

Som Sak spoke before Boon Chu could express his anger. "Don't worry, *Ohn* Vanna," he rasped. "Keep bringing us whiskey, and General Boon Chu will forget your lapse."

The curtain covering the doorway flapped to admit Som Hoktha, freshly bathed and oozing Drakkar Noir cologne. Sauntering to the generals' table with a self-satisfied expression, he tossed a small cloth bag onto the table in front of his uncle. The three undergenerals grabbed eagerly for the package, but withdrew their hands at General Som Sak's hoarse obscenity, *"Joimai, gantuy aing!"*

Hoktha laughed. He loved seeing his elders shame themselves, especially when he set them up for it. General Sak, however was not amused. "So, *Ah*-tha," he whispered without looking up, using the condescending form of address used by superiors to their inferiors. "You have brought me something of interest?" He made no move toward the bag, his eyes narrowing at the faces of the other generals, now glaring with open hostility at Hoktha.

Hoktha was not stupid. He recognized and accepted his uncle's need to put him in his place, to demonstrate his power in front of his friends. Controlling his mirth, he reached gracefully past General Boon Chu's belly to reclaim the bag. He would show his uncle a full measure of respect by properly presenting his gift.

Slowly, he untied the yellow strings that fastened the top of the bag. Holding the bag in his right hand, he spilled its contents onto the palm of his left hand, enjoying the rapt attention of the three generals. His uncle's gaze was still fixed on the ceiling. Moving slowly, deliberately, he transferred the objects into his right hand, grasped his right wrist with his left hand, and reached forward to present the objects to his uncle. "Honored older brother of my mother," he said formally, his head bowed "please kindly accept this unworthy token of my respect."

The General remained immobile, his eyes narrowed in concentration, like a sleek dog thrusting its narrow nose into the burrow of a far smaller animal. Of course, Som Sak treated everyone coldly, so that meant nothing. Hoktha knew, however, that there were degrees of coldness, and felt the tiniest shiver of adrenalin at the sound of his uncle's quiet amusement, the hoarse laugh known as the Phnom Penh death rattle.

Hoktha stood motionless, his hand still outstretched as he waited for his uncle to accept his gift. On his palm were six stones, uncut and of unprepossessing appearance. Each was the size of a large pearl. The entire table breathed a sign of relief when, at last, General Sak leaned forward. He first sifted through the stones with the overlong nail of an outstretched little finger, then reached into his shirt pocket, pulling out a pair of jeweler's tweezers and a small silver cylinder with a magnifying glass capping one end. Plucking up the largest stone with the tweezers, he subjected it to a minute examination through his jeweler's loupe.

Against the light, through the grimy film of the sapphire's rough surface, shone the pure unclouded blue of summer skies. Sak tilted the stone to different angles, holding it now nearer, now further, from the glass. The undergenerals sat impatiently, longing to retrieve the other stones from Hoktha's still extended palm. Hoktha smirked at them.

Finally, the general spoke. "Very acceptable, Hoktha," he said, returning the first stone to Hoktha's palm. "It is of good clarity. There are no occlusions or cracks." Hoktha nodded silently in acknowledgment.

His uncle arranged his tools on the table in front of him, then extended his own hand toward his nephew. Hoktha gently rotated his wrist, allowing the gems to drop, one by one, into the palm of his uncle's hand. Indicating one of the smaller stones, he said, "I believe this is the most exceptional of them all, Uncle."

Their slow, almost ritual actions and formal, measured speech had a certain beauty. Somehow, the cold gems warmed their faces, and both uncle and nephew revealed their intelligence through their expressions of admiration and respect for these stones, the intense blue found only in Cambodia. Mixed with their appreciation, of course, was the satisfaction of knowing what the stones signified to their future.

"So you have a half dozen this time?" Som Sak inquired softly.

Hoktha grinned widely. "Yes, Uncle. All without flaw or blemish, and quite intact."

The other generals sniggered with delight, correctly interpreting the game of *double entendre* the men were playing. Hoktha looked inquiringly at his uncle. "I hope that this gift expresses fully my appreciation for your support in securing my new position."

"You have done well, Hoktha, and your work is timely. These are important attributes in an up-and-coming official of our government. But I'm wondering—how did you manage the cargo with your two guests along?"

"Quite simple, Uncle," Hoktha said, unable to disguise the boasting in his voice. "I met with the villagers on our way into the reserve. I completed my negotiations and payment under the very noses of the foreigners, who have of course not bothered to learn our language. Then, while the Colombian and the woman were admiring the beauties of the Ratanakiri forest, the car was diverted," he coughed lightly, adding, "...an unfortunate mechanical breakdown. While my mechanics studied the problem, I collected my purchases, and—*voila!*—I am now here, delivering these tokens of my esteem to you."

"But what of the guests? How did you manage to return to collect them before coming here?"

Hoktha covered his giggle with the fingers of one hand. "They are still in the forest, Uncle. Although I will rescue them in the morning. You might say it is an extra bonus that they have been obliged to spend the night there. They will have an even greater understanding of the beauty of the nature reserve; perhaps it will increase the woman's credibility with her colleagues who must make the decision to support us."

Sak's voice was tinged with warning. "Take care with the man from Colombia, Hoktha. We still do not know to whom he belongs. He may be here to set up a competition with us. Most likely, though," he said, looking tenderly down at his hand, "it would be with our other commodities, rather than our little gems."

"Knyom youl hauy," Hoktha agreed, before adding in English, "but the woman, she is a naïve creature, easily distracted."

"And what lady would this be?" a voice interrupted from the doorway. The Cambodians swung around to see Major André Balfour leaning casually against the door jamb, the curtains already drawn behind him.

"Your little nemesis from UNOIC," Hoktha answered, laughing. "I imagine she's surveying available accommodations at the new reserve, just this moment." When André's face betrayed no reaction, he added, his smile turning to a leer, "But I have no fear for her. She is with the Colombian. I'm quite sure he will go to great lengths to protect her honor."

The generals sniggered again, one of them emitting a noisy belch.

"You left her alone with the South American?" André asked, annoyance in his voice. "What are you thinking? Do you want to anger UNOIC on your first week on the job? Mademoiselle March is not just another of your local girls, you know. They will not ignore an insult to her."

Hoktha smirked. "Are you concerned for her reputation, André? Surely you know that western women don't worry about such things. They are liberated, not like our little maidens, and they enjoy their animal nature like any man. Besides, we must find the way to reach more influential UNOIC officials than this silly girl."

"Hoktha, you know I disagree with you about the park. You have developed a secure and integrated operation in the northeast. You are hoping the park will allow you to expand your operations, but I fear that the reserve will do just the opposite. And there can be no doubt that it will bring very risky scrutiny to bear on the whole area. The first tourist that gets murdered wandering about on the wrong path will bring all your hopes to an end. Why not delay the park, at least until we have secured another supply line?

That could serve a double purpose by disguising your special interest in this area." Throughout this exchange, General Sak sat quietly, closely observing the younger men.

"Don't be a fool, Major. And please, don't forget about the bureaucracy of UNOIC. It will take them ten years just to figure out how to respond to our request for their support. So we have plenty of time."

"And that is why I am so concerned. The exposure—they will bring in missions, and consultants, and guests, when what you really need is the quiet and seclusion you already have. In any case, just remember, this woman does represent UNOIC. Any insult to her will definitely damage our operations."

André flexed his shoulders beneath the dark blue fabric of his dinner jacket. Turning to the generals, he said, "But I am here not to cross swords with Hoktha. We must discuss our business. What is the schedule for delivery of the next consignment?"

The exchange between the two young tigers seemed to have lifted Sak's spirits. His response to André verged on the playful, although his tone remained flat. "Yee-e-e-e, Major, you are very impatient. Is there, perhaps, a woman waiting for you, her legs already splayed? You must remember, everything comes at its proper time. Yet you insist on talking business. So tell me, your principal—is he ready to buy in or not? We do not wish to waste our time unnecessarily if he is a looker only, and not a buyer."

"He is satisfied with the quality, although still not convinced about the quantity. He liked what he saw well enough, but he is uncertain that you can provide sufficient amounts of the same quality on a regular basis," André said, turning an empty chair around and straddling the seat.

"Does he doubt us?" the General questioned with dangerous quietness.

"I would not say doubt. Let us say he is cautious, a proper response for such an important business, *ne c'est pas*? After all, my friend is willing to pay much better than the Thais, an important factor, now that the AIDS epidemic is making the Thais so nervous. Rest assured, my friend would be disappointed if you were not exercising the same caution as he."

General Sak, mollified by this response, finally offered André a drink. Raising two fingers, he gestured to the Rémy Martin girl. Vanna had remained in the room throughout the discussion, sitting quietly in a shadowed corner. Now, she slipped out through the curtains, returning with two additional crystal tumblers. She poured the whiskey into the two glasses and placed one before André, the other in front of Hoktha. She then circled the table, refilling each general's glass in turn.

André ignored the girl, downing his drink in a single gulp and holding it up for a refill. Hoktha, piqued at his exclusion from the conversation, grabbed the bottle from the girl and poured his own drink, twice the amount she had poured for the other guests. The girl giggled coyly as Hoktha handed the bottle back to her, but she kept a careful watch on the men's hands and slipped back to her chair after a quick glance at the General.

"My friend will have his final answer for you within the next week," André said quietly. "At that point, we must arrange a meeting, possibly in Singapore, where we can finalize our agreement and compare the merchandise and the payment, side by side."

"What don't you understand? Why can't you see how this is a perfect fit with my nature reserve?" Hoktha interrupted. "When your deal comes through, you will need me to supply the raw materials. Then you will be glad I am controlling the entire park area."

"I am responsible for this deal, not you, Hoktha!" his uncle snapped in Khmer. "The Frenchman may be right—UNOIC support for the park may make it more difficult to obtain supplies, rather than simpler, as we anticipated. We may have miscalculated."

Hoktha flushed at the public remonstrance, but said nothing.

André observed this exchange impassively. He considered saying something friendly to lighten the tension, but understood that this was a western approach. Instead, he rose and excused himself, saying he had appointments elsewhere. General Sak nodded, not bothering to ask where. He glanced at General Boon Chu, seated opposite him, through lowered lids. General Boon Chu maintained an extensive intelligence network, with servants placed in the homes of most expatriates throughout the city. Tonight, André would attend an informal dinner at the French Ambassador's residence. Since the butler was in Boon Chu's employ, later that same evening they would know what had been discussed at the ambassador's dinner. Boon Chu was gifted in managing surveillance. Unfortunately, his cirrhotic liver would soon put this activity to an untimely end.

After André had gone, Hoktha said, still smarting from André's words against his plans, "How can you do business with this sharp-nose, Uncle? I have contacts, we can make our own deals. I tell you, we do not need this *barang*!"

Som Sak affected patience. "Hoktha. You must learn to think before you open your mouth. In fact, you have many things to learn. Your education in Europe has perhaps spoiled you, for you are acting as stupidly as a sharp-nose yourself. This man Balfour came to us, remember? You think I trust him? Ha! I reveal nothing to him. His hands now are dirty, my nephew. He has taken the girls we provided him last week across the border into Thailand as samples. We can afford to wait—with our knowledge of his activities, he is in our power as long as he remains in Cambodia. You should help me in this, by doing what I tell you, and keeping your mouth quiet."

Hoktha's face flushed darkly, but he nodded respectfully. Getting up from the table, he made polite goodbyes to his uncle and his fawning underlings, then walked to the door, his hands clenched tightly at his sides. His uncle called to him as he reached the curtained doorway.

"Don't forget to take care of the shipment, eh, Hoktha? Madame Nhu will watch over them for me. See they are sent to her." Hoktha nodded without turning around, and disappeared through the curtains.

On his way to the car, Hoktha gave the parking attendant a vicious shove, and as he sped away from the parking lot, tires screeching, he sent a *cyclo* driver diving into the gutter to avoid the front bumper of the Mercedes.

As he drove, Hoktha reached for his mobile phone. He punched in a precoded number, and at the answer snapped, "Take the girls to Madame Nhu. And be careful, you fool. If their skin shows any marks, it will be the worse for you. I will be waiting there."

While he was talking, he turned down Street 242, the core of Phnom Penh's raunchiest nightlife. Cheap pink lights glowed along the avenue, framing the doorways where girls and women sat chatting in folding chairs as they waited for customers.

Since his arrival back in his homeland two months earlier, Hoktha had begun to think of André as a friend as well as a business partner. Someone more nearly his own age, someone who could understand things better than his uncle, whose character had been fired in another era. It was lonely in this business, after all, and a person of Hoktha's sensitivity needed a confidant, a partner. Max wouldn't do. The idiot was so in love with his trees, he couldn't see the forest, or the treasures it sheltered.

But now André had seen Hoktha humiliated in front of his uncle and the other generals, had even contributed to his humiliation. Was he a child among the adults? Why couldn't they understand that the nature reserve offered the perfect opportunity to expand and link their operations, rather than threatening them? Ratanakiri would be his forest kingdom, a center of international operations. The possibilities were endless—logging, gems, drugs, not to mention his pet enterprise, which thrived on the human products of the hill tribe villages within the park's perimeter. How dare they look down on him!

As his small eyes darted angrily along the street, Hoktha spotted a young girl, her hair tied back in pigtails, the slightness of her body disguised by Chinese lounging pajamas. She was sitting on a cheap plastic chair, playing with a small white dog. The girl's face in the pink light looked ghostly, with its thick coating of light foundation and garish lipstick.

Slamming on the brakes, Hoktha lowered his window, and studied the girl's slim body. Suddenly he laughed, remembering what he had neglected to tell his uncle. He put the car in gear and accelerated, the engine racing as he headed back to the waterfront.

Uncle Sak need never know that a seventh girl had returned with him from Banlung, a girl even younger than the rest.

CHAPTER THIRTEEN
WEDNESDAY, MAY 26, PART IV

This is the right field...?" Lindsay said, turning to Max with some doubt in her voice.

"Definitely," he said, his face serious, but his voice amused at her concern. "Hoktha's probably off checking out another part of the reserve. It's a big area, and there's a lot to see." He pointed ahead to a shaded area. "Let's just make ourselves comfortable, and wait, shall we?"

Max immediately began studying his map, which, Lindsay realized later, probably signaled his own concern over the situation. Determined to stay calm, she refused to listen to the voice in her head that was whispering the warnings of Bopha's fortuneteller. Instead, she pulled out a tattered paperback copy of *The Old Curiosity Shop*, grateful that she'd thought to stick it in at the last minute. Slowly, she sank into the adventures of Little Nell and her grandfather, sipping frequently from her water bottle.

Max's interruption a half hour later dragged her back into the present. "You might want to take it a little easy with that water," he suggested. "We don't want to start dipping into the waterfall unless we absolutely have to. Giardiasis, you know."

She studied him for a moment, wondering if he knew more about their situation than he was admitting. *He's probably just used to contingency planning*, she told herself, determining not to dwell on negatives that she couldn't change anyway.

Dickens held her attention for another hour, and this time the interruption that disturbed their concentration was her stomach rumbling. "Ay-ay-ay, that poor thing. Let me see if I have something for it," Max said, reaching for his pack.

"Thanks, I've got some lunch, too. We could share...but Max, look at the sky," she said, pointing to the horizon, where the sun had already dipped below the mountains. "I don't think we're going to get back tonight." She paused, then added, "What do you really know about Hoktha, anyway?"

He met her gaze, then moved over to sit beside her, wriggling a little to make himself comfortable. "That's better. Well, I met Hoktha through Princess Juliette. It seems they know each other from Paris."

Lindsay ignored the fact that Max had avoided her question, letting herself be distracted by his mention of the princess. "And how did you meet Juliette?" she asked.

"Hard not to, really. The King heard about my work in the Amazon from an old friend of his from the Association of Nonaligned Nations. When he invited me to come here as special advisor on the nature reserve, Juliette was one of the first people he introduced me to. Whenever Queen Monique is away, she serves as a kind of Royal Hostess at the palace, you know."

"She's very beautiful."

"Yes, magnificent. Reminds me of that fishing cat I brought you, wouldn't you say? Could eat me in one gulp, I imagine."

Max's tone left Lindsay unsure whether Max found this an enjoyable prospect or not. "Did you understand what was going on with the governor this morning?" she asked.

"First tell me what you made of it?" he shot back.

"He's no imbecile," she ventured, "no matter what Hoktha says. And... it seemed to me that he knew Hoktha, or at least understood him pretty well, and that he was afraid of him, somehow. Which made me wonder who Hoktha might be when he's not directing a nature reserve."

"You put together quite a lot, on some pretty scarce evidence, Lindsay," Max said, his eyes keen. "But you may well be right. What else?"

"Well, I know that there are dual heads of government in most provinces. Usually, when the governor is a member of FUNCINPEC, somewhere below him there's a Cambodian Peoples Party Deputy who wields most of the power. I was surprised we didn't meet him, because he would probably have a lot more to say about the nature reserve idea. I'm sure Hoktha would know that. If not, he's awfully naïve, and we may run into trouble getting the province on board with the plans for the reserve."

"I don't think he's naïve, Lindsay. He has powerful connections—that's what makes him think he doesn't have to worry too much about following protocol. Even Juliette seems to be a little afraid of him, which surprises me a lot. I suppose I'm expecting his western education—the one he got before his recent dip into the field of forestry, I mean—to make him rational."

Lindsay laughed. "So am I, Max. We're quite the bigots, aren't we?"

Max checked his wristwatch, then reached into his pack. "Enough of that," he said. "Let's grease ourselves up with repellent and take a walk around the clearing. Maybe there's a track leading off from the other side they might have taken."

After applying the pungent lotion to every square inch of exposed skin, Lindsay got up and dusted herself off. As they strolled along the perimeter of the clearing, keeping in the shade along the forest edge, they listened to the piercing whistles and squawks of the birds just within the foliage. A half hour later they had circled the meadow, but there was still no sign of the Land Cruiser or its occupants—and the afternoon had slipped into early evening.

Returning to the top of the glade, they brought out their respective lunches and began a picnic, sharing their food but reserving enough for a second meal. As they ate, Lindsay returned to her questions. "Something else, Max. What was the strange conversation with the driver all about?" she asked him.

"I have no idea," he said dismissively, speaking around a cracker piled high with herbed cheese. "It might have been important, but I'm a lot more worried about those." Lindsay followed his finger, which pointed into the distance where the mountain of cumulous clouds had darkened and lowered.

"Oh great," she said. "I thought Hoktha said the weather would be clear all day up here."

"We need to think about shelter," Max said. "After that, we can plan our vengeance on Hoktha."

Lindsay looked at him, realization hitting her with the impact of a battering ram. "You don't think they're coming back, do you?" Several terrible possibilities crossed her mind in rapid succession. Their car had been waylaid by bandits! Hoktha's so-called guards had turned on him! The villagers had taken the Land Cruiser hostage!

Max's voice intruded, reading her thoughts of disaster. "I'm sure its nothing, Lindsay. Hoktha probably took his boys off for some booze, to reward their loyalty or something, and drank too much himself. At some point he'll remember to send the driver out after us. But in the meantime, well, let's just be sure we're prepared."

He got up and studied the area. "That looks like a good place," he said pointing to a spot at the top of the clearing. "High ground, so there'll be good drainage when the storm hits, and the trees will provide some shelter. Let me see what I can rig up."

"I'll scout around for some firewood, then," Lindsay said. "I'd like a campfire, and it will help them find us. Just in case they're looking."

"Good idea. It's probably pretty cool here during the night, anyway. You don't happen to have a poncho with you, do you?"

She did, since it was part of UNOIC's regulation kit for fieldwork. She handed it to Max and headed into the forest. Gathering dead branches and twigs as she went, she began to hum. *It's surprising,* she thought, *how quickly a strange situation begins to feel normal.* She laughed, remembering the affirmation she'd practiced in college. *I am in exactly the right place, doing exactly the right thing, at exactly the right time*, she whispered, bending over to grasp a particularly large branch. Glancing back to see Max hard at work on their shelter, she added thoughtfully, *...with exactly the right person.* Although she felt less certain about the last bit.

It took a surprisingly short time for Lindsay to amass an impressive pile of firewood in a neat stack right beside their campsite. As she returned with the last armful of branches, Max was just covering the shelter with the second poncho. He'd used the first to line the floor of their makeshift tent.

Stepping back to survey his work, he announced proudly, "Just the right size for two, *querida*. Although now that it's done, they'll probably be showing up any minute."

Lindsay cocked her head, hearing a distant rumble, but it was only the growing roar of the wind in the trees—and an echoing crash of thunder. She thought she'd come to an acceptance of their predicament, welcomed it even, while she'd been gathering wood, but out here in the clearing, the sky was wilder, more powerful and threatening. She shivered.

Max looked concerned. "You're cold?" he said.

"No, just expecting to be," she laughed.

He bent down to her woodpile, selecting some small pieces and arranging them in a neat cluster just outside the gap he had left as an entrance to the tent. "You're a bureaucrat, you must have paper," he said.

She scowled at him. "Don't stereotype me, Max, and I won't typecast you. But...I do have some paper." When she looked back at the sky after digging some scraps of paper from her pack, she realized with alarm that the storm had arrived.

The wind swelled to a roar, the canopy of trees thrashing in a frenetic dance. Lightning flashed in jagged spears that jabbed into the earth. Their position at the top of the clearing provided a front row view of the majesty of the storm.

"This is going to be fantastic," Max said slowly, his eyes on the gathering heavens. "Come on, Lindsay. We might as well stay dry." He crawled through the opening into their teepee, and, pivoting, held out his hand to her just as the first drops of the storm spattered to the ground. Clutching his hand for balance, she crawled in after him, twisting to avoid landing in his lap. As it was, there was no way to avoid the contact of their legs and shoulders, although it was surprisingly roomy inside. Lindsay realized that she could probably stretch out comfortably if they ended up spending the night here. Max would have to leave his feet outside, she thought, giggling at the picture this would present to any nocturnal visitors. The image of their bodies stretched out in the tiny teepee made her wonder exactly how they would spend the night, whether it would seem awkward or natural.

She flinched as Max brought his hand to her face, gently wiping the raindrops from her cheeks. As the storm increased in force, they craned their necks to watch the show. So far, at least, the inside of the tent was perfectly dry. The ventilation Max had arranged by interweaving branches kept the plastic from feeling stifling, and Max had fastened everything together with almost military precision.

The pounding of the storm was deafening. Lindsay leaned against Max to speak directly into his ear. "Thanks, Max," she murmured, but he just shook his head and smiled, unable to hear her words. Then he held up one finger, signaling her to wait, and reached into the bottom of his pack to pull out a chased silver flask. He opened it and held it up for her inspection. Bending over the neck of the flask, her nose was hit with the heady scent of brandy, very good brandy. She took a swift swallow, feeling the mellow fire burn and numb all the way down. "Perfect," she mouthed, handing the canteen back.

They passed the canteen back and forth, consuming most of its contents before the storm abated to a steady drumming on the roof of their teepee. Max had stretched his body into a loose curve, conforming to the inner perimeter of the teepee, his head propped up on his elbow. "There are very good ghost stories in the Amazon, Lindsay," he said, his voice deepened and slowed by the brandy.

Lindsay sat cross-legged against the opposite wall. She looked down at him. "*Digame*," she said, still aware enough to know that the brandy that had slowed Max's speech was filling her with a sense of infinite well-being.

He told her five different stories in all, each one a path for inane conversation, although the last two were decidedly lascivious in nature. Throughout the night, the rain pelted down and the wind howled through the forest. At one point, the lightening struck close enough that they smelled ozone, followed by an instantaneous and violent crack of thunder that sent Lindsay into Max's arms. He squeezed her tightly, then released her and went on with his story.

They continued to sip from Max's flask, achieving a companionable and whimsical drunkenness. He sang a song, a folk song of the Andes, and applauded when she reciprocated with an aria from *Nozze di Figaro*.

By the fifth story, they had reached the dregs of the flask, forgotten their missing vehicle, and were at peace. He fell asleep first, pulling his shirt off and curling up like cat, his pack under his head. The storm had passed, and Lindsay crawled from the shelter to appease her brandy-swollen bladder. Outside, the stars were emerging from the clouds. *I could stay here forever*, she said aloud, before returning to Max's side in the teepee.

The starlight outlined his tousled hair, the rise and fall of his chest. In wonder that even half a flask of brandy had not dulled her libido, she reached out to run her hand over his smoothly muscled torso, the sculpted marble of his chest and shoulders. When she found her hand wandering further, she stopped and spoke sternly to herself. *Take it easy, Lin*, she thought. *In case you've forgotten, you're not supposed to take advantage of the guys you get drunk.*

Oh, all right, you old fuddy-duddy, she responded to her conscience, this time speaking aloud. *Go ahead then, go to sleep, and throw away the best opportunity you've had in years.* She giggled slightly as she curled herself into the hollow of Max's shoulder, realizing the humor in being torn between gratitude for

Max's courtesy—and her frustration that she wasn't being swept up into that magnificent chest.

They were both awoken by furtive movements just outside their shelter. As can happen in the wilderness, Lindsay found herself immediately alert despite having only a few hours of sleep. Looking up, she saw that dawn was just breaking, the gray tones of the early morning sky tinged with delicate pinks and golds. Already, the earth and the air were growing warmer. Looking around, she saw that Max was awake as well, his head tensed and listening.

Moving soundlessly, he shifted toward the entryway and looked out. Joining him at the door, she gasped. Three feet away sat a sunbear, studying their pile of firewood. He looked like a loveable little teddy bear, but Lindsay knew that the sunbear was another endangered animal prized by the Chinese for its medicinal powers. The bear sat sedately, cleaning itself with an incredibly long tongue.

"They can catch termites with that tongue," Max whispered, his breath warm in her ear. "That firewood you brought in was probably full of bugs; that's what brought him here." They sat motionless, watching, but the bear had sensed them. It turned, looked them straight in the eyes, then rolled onto all fours and lumbered off into the forest.

Lindsay stretched luxuriantly, feeling as rested as if she'd slept on a down duvet. "I don't even miss my coffee," she said.

Max was sitting up, pulling on his boots. "Come on, let's get to the waterfall before they come back," he grinned. "Can you imagine how gorgeous it's going to be in this magical light?" He scrambled from the tent, extending his hand to help her. He pulled her from the tent easily, without wrenching, and kept her hand clasped firmly in his own as they retraced their steps to the waterfall.

Max looked great. The body she'd traced blindly during the night was even more appealing in the dawn light. His skin glowed with good health and well-toned muscles. The hand holding hers was gentle and strong at the same time.

With a final scramble up the bank, they were there. Max was right—the place was enchanted in the early morning light. Mists swirled above the pools, and a small rainbow wavered in the single ray of sun that fell on the spray rising from the falling waters. They stood mesmerized until the rising sun caught them full in the face. Max whooped with exhilaration. "Race you to the bottom!" he cried, clambering over the rocks to the first pool. The mist, rising from the pool, felt warm against Lindsay's skin, warmer than the ambient temperature, a strange sensation.

"I can't wait to get into that water," Max shouted, pausing on a damp rock just above the water to kick off his boots and socks. For a minute he dangled his toes into the water, seeming to ponder something. "Lindsay...I hope it's okay with you if I swim?" he asked politely.

"I'm right behind you," she said, watching Max as he nonchalantly stripped off his pants. She watched his powerful muscles stretch as he leapt from the rocks, landing in the water with a resounding splash. Surfacing, he turned onto his back and floated low in the water, with just his head above the surface.

But Lindsay was no longer watching, suddenly feeling shy. *Oh, no*, she thought. *None of that. This moment will never come again, and you are going to live it.* After pulling off her own shoes and socks, she tugged her t-shirt over her head, then reached back to struggle with the snap of her bra. She had worn, as always, black French lace lingerie, a matching set. It was a conceit and she knew it, but at least it was a hidden one. Usually. While she didn't dare to look directly, her peripheral vision told her that Max was watching her struggles with appreciation.

Suddenly, it seemed that the past twelve hours had prepared her for this new level of intimacy. She became acutely aware of her body and of his, and her awareness translated into a new grace in her movements. Turning to face the pond, she arched her back and reached up, stretching languorously, a soft smile spreading across her face. Slowly, her breasts straining against the lace cups of the bra, she released the clasp and let the bra fall to the ground. Then her hands moved to her belt, smoothly unbuckling it and unfastening her khaki trousers. These, too, she allowed to fall to the ground, raising each leg in turn to release it from the binding fabric. Hooking one finger around the elastic of her panties, she slid

them to the ground, fully aware of the slim firmness of her body
and the glowing paleness of her skin.

Moving closer to the water's edge, she executed a shallow but
graceful dive. The water was delicious against her skin, cool but
comfortable, like crisp clean bed linens. In a moment, Max was
there. He was standing, she realized, although the water was well
over her own head. Leaning back to submerge her head into the
water, she felt his touch on the back of her neck. As his hand
drifted over her shoulder and down her spine, setting her nerves
tingling, she watched his face descending. Her last thought, as she
felt his mouth moving on hers, was that his lips were softer than
the fur of the little *chmar prei*. For those few moments, the world
contained nothing but their two mouths, teasing, biting, tasting
each other for the first time in many long years.

When she finally opened her eyes, she found him looking down,
a somber expression of awe on his face. "You are very beautiful,
Lindsay March," he said simply.

"So are you," she said without thinking, trembling a little,
yearning for his touch. That special link had definitely not
disappeared during the night. She felt Max's hand sliding across
her skin, propelling her into shallower water. He guided her around
like a floating boat, one hand at her neck, the other now low on her
belly. As he came to a halt in the chest-high water, he set her
upright and brought both arms swiftly to her back, cupping her
buttocks before moving further down the backs of her legs. Gently,
knowingly, he pulled her legs toward him, parting them and
guiding them around his waist. From below, she could feel his
insistent erection nudging against her.

Lindsay arched her back, biting off the quick intake of breath as
he moved his palms up over her ribs and cupped her breasts. She
held her breath, keeping herself high in the water until his arms
went around her again and his strength pulled her up from the
water, her breasts level now with his mouth. His lips and tongue
were hot against her nipples, and she tightened her legs around
him, sensing the hardening of her own erection as she felt the tip of
his penis against her. Cradling Max's head against her breast, she
moved with him as he guided her body down to join with his, his

hands urging her hips steadily forward until he was entirely, fully, inside her.

They were both ready. The tension that had been building since the King's reception, when they'd seen each other for the first time in over a decade, had reached the boiling point. Now his hands set the rhythm, his mouth fastened on one breast, as they danced the world's oldest dance beneath the spray of the pounding waterfall. Their mutual explosion came as the sun's full glory burst through the canopy above.

Finally, Max released her, raising his hands into the air with a victorious whoop, then collapsing backward into the water. Lindsay's knees were shaking with her own release, but a sense of wellbeing flooded her as she remembered her mantra of the previous evening: *the right time, the right place, the right person—and doing the right thing.*

But as she slowly returned to earth, she become aware of the fading mist, the warming air, the buzzing insects, the vanished rainbow—and the reality of their predicament. A battered Pepsi can bobbed up in the water beside her, and her eyes were drawn to the algae scum floating around the edges of the pond. What had she done? She tried to suppress her growing unease. Max, too, seemed restless. Standing, he took her hand and pressed it to his lips. "Thank you, *querida*, for bewitching me," he said.

But to Lindsay, the words did not ring true. They sounded like a packaged pitch, words grown weary through repetition. For the moment, she ignored the warnings flapping in her brain, instead reaching up to kiss him, lingering a last moment before swimming for the bank.

By the time they had dressed, gathered their belongings, and returned to the clearing, another hour had passed. Lindsay's fatigue was catching up with her, and she was wondering yet again what would happen to them, when the sound of an approaching vehicle reached her ears.

Before it arrived, Max drew her to him in a tight hug. "This will be our place, *querida*," he whispered, kissing her ear. "We can be together here. But Lindsay, no one must know."

Lindsay was puzzled. "Why would we worry about that, Max?" she said, tracing his jaw line with an uncertain finger. "If we want to be together, why would we want to keep it a secret?" But her true thoughts went unspoken. For she was ashamed to realize that she, too, would rather keep this adventure secret from the rest of the world. And her question to Max went unanswered, because at that moment the Land Cruiser roared into the clearing.

Moments later, Hoktha was climbing down from the driver's seat, his face plastered with an insincere smile. He was dressed in an outfit even more trendy than that of the previous day, and his hair was again styled immaculately.

"*Mon Dieu!*" he said. "Are you all right?" He'd expected to find Lindsay and Max tired, dirty, hungry, and thoroughly annoyed. But here they were, full of smiles and glowing with health—or something.

"Actually, we were worried about you, Hoktha. What happened?" Max demanded.

"Oh, it was ridiculous. I was taking the boys into town, giving them a lift, you know, and the damn car broke down. A military truck came by and gave us a tow, fortunately. But by then it was after dark. I was able to stay at the governor's house, but I couldn't sleep at all, knowing you were up here without any supplies or shelter. I wanted to send someone after you, but I had no one to send."

He glanced around, spotting their small shelter. "But it seems you've managed to take care of yourselves," he said, his voice changing into a leer as he pointed to the teepee and directed a sly wink at Max. "I see you even constructed your own virgin hut for the night," he said, clapping Max on the shoulder. Max's answering laugh was hearty, and Lindsay looked the other way, wondering again just what she had done—and what it had meant to Max.

Hoktha helped them load their packs into the Land Cruiser, and with no further conversation they set off on the road back to Banlung.

CHAPTER FOURTEEN
WEDNESDAY, MAY 26, PART V

A ndré lounged at the French Ambassador's table, flirting over coffee with a slender blonde dressed in a sophisticated sheath of blood red linen. His long fingers caressed his demitasse spoon, stroking its curves with slow intimacy as he discussed the merits of different forms of traditional massage in Southeast Asia.

Seemingly oblivious to the Khmer waiters hovering behind their seats, the woman said in a low voice, "You have convinced me, Major. In fact," she added, joining his fingers in their sensuous exploration of the spoon, "I demand a demonstration."

"That could be arranged," he suggested slowly, his dark blue eyes gazing deeply into hers. "Perhaps this evening?"

The dessert plates had been cleared and the last of the wine had been poured. Madame Ambassador's eyes were noticeably glazed as she nodded in uncomprehending accompaniment to a chubby little Hungarian priest who was explaining in detail the curriculum of his training program for bicycle mechanics. Pulling herself together, the woman exchanged glances with her husband and rose, signaling the end of what had seemed an interminable evening.

Shortly afterwards André, arm-in-arm with the blonde, exchanged farewells with the host and hostess and departed into the night in his vintage Citroën. The waiter who'd been observing them watched the car disappear, speculating baldly to the butler on the sexual adventures awaiting the Frenchman.

Following the blonde into her suite at the Cambodiana, André closed the door, keeping his hand on the knob. "Turn on some music, *cheri,*" he advised, completing a quick scan of the room before adding, "It will put me in the mood for love."

Her face twisted into a sardonic moue, but turned to the radio on the bedside table, flicking through the stations until the mellow notes of a jazz saxophone entered the room. "Is that romantic enough?" she asked, her expression deadpan. At André's answering grin, she tugged up the hem of her long gown and sat cross-legged on the bed. "Quickly, give me a rundown on how the negotiations are going. Is Sak biting?" She asked.

He sighed in frustration. "I think so. My sources tell me that the Thais truly are getting nervous on the AIDS issue. Apparently they read the World Health Organization survey reports with great interest. But the generals are nevertheless refusing to lower their prices. I fear a trap. If I seem overeager, they will be suspicious. It is a murky business," he added, stretching out on the bed beside his Interpol contact, Solange Dumaurier.

"You cannot imagine how tiresome these reformed Khmer Rouge are. Living off the forest for so many years has turned their brains to humus, I think." André was restless, moving from the bed to the minibar in the entryway, picking up the tiny bottles, one by one, to examine their labels. "I think cognac is in order, although I doubt it's up to Embassy standards," he remarked, opening a bottle and deftly dividing the contents between two snifters. "As for the generals, they are now far too busy worrying about their Swiss bank accounts to attend to business."

Solange accepted the glass he held out to her, and they sipped in companionable silence. André removed his shoes and loosened his tie before again stretching out on the bed. "You managed to steer them onto the proper subjects, then?" Solange said, watching André's lean features relax.

"*Mais oui*, although I've had to run up a few bills at the casino. I hope they will be covered. As if I could afford the VIP salon on my consular salary!"

She chuckled. "Well, I suppose it depends on the outcome. You are deliberately leaving me in suspense," she chided, her husky voice soft.

"Well, we did make some progress tonight. I have agreed to buy, made a final commitment, in fact, and we have scheduled an exchange—my nonexistent principal, the generals, myself, and the goods. And I goaded Hoktha into admitting that he will indeed use the park as a cover for what he considers an integrated ecological system—buying village women and children, selling them—to people like me or the Thais—for drugs, and bringing drugs back into Cambodia to trade to the loggers and miners in exchange for their gems and logs, and more women and children. Once he's got his hands on their legitimate resources, timber and gems, he'll offer those for sale abroad. All we need now is an actual exchange, and we'll have them. Unfortunately, Hoktha is completely unpredictable. I fear that he will do something reckless that will upset everything. In fact," he sighed, turning to lie on his side to face her, "Do you know what that idiot has just done?"

Solange laughed. "No, André, how could I know?"

"He deliberately stranded the UNOIC woman and the Colombian environmentalist overnight in the jungle. If he's as stupid as that, what else will might he do? Sak was annoyed, and scolded him in front of his underlings. Dangerous, that. Hoktha is not a man who likes to lose face. But I am worried about Lindsay. She seems so innocent, and distrusts me completely." He grinned in response to the question in Solange's eyes. "Yes, it's true. I wish that were not so. But—"

They both froze as the telephone chimed, looking at it in horror. Finally, Solange picked it up. "Hello?" she asked cautiously. After

139

listening in silence for a moment, she turned to André. "Are you expecting someone?" She hissed.

He looked at her for a moment, his puzzled expression slowly changing to elation. "But it is incredible. It is a woman, right? A Khmer? Yes, tell them to send her up," he said.

Solange nodded, speaking softly into the phone before replacing it on the bedside table.

"What's this all about?" she said, concerned.

André laughed. "An amazing feat of bravery, a moral tale of good and evil, the prevailing of right over wrong—"

"Have your fun, but you cannot put me off long with that bullshit."

A light knock on the door set them off again, and they laughed at each other's jumpiness. This time, André got up. He pulled the door open to find a Khmer girl standing patiently, her arm firmly gripped by one of the hotel managers. His expression carefully neutral, he said. "Sir, this lady is asking for you. Is it correct that she has an appointment?"

"Yes, that's right, son," André answered heartily, loosening the man's fingers from the girl's arm and gently pulling her into the room. He reached into his pocket and removed a 100 baht note. "Good night," he said handing the bill to the manager.

The man pocketed the money, leering as he backed away. Solange stayed seated on the bed, studying the girl from her perch. "What exactly does she have to do with the battle between good and evil?" she asked.

"This girl has already risked her life once tonight, and now risks it again by coming here," André said.

The girl appeared to be in her early teens and was dressed in the Southeast Asian version of American sportswear—a neatly pressed t-shirt, awkwardly cut denim jeans with heavy white topstitching, and red platform sport shoes. On her back was a puffy blue plastic backpack, like a giant Barbie Doll accessory. Her hair was tied back with a simple elastic, the ends elaborately curled in ringlets that had been so heavily sprayed they shone like obsidian.

The girl looked anything but brave at the moment. Her face was modestly averted, and her fingers were strangling each other.

André gestured for her to take a chair near the television, and offered her bottled water from the stand beside the television. She accepted a glass and sipped repeatedly.

"André, tell me what this is about," Solange said impatiently.

The girl looked up at André. "This is a friend?" she asked. He nodded, and she began to talk. "Madame, my name is Vanna. I work at the Hu Fang," she said in clear English. "My brother was a soldier, he was *kohn jao* to Ta Sak—" referring to the system by which military officers expect familial loyalty from their men, and are in turn addressed as grandfather "—and he was blamed for stolen money from the payroll. Ta Sak sent him to the frontlines, even though he did not take the money. He was killed less than a week later." There were worlds of hurt behind her simple statement.

"I'm so sorry," Solange said, looking at her for the first time. "And now you want to help us."

"I want to revenge my brother," Vanna answered simply, wanting to be sure they understood her reasons for helping. "Mr André promised to help me, if I helped him."

"She was working at the Samaki Hotel, where I'd been staying," André explained. "She told me her brother's story when it happened, and I suggested she try to get a job as one of the drinks girls at the Hu Fang."

"Because I am tall, they let me be the whiskey girl," Vanna interrupted.

"And being the whiskey girl, Vanna has the honor of personally serving the generals when they meet there in the restaurant's private room. They don't even notice her, talk in front of her as if they were alone. If they knew she was listening—"

"They would kill me." Vanna had a devastatingly direct way with words.

Solange downed her brandy, all playfulness gone. "Oh God, André, this is how you've been finding out about Som Sak, isn't it?" she said. "Well, I hope it's worth it," she added. But her expression was dubious.

Vanna began her report, relating what the generals had discussed prior to André's arrival. She described the gems Hoktha had delivered, and the puzzling conversation that had accompanied them. At the mention of Madame Nhu, André asked her if she had ever heard this name before, and she nodded tentatively. "I think this is the woman that Ta Sak set up in the squatter camp on the river," she said. "He was complaining about the rent for such a bad place. But the location is necessary, Hoktha told them. The boat can come directly to deliver the girls."

"Yes, we know they come down the Mekong," André said. "But what we don't know is where they go from there. Were you able to learn anything at all?"

"The generals were saying about Thailand," Vanna said. "And General Rith Ken is the one that Ta Sak looks at when they talk about the girls."

"General Rith Ken, when he's not drinking in Phnom Penh, is the commander of armed forces in the southwest of the country, from Pursat to the Thai border," André explained to Solange. "So it's very possible that he's moving the girls out through his territory. For sure they're not going through Poipet. We have informants there—we'd hear about it. Anyway, they are especially careful with these girls. They have special value because they come from Ratanakiri and their keepers guarantee that they are virgins, disease-free virgins with protective powers."

Turning back to Vanna, André said, "We have to know for sure though, Vanna. We need a specific place."

"I will try, Mr André," Vanna said.

"It better be soon," Solange cautioned. "This is a dangerous game, especially for you, Vanna."

"I don't care. I am not afraid," Vanna said bravely.

"I know you're not," André told her, his voice gentle, "but I wouldn't want you to find yourself part of their next shipment out of the country. Hoktha is another problem," he said to Vanna. "What do you think of him?"

Vanna shivered. "I am afraid of him," she said stolidly, looking younger and more vulnerable.

"You're right to be frightened," André told her. "You stay as far away from that man as you can."

At this advice, Vanna rose to her feet. "I must go," she said nervously. "My father will be worried if I am later."

André saw her out the door, then turned to Solange. "This stupid nature reserve is a nothing but a complication. If only the King had waited a few more months to make his proclamation. Because I'm afraid that once he's got his own little kingdom up there, Hoktha will go completely crazy. Not that he has far to go. We've got to stop him before that happens. And this Colombian has his own plans, I'm sure. Probably drug running. They're both using that UNOIC woman for cover, the bastards. It is all I can do not to lose my temper with those fools. How can they be so blind? Max thinks he can control the Khmer, while all the time the Khmer are leading him by his *zizi*, and they both think they can manipulate Lindsay."

Solange thought a moment about these remarks. "Do you think that Som Sak is deliberately planting Hoktha on you, because he suspects you?"

"Anything is possible, but I don't think so. Well," he said, looking at his watch, "do you think we've allowed enough time for a believable seduction?"

Solange's lips curved into an appreciative smile. Her eyes swept down the length of André's compact body. "Surely not," she said seriously. "Perhaps we should try it and see how long it really takes. Don't you think it's the best way to avoid suspicion?" she added, sliding down beside him on the bed.

André's arm seemed to have a life of its own, wrapping itself around her shoulder and pulling her close. But his lips landed lightly on her cheek. "Oh, Solange. You cannot imagine how tempting that offer is. Coming from you, it's not easy to refuse," he said, moving away from her impending embrace. "But I'm afraid I must decline."

Solange shrugged with good-natured resignation, reached down into the bodice of her loose dress and pulled out a small package the size of a matchbox. "You take your work too seriously, Major. I'd thought you might enjoy discovering this for yourself. That's why I didn't give it to you earlier."

"I was wondering when you were going to hand it over."

Solange clicked open the small box. Inside was a crumpled piece of fine silk. She carefully unfolded the cloth to reveal a pear cut emerald, at least 15 carats in size.

"*Mon Dieu,*" André breathed. He studied the emerald, which shimmered with the brilliance of morning sun on newly planted padi, finally looking up with an expression of almost religious wonder.

"Evita's Teardrop?" he said.

Solange nodded. "If you lose this, André, your career is finished."

André moved away and she heard him say softly, almost to himself, "It is worth even more than our agreed-upon price. And if I lose it, it will be more than my career that is finished." Turning to face her, he said, "I'm sure that this stone will convince him, Solange. It will prove to him that we are serious, and that we can be trusted. That means that by this time next week, we could be back in Paris."

"*Il ne faut pas vendre la peau de l'ours avant de l'avoir tué,*" she said, her lips tight. "It's never that simple, and you know it."

"Solange, we are not speaking of bears or of selling their skins. If the nature reserve becomes reality, it will mean a personal fiefdom for Som Sak and his nephew. It will have nothing to do with conserving the environment, that is evident. But they will gain power, legitimacy, and incredible wealth. The area is huge, and it is filled with natural wealth of many kinds, not just the gems, and not just the girls. It sickens me, this using the King and UNOIC as fronts for such meaningless greed. I don't understand how the King has let this get so far, why he has given this travesty his blessing. I mean, I can understand a young innocent woman trying to make her career, but not the King. He should know better."

"Oh, *cheri*. You are a true royalist, aren't you? But I still think you are more bothered by the woman than the park."

"And you are trying to flatter me by making me think you are jealous," André laughed, pressing his lips to Solange's cheek again before heading out the door.

CHAPTER FIFTEEN
THURSDAY, MAY 27, PART I

By morning, the skies had cleared. The early morning sun sparkled on the wet leaves of the Ratanakiri rubber plantations, on the puddles in the packed mud yard around Bopha's modest home north of Phnom Penh, and on the hand-made wind chimes tinkling above the porch where Sam and Olga sat drinking their second coffees of the day. In Ratanakiri, Hoktha had arranged a helicopter from the fleet left behind by the Russian UNTAC team for their flight to Phnom Penh, the King's Cessna having already returned to the city.

As if reluctant to surrender to its abandonment, the interior of the copter's cabin still sported pornographic photos, captioned in Cyrillic script, taped along the inside of the cabin. Lindsay concentrated on ignoring her surroundings while she covertly studied Hoktha.

Something about him made her distinctly uneasy, not least because his actions over the past two days had maneuvered her into an extremely vulnerable position, both with UNOIC and with the Cambodian government. She glanced at Max and sighed. More confusion there. Her encounter with Max had been in direct conflict with her struggle for validity in a male-dominated professional environment. And as she looked at him from behind the dark lenses of her sunglasses, she admitted that it had also been out of alignment with her own personal standards.

Closing her eyes, she projected the interpretation that would be placed on her unexplained absence. Through the loud drone of the blades and engine, she heard Hoktha's high-pitched voice and opened one eye to see him grin wickedly and grab Max's thigh. "It was very rough for you last night, Max? And perhaps very rewarding, yes?"

Lindsay stiffened in anticipation of Max's response, flooded with the sudden realization that the entire adventure—up to and including the waterfall—could have been nothing more than Max and Hoktha's well-orchestrated strategy to ensure themselves of her support for the park. But Max made no reply, behaving as if he hadn't heard or understood Hoktha's meaning. Lindsay exhaled, suddenly realizing she had been holding her breath in anticipation. Was there no one she could trust, nothing in this country that was as it appeared? How dangerous was Hoktha, really? The small voice at the back of her mind, the one she relied on when no other information was available, told her that where Hoktha was concerned, she was definitely at risk, both professionally and personally. Unfortunately, the little voice was not adding any useful instructions on how to deal with these threats. Perhaps she should ask Bopha to take her to Wat Phnom to ask for more details on her future. Hoktha was, after all, a dark man, and so was Max. And Ratanakiri was even more of a faraway place than the rest of the country.

She was jolted from her reverie by the descent of the helicopter. "Where are we?" she shouted over the roar of the engine. Surely they hadn't been airborne long enough to have reached Phnom

146

Penh. When Hoktha didn't answer, Max repeated her question, leaning forward to yell into Hoktha's ear.

Hoktha shouted back. "Kampong Cham. We'll take a boat from here. The helicopter is needed back on the border."

Remembering her last trip on a boat, Lindsay glanced at the sky and was relieved to see the clouds huddling passively along the eastern horizon. They quickly disembarked onto a small air field. After a quick coffee, white with the thick creaminess of sweetened condensed milk, they boarded the boat and sped downriver toward Phnom Penh. Hoktha sat beside the pilot, using the high frequency radio set near the wheel for heated conversations in Khmer through much of the first half hour.

The trip was quick and mercifully uneventful. Lindsay awoke two hours later to find her neck cramped at an angle and the temple spires of Phnom Penh looming ahead. It was just after noon as they passed through the shadows beneath the Japanese Friendship Bridge and zoomed on, leaving a scattering of small craft rocking in their wake. On the floating dock, a small group of people waited.

As they approached, Max gripped her shoulder to shout into her ear. "So, *querida*, you will support the park?"

Lindsay shrugged, then shouted back. "I can't promise, Max, but I'm feeling that it is a great idea, and I'll certainly make that clear in my report to David."

"Good girl, Lindsay," he laughed, releasing her shoulder and turning to face the welcoming committee.

Lindsay caught her reflection in the chrome fittings of the boat—thoroughly bedraggled—and laughed. What fun Hoktha must have had setting up this welcoming party just for her discomfort. But the humiliation was greater than she'd expected, for as they docked she identified the extraordinary profile of Juliette Sovannalok, waving avidly and crying, "Max, Max, welcome home, darling!"

Hearing these words, Lindsay gulped, a knife twisting in her guts. Darling? It seemed like proof enough, all the proof she needed anyway, that what they'd experienced together in the raging of the storm had been nothing more than a ploy.

Juliette wore silk, an antique gold that shimmered along every curve of her sinuous body. "Darling, I thought you would never come back to me, I was so worried when I heard you were lost," she gushed. "Oh, I see that you brought the little UNOIC girl with you," she added, turning to Lindsay. "Oh, my dear, do forgive me, I've quite forgotten your name. But I'm sure it's you that I've just been reading about."

Lindsay's survival instincts were on full alert. "Lindsay March, your highness," she said, holding out, then quickly withdrawing, a grimy right hand. "I had the honor of watching your dance at the reception last week. But you say you've been reading about me? Perhaps you have me confused with someone else?"

"Oh, no no no, I am quite sure it was you, *oui, je suis certaine.* But I am being so silly! Of course, you have been in the wild forest, you have not seen the latest news in the English paper."

Ignoring the confusion and dismay on Lindsay's face, Juliette turned back to Max, using her fingers to rub a smudge from the thicket of bristles sprouting on his chin. "But darling, I really must whisk you away. You look in a dreadful state. I can see you badly need the attention of a woman." She glanced quickly at Lindsay, gauging accurately that her last words had hit their mark as she tucked her beautifully manicured hand into the crook of Max's elbow.

Max, Lindsay tried not to notice, made no effort to extricate himself from Juliette's grip. Instead he smiled charmingly down at her. "I think we could all use a bath, my princess. Do you have transport available for us?"

"Oh, darling, you are coming straight to the palace with me." She shifted her head toward Lindsay and said negligently, "Hoktha will take the UNOIC girl home, won't you, Hoktha?"

Lindsay thought fast, ignoring Hoktha's appraising stare. Before he could answer, she found herself saying coolly, "No worries, my office is just up the road. My driver will take me back home from there." When no one, not even Max, replied, she steeled herself and said her farewells. "Well, good bye Max, Hoktha. It has certainly been interesting. Your Highness, a pleasure to see you again." As she turned to go, Max stepped toward her. "Lindsay, we'll talk soon," he said. For the first time she noticed that his eyes were just a tad too close together, and that his hair began just a bit too low on his forehead. She barely heard his words as he continued. "But if you don't hear from me, don't wait. Get that report on David's desk as soon as you can." He winked, she winced, and imagined the gloating expressing that the princess must be wearing. Turning away, Lindsay walked steadily toward the office, clutching the shreds of her dignity.

Two blocks and five minutes later, Lindsay entered the deserted UNOIC compound, waving hello to the armed guards outside the gates. Inside, she found a neatly printed note from Bopha on her desk, written the previous afternoon. "David is back. He would like to see you as soon as possible."

Shit, thought Lindsay, *Why couldn't he have waited until I got this sorted out?* She climbed the stairs to David's office, preferring whatever she might find there to her own imaginings. But David had not yet returned from his lunch, and she was flooded with relief.

Waiting for coffee to brew, she spotted the most recent edition of the Phnom Penh Piper among the UNOIC propaganda publications on the table in the middle of the reception area. Grabbing it, she threw herself onto a chair and leafed through the tabloid until she reached the Letters to the Editor section. The title words stared up at her from the page.

Innocence Abroad

Open Letter to UNOIC:

Regarding your recent spate of articles on the proposed northeast nature reserve, it is clear that you are missing certain key pieces of information. I speak from years of experience in Cambodia, much of it in the northeastern provinces. Based on my recent trip to Ratanakiri, I would ask you to consider, and answer, the following questions.

1. Are you aware that the reserve is nothing but a front for Cambodia's most powerful generals to continue their wanton rape of the forest?

2. Why is UNOIC colluding with this rape, through its whitewash campaign promoting the nature reserve while ignoring all evidence of environmental degradation?

3. Why has UNOIC appointed a naïve and inexperienced young woman as the Public Information Officer responsible for working with the government on this proposal?

4. Where are the Environmental Impact Reports, timber surveys, and anthropological studies to support this project?

5. Has UNOIC considered who stands to gain from this ludicrous proposal? Who has authority and responsibility for this project?

Tell me, UNOIC! And study the aerial photographs. It is obvious that logging has already reached deep into the so-called nature reserve.

A True Friend of Cambodia

Editor's note: the photos referenced in this letter were received by the Post, but were not published due to lack of technical corroboration. The Post would like to assure its readers that we take these issues seriously, and will continue to investigate the nature reserve proposal.

Lindsay stood to retrieve her coffee, setting the paper down carefully, stifling the impulse to tear it to pieces and stomp on it. Rationally, she knew the attack was on the proposal and not on her, personally. But she'd been made to look ridiculous, and would now be an object of either derision or pity. *Maybe a quick trip to Singapore?* she thought longingly. No. She'd accepted this job because she wanted to be challenged, and she wasn't going to run away the first time a challenge appeared.

But before she could pursue the topic of just how she would confront this ordeal, the door of the office opened and an unlikely couple stepped into the reception area. The man was tall and very thin, his sunburned face contrasting with sandy blonde hair and the most tranquil gray eyes she had ever seen. The woman was large and statuesque, as tall as the man and a good ten years older. A thick plait of dark auburn hair trailed down her back, and high angular cheekbones suggested a Slavic or Scandinavian ancestry. Both the man and the woman were underdressed by UNOIC standards, clearly members of the sandal-and-ethnic-fabric crowd, as an unsympathetic colleague called them.

Lindsay sighed and stumbled a bit as she stood up. "I'm sorry, but the office isn't really open," she said, gesturing to the darkened rooms and blank computer screens around her. "Is there something I can help you with?"

Sam and Olga stared at Lindsay, their expressions puzzled. Then Sam said gently, "Hey, are you all right?"

"Me?" she asked, not wanting a response, knowing it was her disheveled appearance that had shocked them. "Oh, I'm just a bit tired. Long field trip. So, are you looking for someone in particular?"

Olga spoke with exaggerated slowness. "We are here to see Lindsay March about the proposed nature reserve in the northeast. There are some serious issues around that area that UNOIC may not be taking into consideration. It is very important," she added more quickly, sensing Lindsay's imminent dismissal.

Lindsay looked at her, finding herself returning to what seemed a constant preoccupation these days. How much to trust whom? "You're talking about the logging? I am Lindsay March, by the way."

"Nope. Logs are logs, but this is about people, and it's appalling." The man couldn't wait to tell the story properly, to make his case. "Ms March, here in Phnom Penh we're finding more and more girls, young girls, on the streets. Most of them seem to be coming from Ratanakiri." Sam's voice was low and intense, willing her to take him seriously. "As you know, that's the location of the proposed nature reserve."

But Lindsay was too tired to notice. Her hand strayed to her forehead to rest her head a moment. Olga, misinterpreting Lindsay's fatigue as boredom or disbelief, placed a hand on Sam's arm. "Let's just go," she said. "We are wasting our time."

Lindsay opened her eyes and glared at them. "Great. First it's raping the environment, and now it's children that are being raped. This place is beginning to sound like the House of Usher. Don't you dare leave this office without telling me what you know and what you think UNOIC ought to be doing about it."

Olga caught the telltale catch in Lindsay's voice. "You have seen page five, then," she said with a carefully neutral directness.

"Hard to miss," Lindsay said bitterly.

"You will come with us, and I will buy you a strong drink." Lindsay, watching from some remote part of her brain, amazed herself by saying yes.

She left the room to scrub the dirt from her face and run a comb through her tangled hair, then reported her return to Kimson in the radio control room, picking up a fresh radio battery on her way out the door. Rejoining the couple in the reception area, she found them bent over the Royal Bulletin, a slick monthly digest of news articles covering the King's activities, thoughts, and accusations.

"Do you know who this is?" Sam demanded, jabbing a finger at a color photo on the cover of the journal.

Peering down, Lindsay said, "Yes, I'm sorry to say that I do. That's the new director of the nature reserve. I'm just back from an entirely too long trip to Ratanakiri and the park site, and he was one of my traveling companions. I've left him back at the dock, right before you two walked in. Why do you ask?"

"I saw him," Sam announced, stabbing the page with a thick forefinger, "in the royal compound two days ago."

Lindsay laughed. "Well, he probably has more right to be there than you do," she said, picturing Sam attending a royal reception in his tie-dyed farmer pants. "He's related to some mucky-muck or other, and that's why they've appointed him to this position. Supposedly he just finished a degree in Tropical Forestry in Indonesia, but after listening to him over the past two days, I suspect the degree was purchased. It certainly wasn't earned."

She glanced at Olga, waiting for her to add to the discussion, but her eyes were focused on the bulletin boards lining the wall.

Lindsay shrugged and said, "Who are you guys, anyway? Guardian angels?"

Olga came back to the room with a snort of laughter. "I doubt many NGOs would see me in that role."

"Oh, I don't know, I think it suits you," Sam countered. Olga didn't respond directly, but a faint smile softened the strong lines of her face, revealing a tenderness between the two visitors.

Sam spoke first. "I'm Sam Jarrett, and this is Olga Herrin. We both work with street kids here in the city. And at the risk of

152

sounding like conspiracy nuts, we believe that young tribal girls from Ratanakiri are being abducted for sexual trafficking. It's got to stop. Proclamation of the area as a nature reserve could put an end to it, if it were legit—or it could provide someone with the perfect cover for expanding the business. I'm guessing it all fits in with the gem mining and the logging somehow, but I don't even care about that. Because there's more..."

But Olga's hand on Sam's arm interrupted, warning him to silence as a trio of local staff members arrived back from their lunch break. "Later," Olga said softly, and the three of them stood to leave.

They headed for a small café on the river, nondescript but comfortable. Taking seats around a secluded rattan table on the deck above the rushing current, they ordered a bucket of beers on ice with three glasses and a basket of bread, after Sam laughed and said he'd had all the coffee he could drink for one day.

Lindsay sipped the cold beer appreciatively and glanced at her watch. Still not one o'clock. She made a mental note to have beer for lunch more often, forced herself to relax, and said, "Okay. Tell me."

Sam opened his mouth, shut it, then said, "Olga, you're the one who knows the most about this. Please, you start." Although the two of them had prepared for this visit by putting together a list of incidents, evidence, questions, and plans of action, Olga was still the one with the most personal knowledge.

Lindsay looked at Olga with curiosity. The older woman seemed kind enough, but there was an edge of street-toughness about her, and she was superbly self-contained. Not a woman to be taken lightly.

Olga compressed her lips for a moment, organizing her thoughts. Then, step by step and month by month, she described the events she had witnessed in her controlled voice. There was no elaboration, not even over the unsolved murders. Finishing her recital with the latest incident, the attack on the tribal girl who'd been dropped off at the orphanage just two days earlier, she sat waiting for Lindsay's response.

Lindsay's jaw had dropped with disbelief, even as her brain was spinning with questions. "This is a hell of a story," she said. "Do you have any evidence, other than the girls' accounts? Names, dates, that sort of thing? Not just for the girls who were murdered—for any of them. I think that's what we need to put together first."

Olga sighed. "Lindsay, you do not want to hear this, but there is some truth in that letter. You are still young, and idealistic. You must know that evidence is useful only if there will be an investigation? And in a situation like this, with high-ranking officials and money involved, there will never be an investigation. What reason would they have to do an investigation? But any corroborated evidence that did get into their hands could put a lot of innocent people in danger."

Lindsay's smile was rueful. "It is hard to be too angry about the letter. Even I know I was selected for this job because UNOIC has been hiring too few women. But still, I'm no lightweight. I take my responsibilities seriously—both my responsibilities to UNOIC, and my responsibilities as a human being. If you can substantiate the facts that support your suspicions—I can promise you that I will not allow this atrocity to be shoved out of sight."

Sam and Olga were impressed by the strength and commitment of Lindsay's response, and listened carefully as she continued. "I have a few questions. First, what's the deal with Ratanakiri? Is there some reason why girls are being taken from this province rather than some other rural area?"

"You are right, rural poverty makes prostitution a reality all over the country. But I think we can show that too many prostitutes in the city, especially the young ones, are coming from the northeast. And I know for a fact that all of the bodies we have recovered, and the young girl who came to us this week, are from Ratanakiri. They were all marked with the peculiar tattoo of their tribe, a curving vine that crosses their breasts and is applied when they enter puberty. On some girls, the tattoo had not even healed. It is very distinc—."

"Wait," Lindsay interrupted. "What does it look like again?" she demanded, impatience in her voice.

"I am guessing it is a stylization of the lianas that grow around the giant forest trees. The vines encircle each breast, and appear to be binding them to each other. Why do you ask?"

"Because I've just seen it! On the trip yesterday, Hoktha stopped at a Tamin village, and there was a woman there with a tattoo just like the one you're describing. And you're saying that girls with that tattoo are showing up here, on the streets of Phnom Penh? Well, assuming they are being abducted for prostitution and worse—who's behind it? Do you have any idea?"

Sam and Olga looked at each other, silently asking whether they should respond. At Olga's nearly imperceptible nod, Sam finally spoke. "The man we spoke of earlier, the one you said had been named the new director of the reserve?" Lindsay nodded, and Sam continued. "Well, we didn't know until this morning that he'd received that appointment, but it all fits together. You see, your Hoktha is the nephew of General Som Sak, a high-ranking general with a suspicious amount of wealth—unusually wealthy, as the Thais so quaintly put it. People say Hoktha's involved with trafficking—and the scariest part about it is that he also has a reputation for being, well, rough on women."

For a moment, the table fell silent as the three of them sipped their warming beer. At last Lindsay spoke. "Well, it's dynamite, this is. Dangerous. And especially risky, since there's really no proof." She gazed down at the water moving beneath them, tracing a split along the grain of the wooden railing with one finger.

"I wish there was something I could do, myself, but UNOIC can't become involved in anything without the direct invitation of the government. However... we can certainly do something less direct. The Beijing Women's Conference called for legislation against exploitation of women and young girls, and it's our job to promote that kind of protective legislation."

"Yes, in the long term. I agree with you," Olga replied. "Legislation first, then action. But what do we do in the meantime, how do we keep more girls from being killed?"

"Exposure," Lindsay replied promptly. "International donors of humanitarian aid won't like this at all, and the international press is the way to let them hear about it. If it were done in a really loud and splashy way, the government would have to shut it down, especially if it is the work of a single person."

She felt a wave of emotional and physical exhaustion threatening to drown her. "Give me a little time to think about this. I know it's urgent, and I can't tell you how much I appreciate your coming to me. I understand how you might not expect a warm response from UNOIC."

Olga smiled appreciatively. "I can see we made the right decision. I admit, coming to see you was Sam's idea. You see, it is difficult to trust that people will understand the situation here. The Cambodian people have suffered much trauma, and it has left them, some of them, with very little in the way of normal notions of morality."

Lindsay nodded, still focused on the problem. But her exhausted mind, topped off by too much beer, refused to work. She stifled a yawn. "I've got to get home," she laughed, "before I fall over." Saying goodbye, she rose from the table and walked toward the door.

"Wait!" Olga called after her. "Take Sam's card so you can reach us when you are ready." Sam handed her a hand-lettered card with Boun Thong's phone number, and Lindsay headed for home.

CHAPTER SIXTEEN
THURSDAY MAY 27, PART II

W hile Lindsay slept the dreamless sleep of the exhausted, blankets shielding her from the icy blasts of the antique air conditioner, Princess Juliette Sovannalok amused herself with dreams of sleepless exhaustion. Leaning her glossy head closer to the trifold mirror of her dressing bureau, Juliette studied the fine lines that were becoming all too visible around her dark almond eyes. She lifted her eyebrows, studying the smoothing effect of that action on her forty-five year old face and remembering how it came about that she, a woman of royal blood who should never have been exposed to any wrinkle-causing stresses, had ended up like this—an aging and all too ordinary woman.

She brought her brows back down, not allowing them to frown, but closing her eyes into a squint that blurred her reflection and allowed her to see herself as she once was. In 1977, Juliette, a glamorous and idealistic member of the wealthy radical class, returned to Cambodia to participate in Pol Pot's great experiment, the building of a new society beginning at ground zero. It didn't take long for Juliette to understand that the revolutionary society, her idyllic dream, was a hellish nightmare.

Within weeks, she'd been plucked from the ranks of those who were in charge and placed among those whose very lives depended on following orders. The work camp was too horrible to endure—the dirt, the vermin, the fear of betrayal. When she was approached with an ignominious offer, Juliette had accepted, believing it her only hope of survival.

Juliette's musings were interrupted by a knock at the intricately carved door of her boudoir. She waited a moment, then called imperiously, "Come!" The door swung partially open, just wide enough for a balding old man wearing nothing but a pair of ragged short pants to edge his way into the room.

"Your Highness, about the *barang...*" he began, his head lowered obsequiously.

"What? Is he not sleeping?" Juliette demanded fiercely.

"He sleeps yet, my Princess," the old man mumbled. "But what must I do when he awakens?"

Juliette's hesitation lasted only second. "You will provide him with towels and soap," she said. "But do not bring clothing or robes for him. Ensure that the cistern in his bathing room is empty, and that both hot and cold water taps are closed from outside his room. Inform me when he has entered the bathing room. That is all."

The servant's bald head reflected the twin rows of lights that bordered Juliette's dressing table mirror as he bowed his way out of the room, his hands held high before his face in the traditional *sompeah* gesture of respect. Juliette's eyes were again far away, still focused on the past.

She had accepted the offer of that Khmer Rouge cadre. What should she have done, die of starvation? The man who had enlisted her—a rising young star she knew only as Sak—brought her into the Royal Palace. Once there, she was instructed to observe and report on every word, every glance, every smallest habit of those remaining members of the royal family living there under house arrest.

Yes, I was a spy, she said to her reflection. *And why not? Were they any better than I?* And in any case, the information she'd provided had hardly been of strategic value—that this prince suffered hemorrhoids, or that prince had managed to conceal a pair of reading glasses and was studying the ancient Sanskrit texts found within the palace walls.

Of course, that didn't change the fact that she had made a bargain with the devil. Oh, how she had prayed that Sak would fall to one of the periodic purges of the Khmer Rouge. But he had survived, had prospered even, first by defecting to the Vietnamese at just the right moment, and then by joining the new Cambodian government.

Now, although the Khmer Rouge era had come to an end, she remained the tool of her tormentor. Sak, as the cadre had called himself back then, was now General Som Sak, a powerful figure in the new Cambodian administration. And he continued to pull the strings, continued to force her compliance by "allowing" her to assist him with his business endeavors and commanding her to obtain information from both Cambodian and foreign men by using her body to gain their trust.

Today, she must again do the General's bidding. Just three weeks earlier, Sak had visited her here in her chambers with the terse instruction that she must secure the confidence of the South American, Maximiliano Vega y Ortega, and learn the true purpose of his work in Cambodia. The orders were clear, although the methods were left to her own creativity.

How ironic life was, she mused, frowning at her reflection. Max was certainly attractive, and she would have pursued him happily for her own amusement. Although he was a bit of a bore, arrogant and single-minded about this nature reserve. So far, though, her efforts had been unsuccessful on both fronts. Max was happy to flirt, but he had yet to succumb to her charms. And without reaching that level of intimacy, it could not be expected that he would begin sharing his secrets with her.

In fact, it's been rather fun, she sighed aloud, replaying the time she'd spent softening Max up. But now it was time to move from softening to hardening. General Sak's visit late the previous evening had made it clear that she could no longer afford to take it slowly. "You must find out who he is, why he is here, and who he is working for," the general had growled, before forcing her down onto her bed.

All in all, though, she was not unhappy about the General's new orders—she had her own plans for Max, and the General's orders fit nicely with them. It was these plans that had motivated her to meet Max at the dock upon his arrival from Ratanakiri. *I wonder,* she thought with some irritation, *whether he realizes how significant it is for a member of the royal family to greet him in such a low setting?* Perhaps not. After all, Colombia had no royalty.

And what was the significance of that insipid little UNOIC girl? Her informants had told her that Lindsay was unimportant, not to be taken seriously. But the way Max had looked at her... And he'd offered to accompany her home, surely just a meaningless courtesy—but had the look in his eyes suggested something more? *She cannot compete with a princess!* Juliette said to her reflection, which smiled back in a knowing way. *The South American will not know what hit him.*

***

The old man's words were true. Max had indeed spent the morning sleeping. Awakening with a start at the rap on his door, he'd watched sleepily as the aging servant had silently carried a pile of towels into his bathroom, then bowed himself out of the room. He'd slept naked as always, and stretched languorously as he sat on the side of the bed. His searching glance around the room revealed that his clothes were missing—*off to the laundry, I suppose,* he thought with annoyance.

Well, can't be helped. Max was possessed of a happy pragmatism that dwelt wholly in the present. For Max, the possibility of future unpleasantness did not exist. Standing and stretching again, Max followed his manhood into the bathroom with happy anticipation, sighing with pleasure as he relieved himself into the porcelain fixture. Humming softly, he turned the tap, anticipating the refreshing blast of cold water. When nothing but a few rusty drips emerged from the showerhead, he turned the knob further, increasingly irritated. Nothing happened. He was still standing naked in the shower, cursing softly, when the telephone buzzed in the other room.

"Max, *cheri*, are you awake? And have you bathed? I hope I am not interrupting," Juliette murmured over the internal palace line.

"I am awake, Juliette," Max said emphatically. "But bathing appears to be impossible. Why is there no water?"

"But there must be water, Max," Juliette responded breathily, stifling an impulse to giggle. "I'm so sorry. Let me just check."

Biting her lip with amusement, Juliette held the phone in her lap, waited a moment, then said, "No, Max, there is no problem with the water. Are you sure you've turned the taps far enough?"

"Juliette," Max said patiently, "I may not be a genius, but I do know how to turn a faucet. There is definitely no water in this bathroom."

"Poor Max. You must have gone straight to bed exhausted this morning. So you haven't bathed since Ratanakiri?"

"No."

"Give me a few moments, *cheri*. I will speak to the chief of the household staff and see what can be done."

"Thanks," Max said glumly, and hung up the phone.

Moments later, there was a soft knock at the door of his room. Wrapping a towel around his waist, he opened it to find the same servant he'd seen entering his room earlier.

"So sorry sir," the servant stammered. "No water this room. Please, sir, you come with me."

Max started to explain that he had no clothes. But looking at the servant's worried face, he held up his hands in disgust. "Okay, *viejito*," he said, closing the door behind him with one hand as he stepped out of the room, keeping a grip on the towel around his waist with the other.

The servant led him through a maze of landscaping and a guarded gate to a tiny house set in the middle of a miniature bamboo grove like an exquisite stone in a golden ring. At the door, he gestured for Max to enter, then scurried away.

Before knocking on the door, Max studied his surroundings. In spite of the weeks he'd spent working within the royal grounds, the miniature palace was new to him, so well was it camouflaged by the leafy shadows of the bamboo. He tapped softly on the intricate carving of the solid teak door, only to have it swing slowly open beneath his fingers.

Inside, Max blinked to adjust his eyes. The windows were thickly curtained, admitting no light, and candles glimmered from hundreds of sconces. In the center of the room, shimmering in the flickering light, stood Juliette. A long satin kimono robe of brilliant green clung to her body, and her hair hung loose and glistening on her shoulders. The candlelight was kind, disguising all trace of the wrinkles she'd been lamenting earlier.

"Max darling, come in," Juliette purred, her smile slow and beguiling. "Make yourself at home—quickly, before you are seen in such dishabille. These are my personal chambers; I wouldn't normally bring you here, but you must bathe, mustn't you?" she said. Gesturing to the rear of the room, she added, "You'll find the bath just through those doors."

"Thanks, Princess," Max said, "I feel like I haven't bathed in a year." But his nonchalance required an effort of will. *What could she be thinking?* Max wondered. Or was the explanation all too obvious? "You're too kind," he continued, moving around her toward the bathroom.

The french doors swung open on a large chamber lined completely with black marble. Steam rose in a warm fog above the sunken bath. Shedding the towel, Max stepped into the scented water, his skin cringing from the momentary sting. As his muscles relaxed, Max thought about Juliette. What was it that had brought him to this moment, in this tiny apartment, in the Royal Palace of the Kingdom of Cambodia? And to the beautiful princess who stood in a satin kimono just beyond the door—a kimono that probably covered nothing more than her bare skin. For several weeks, he'd wondered just what the Princess' interest in him could be. Now, he knew. *Poor Lindsay,* he thought, remembering her bedraggled dismay when she'd seen the impeccable Juliette waiting for them at the dock. *But she can't compete with a Princess!*

Max closed his eyes blissfully and let his hands stroke his body, smiling softly in anticipation as his fingers lingered at his groin. As the water slowly cooled, he realized with a start that he'd been expecting Juliette to join him. Why else had she brought him, wearing nothing but a towel, to her private chambers? He waited a few more minutes, stroking his erection, but the door remained shut. It seemed he was to complete his bath alone.

Shrugging, he finally rose and reached for the towel he'd dropped on the floor before stepping into the tub. But it wasn't there. He looked about for a linen cupboard or other storage space, but there was nothing, nothing but the solid black marble. At last, he opened the door a crack and called out. "Princess... um, Juliette, I don't seem to be able to find my towel."

Her laughter tinkled like small bells. "How silly of me! The maid must have neglected to bring clean towels for you. She is accustomed to drying me herself, rather than leaving towels beside the tub. And," here her laughter chimed again, "I'm afraid I have absolutely no idea where she keeps them."

Max waited, hearing Juliette rustling about in the outer chamber. Moments later, the door swung open. "This cloth will have to do, I'm afraid," she said, her laughter still tinkling as she handed him a finely woven sarong of lustrous burgundy silk. Taking it from her, his fingers brushed her hand, and he again felt his member filling, swelling—and he felt Juliette's eyes fixed on the movement of his loins.

Wrapping the sarong loosely around his waist, he walked toward Juliette, his hands reaching for her as he apologized in a soft voice, "I'm afraid I'm going to get you wet, Princess. This thing isn't very absorbent..." Feeling the sarong loosening from his waist, he turned away to readjust the fastening. When he looked up, Juliette had disappeared.

"What's that, *cheri?*" Juliet's sultry voice came from behind a narrow louvered door at the opposite corner of the central room. Pushing through the door, Max found himself in a darkened room with a single candle, its flickering light outlining a female form reclining on a large bed, surrounded by pillows and bolsters of all sizes and shapes. One arm was raised, beckoning him to enter the room. The scent of jasmine hung in the air. "Come, Max," Juliette commanded, her voice the merest whisper.

Max couldn't speak, the intensity of his physical desire seeming to engorge his entire body. Moving toward the bed, he took Juliette's outstretched hand and sank down onto the cushions. Her fingers caressed his palm, bringing it to her lips. He shivered in exquisite agony as her tiny tongue explored, one by one, the tender webbing between each of his fingers. When the soft hands moved to his shoulders to draw him near, Max groaned and relinquished his remaining shreds of control, pushing himself into the acquiescent body beneath him.

***

His exertions complete, Max was still breathing heavily when he found his mind wandering away from Juliette to the jungle hut of the night before—and Lindsay. How was it that Juliette, at least 15 years older than Lindsay, retained the suppleness and innocence of a teenager? He heard a polite cough at the far side of the room, and then the sound of curtains opening. Squinting against the light flooding the room, Max opened his eyes to see Juliette standing, still sheathed in her kimono, beside the bed. "What's going on?" he gasped, tearing his eyes from Juliette's half-smile to the woman still lying on the bed beneath him. The woman, whom he could now see was a mere girl, immediately averted her eyes and slid away, wrapping the bedsheet tightly around her breasts and gliding primly from the room.

"Get dressed, Max," Juliette said. Her voice had lost the huskiness of seduction and was now strident with command. She motioned to a neatly folded pile of clothes on the bedside table. "We must talk. And by the way," she trilled, smacking him lightly on one bare cheek, "Let me congratulate you on a magnificent performance."

CHAPTER SEVENTEEN

FRIDAY, MAY 28, PART I

David Bullford was back. He'd been back for two days now, although Lindsay had yet to see him. The telltale signs were all there, easy to read—Bopha's increased formality, the fresh cut flowers tastefully displayed on the coffee table in the reception area (some bosses brought candy for the staff after a trip—David brought flowers for the coffee table), and the stressed look on the face of the receptionist.

Lindsay poured herself a cup of coffee, doctored it liberally with cream powder and sugar, and bit the bullet, moving down the hall and through the open door of David's office. "Helloo, David. When did you get back?" Lindsay said, her voice cheery. "Bopha left a note saying you wanted to see me. Would you like to make it now, or shall we set a time for later?"

David frowned. Even frowning, though, David maintained a cool elegance that made her feel like one of the great unwashed. "We were somewhat concerned," David chided, finally speaking. "You were out of radio contact for over 24 hours. Could I have forgotten to inform you of the policy?"

"I'm really sorry, David. I'm afraid it couldn't be helped. I was stuck out in the forest, beyond radio contact."

David cleared his throat, looking down at the Phnom Penh Piper spread out on the desk in front of him. "Look, Lindsay, we've got a lot of catching up to do, but I'm afraid I haven't the time just now. We'd better make it this afternoon," he said, after squinting at the pages of his diary, "say at 11:00."

"You got it, boss," Lindsay said, still cheery. David's face stiffened. She knew he hated her breezy American persona, but using it kept her from feeling quite so intimidated.

She'd just gotten settled behind her desk when the door opened. "How was the trip, Lindsay?" Bopha asked quietly, stepping into Lindsay's office and closing the door behind her. *If you only knew,* Lindsay thought, as she began to describe her adventure.

"It was incredible, Bopha. The area is gorgeous, rain forests and a waterfall that are magic, the place is bursting with life. I've never been anywhere like it, ever," she said honestly, then added, "I wish you could have come along." And she did, for a number of reasons. "There is an issue with the tribal people up there. We need to look into it. They're called the Tamin, if I understood right. They're minority people, and they live in the park area."

"Yes, Tamin," Bopha said, studying Lindsay's face for more information.

"There aren't many of them left. The village we saw looked terrible. It was neglected, and a lot of the huts were abandoned. Everything was falling apart, and the people looked hungry. But at the same time, there were signs that there was money around. Maybe you could do some research on them for me.

"And another thing. This man Som Hoktha we went with has been named director of the park, but how did he get chosen so quickly? He was passing out money to the villagers, which was a little surprising. And when I tried to explore the village, he made some excuse about it not being culturally appropriate. The really shocking thing is that I've just heard a rumor that he's been involved with trafficking in women and children. I don't know if it's true, but it would be a horrible mistake to give him our support if it is. So as you can see, I need to understand the background a lot better."

Bopha nodded, thoughtful. "The hill tribe people are very special, and they got hurt so much. The war, and then Pol Pot taking them away from their homes. They are very strong though, and they survived all that. And now maybe we will kill them with development. If they can't hunt, or do the things they know, then they are destroyed."

"What can we do?" Lindsay asked

"Let them alone." It was a very Buddhist solution.

Too late, Lindsay thought, and wondered if this tribal group should be the center of their concern, rather than the forest itself. Bopha returned to her work without commenting on Som Hoktha, and Lindsay found her mind wandering, her stomach churning with memories of the night in the park—and the morning beneath the waterfall. It was a startling rush of pleasure, wonder, and shame, and within it she recognized both the lurch of desire, and the shiver of self-loathing.

Everything had flowed together so seamlessly from the moment they arrived in Ratanakiri to the morning of their departure. And everything had turned so sour within minutes of the amazing climax beneath the shimmering rainbow of the waterfall. Why had Hoktha abandoned them in the forest? Intuitively, she understood that it couldn't have been an accident, was convinced, in fact, that it had been planned. Surely Max had not been simply playing a part. But could she be certain? And there was another thing worrying her—in the heat of the moment, neither of them had considered the need for protection. It was simply stupid. And why hadn't he called her, anyway? She needed to hear his voice, to sort out exactly what had happened and how she wanted to proceed. She flipped through her Rolodex, found Max's number, and was reaching for the phone when it rang beneath her fingers.

She heard Bopha go through the lengthy process of identifying the caller, then ask them to hold, please. "Lindsay, for you."

"Who is it?"

"Maximiliano," she said, pronouncing each syllable separately.

Lindsay picked up her phone and punched the flashing button. "Good morning, Max," she said, "I was just thinking about you. I think we need to—"

But Max had interrupted. "Listen, Lindsay, I've got some great news!"

"You do sound happy. What's up?"

Max snorted. "Happy is an understatement, Lindsay. This morning the King was enthusing about the park, and gave Hoktha clear instructions that he's to listen to my advice—after all, he said, why have a Special Advisor if we don't take his advice? Makes sense to me! Anyway, even though I couldn't shower under a waterfall with you this morning, and I haven't had breakfast, I'm still happy."

"Listen, Max, I've been thinking about the best way to present the nature reserve to David," she said, tentatively. "That map you had with you on the plane. I'd like to get an enlargement of the reserve section scanned into the computer, so I can add details to it as we develop the project. It would be great if I could have it for my presentation to David this afternoon, too. The other thing, of course, is photos. Why in the world didn't we take a camera?"

"You will not need a map to convince David," Max said, "or pictures, either. Just smile that crooked little smile, and cross those beautiful legs of yours, and he'll be yours to command."

Max's tone confirmed all of Lindsay's newly forming doubts about him, but she ignored them, wanting to get their collaboration back onto a more professional footing.

"We really need to meet to discuss the next steps, Max. What about an early lunch?" she suggested.

There was a pause. "Uh, I don't think it's such a good idea, *querida*. Remember what I said about the park being our special place? Let's keep it that way."

She sighed. "Max, I think there must have been pheromones in the air up there. Or something, because back down here in Phnom

Penh, I don't feel like I even know you. I'm not trying to get you into bed, I'm just trying to do my job. Once again, it's time for us to put our past behind us—and this time we need to leave it there."

"Well all right, if that's the way you want it." Lindsay heard his voice change subtly, becoming sly as he continued. "It's your loss. The Princess Juliette seems to enjoy my company well enough."

Lindsay realized with a start that Max needed her much more than she needed him. Why else had he bothered to seduce her? Because she saw, very clearly now, that that was exactly what had happened. What a fool she'd been. "At least you won't be lonely, then," she said.

Max's voice was calm, "You just focus on getting through to David, and let me know when you do. Got to run, Lindsay." And the connection was broken.

Lindsay stared at the phone. *Prick*, she said softly. She was shocked, not because Max had hung up on her, but because she realized, in a flood of shame, that she had just repeated her past. The first time, she'd been young—a fairly good excuse for making bad decisions about men, but one that no longer applied. Why had she let this happen? Had she been trying to change the past, to make it all come out right? *I certainly failed, if that's it*, she told herself ruefully. *But the difference is that this time, I will not let time stand still while I get over it.*

CHAPTER EIGHTEEN
FRIDAY, MAY 28, PART II

S peaking of which, what time was it? *Omigosh*, Lindsay whispered, seeing the hands of her watch pointing to ten minutes past eleven. She rammed her hip painfully into the corner of her desk as she raced for the door. Yanking it open, she found David standing at the coffeemaker, filling his mug. His expression was hard to read. Annoyance that she was late? Delight at having caught her out and put her on the defensive? Boredom with having to deal with her at all?

"Why don't you come on into my office whenever you're ready, Lindsay," David said calmly as he headed back to his office. "If we don't get this over with soon, you'll have forgotten your trip, and I'll have forgotten why I care."

"I'll be right there, David," Lindsay called after him. "I'll just grab my notes."

When she entered David's office, Lindsay found to her relief that David was seated on the batik-covered settee, rather than behind his desk. The less formality the better. Settling herself beside him, she riffled through her notes, than began to talk. Throughout her report—the early rumors she'd heard of plans for a big announcement, the reception itself, the developing (professional) relationships with the South American and the Frenchman, their attitudes toward the park proposal, and, finally, the trip to Ratanakiri itself and her concerns about the Tamin— David sat quietly, silent but not still. At times he doodled fantastic shapes on the pad in front of him, but for the most part he sat leaning forward, his attention focused on her face. As she spoke, he gave sharp, quick nods that suggested he knew what she was going to say long before the words even left her mouth.

When she finally wrapped up her report with the rationale she'd developed for handling this project herself, David spoke. "I should not have designated you Officer-In-Charge, I can see that," he said quietly. Lindsay's heart sank, but she did not allow her dismay to register on her face. "You have neither the experience with UNOIC nor the background knowledge of Cambodian politics, and it was unfair of me to expect you to face the machinations of the royal family and the Cambodian military all at once and on your own. I hope you will accept my apologies?"

Now Lindsay was confused. "David, I am perfectly willing to share responsibilities here, just like every other member of the staff. I am young, but I am qualified for this position, and the more responsibilities I have, the faster I'll learn." Lindsay knew that her Public Information Officer post had been created in response to UNOIC's prominent position in the country's affairs. And she knew that, in spite of her double major in international communications and political science, it had been her family background and the fact that she was female that had won the post for her. After nearly 50 years, someone at UN headquarters had finally noticed the dearth of female staff in the agency, and now the pressure was on to find qualified women to fill every job vacancy possible. But she also knew she was capable of the job, and she truly cared about the principles that brought her to the United Nations in the first place.

"Well, Lindsay, you may be right, and in any case this particular episode is now behind us. At this point, you certainly know much more about the nature reserve than I. I agree with you that, for now, you should indeed continue to coordinate with the palace and its Special Advisor to assess the potential for our involvement in the project." Seeing Lindsay's smile of pleasure, David shook his head. "Just for now. With the understanding that I may take over at a later point. And that I find a Note for the File on my desk at the end of each week, updating me on what is happening with the proposal and what you've learned."

"Thanks, David," Lindsay managed. "I'm going to find out as much as I can about what is really going on with this proposal— because I'm starting to realize that there is a lot more to it than saving the forest and the animals." Getting to her feet, she added, "And I will definitely keep you informed—."

"Oh, and Lindsay," David interrupted. "You do understand that since you traveled without an approved Travel Authorization, your F-45 Travel Claim cannot be reimbursed?"

"No problem, David," Lindsay said with a sigh as she left David's office. Unfortunately, her expenses had been wholly emotional. Sometimes UNOIC's plethora of forms and regulations made her wish she were working for a smaller organization, like Sam and Olga. Sam and Olga! She had totally forgotten to update David on the story the two of them had brought to her the day before. She hesitated a moment, then moved across the foyer to her own office. *I'll put it in this week's report,* she decided.

Placed squarely in the middle of her desk, Lindsay found a Post-It note decorated with Bopha's neat handwriting. Earlier she'd given Bopha a list of names—Rex Branson at WFP and Nick Graham, her speedboat rescuer, for two—and asked her to set up appointments with each of them as soon as possible. Glancing at her watch, she saw that Bopha had cut things close, but that, with a reasonably fast *moto* driver, she could just make her two o'clock appointment. The next appointment wasn't until Sunday, when she would meet Nick at the Foreign Correspondent's Club.

Bopha made the right choice, Lindsay thought as she straddled the seat of the motorcycle. Although she hadn't spent a lot of time with Rex, he seemed the most knowledgeable and most trustworthy bureaucrat she'd met yet. If anyone could clear up some of her confusion around the king's proposal, like who stood to gain from such a project, it was Rex.

***

Rex's extroverted charm swept away the cobwebs of romance that still clouded Lindsay's mind. "Now, you know we're not directly involved with anything in the northeast, Lindsay," he said, after hearing her bowdlerized synopsis of the events of the week. "But that doesn't mean I don't have opinions."

Despite the excellent coffee cultivated in Southeast Asia, Rex insisted on drinking watery Maxwell House. Lindsay stifled her shudder of distaste and took the flowered china cup from Rex's hand with a smile. "That's what I'm here for, Rex, so fire away."

"Well. I'm afraid you're going to feel like you're back in the classroom, but hear me out, and take it in the spirit it's given. First off, UNOIC isn't like the NGOs or the bible beaters," Rex said, stroking one handlebar of his giant moustache with his little finger. UNOIC doesn't have their freedom of action, not by a long shot. Once the government lets them in, the NGOs can do pretty much whatever they want. UNOIC, on the other hand, is legally mandated to assist governments—but only if they ask for it, and only with their priorities. As the UNOIC Public Information Officer, your job is to inform, not to advocate. But your instincts are right—you can't provide reliable information without first making sure you've got reliable information.

"Second, every single issue, every single problem in this country is affected by its politics, which are a disaster. Name an issue, and you'll find one of the major factions in favor of it, and the other opposing it. Those with less powerful roles, the small fry, wait like hyenas to fight over any scraps that might slip from the grasp of the big guys.

"In order to do your job, you need to know everything every one of these factions is up to, and what everything they're doing means in terms of alliances and shifting positions."

"Sounds impossible, Rex!" Lindsay interrupted.

"Almost impossible, Lindsay, but there are ways. Get copies of all the local newspapers, and have your Cambodian assistant skim them every day. You'll have to guide her on the kinds of information you're looking for, or you'll both be too overloaded to do anything else. Not that you should believe everything you read, by any means. But knowing what's happening and what's being said about it, true or false, puts you in a position of power. Another thing you can do is network with some of the wire folks—UPI, AP. Ask them to let you know what's not showing up in their stories.

"Finally—I'm probably out of line in saying this, but it's for your own protection. Put everything, and I mean everything, you see, hear, and do, in writing. Notes from meetings, statements, everything. If the flak starts flying—and it will—you need to have something solid to support your opinions and recommendations. So. That's the general orientation spiel. Am I being just too pompous?"

Lindsay laughed. "Truth is, Rex, I never had any orientation to this job at all. It's embarrassing to admit how little I know about UNOIC, so this is great. And don't worry, I can't be offended."

Rex sipped his coffee, put his boots up on his desk, and leaned perilously back in his swivel chair, his weary eyes examining the plasterwork scrolling on the ceiling.

"I hope you mean that, about not being offended. Because I'm about to get a little personal. I can understand your interest in the South American, Lindsay. He's got genuine magnetism. And the word around town is that he's focusing some of it on you."

So, Lindsay thought, her attempts to sanitize her story had been wasted. She studied Max's over-sized black cowboy hat, which nestled on the bottom shelf of his bookcase, and waited for him to continue.

"Speaking frankly," Rex continued, still intrigued by the light fixture, "it's in the Colombian's interest to do whatever it takes to get you involved in this project, and keep you sympathetic. I'm not sure how far he would go to make that happen..."

Lindsay forced herself to meet Rex's hooded eyes. "I don't think there is a limit to what he would do, Rex, because he's already done. I may be slow, but once I learn, it sticks. What else?"

"Well, I do have a bit of perspective on the Frenchman, André Balfour, since I play racquetball with the first secretary at the French Embassy. It seems that André is something more than he seems. He is the military attaché, true enough, but that's only part of it. How is he involved with the nature reserve? I don't know, but I'd be surprised if there weren't something more at stake than just a personal prejudice. André plays cards with some of the worst characters in Cambodia, senior members of the military who are still wearing their Khmer Rouge underwear. Maybe he's currying favor for the French Government, or maybe he's trying to accomplish something else. I don't know. But he's a serious man, and I think he can be trusted. So when he says the nature reserve is a bad idea, it's worth finding out why.

Lindsay reluctantly added André to the list of people she needed to meet, and then asked Rex the question that had been skulking around the edges of her brain since Hoktha's boy soldiers had shown up in the forest. "Do you think I could be in real danger, Rex, if I don't recommend UNOIC's support?"

Rex didn't answer. His lips pursed, he looked at her, considering how to reply. When he finally spoke, his voice was serious and his words a surprise. "Tell me again where you live, Lindsay?"

"I rent from a senior government official behind the old tile factory, down near the Monivong Bridge. It's a bit out of town, maybe too far." Lindsay told him about her traditional-style wooden house hidden away in the back of the Chinese tile factory. Built during French colonial times, the house was a tribute to the family fortune. Spacious high-ceilinged rooms, gleaming dark hardwood floors, dark massive teak furniture, all set in a tropical paradise overlooking the reversible waters of the Bassac River.

The catch was the isolation. Located on the edge of the city, far beyond the expatriate ghetto, Lindsay knew she was taking a certain amount of risk. Robberies, particularly of homes occupied by foreigners, were a daily event. But the elderly couple attached to the household through some obscure familial relation with the landlord had welcomed her like a long-lost grandchild, and they'd assured her in their broken French that the status of the owner would protect her from harm.

"That's old Kim Aun, Lindsay. Aun's all right, he's tied up in customs revenue, and won't have any interest in this nature reserve. The people to watch out for are the ones like this Hoktha character, people who are trying to build their empires. At the moment, Hoktha's in the same position as Max—his interests happen to coincide with yours. But if that changes, well yes, he'd be someone to watch out for.

"You've gotta keep an even keel, Lindsay, and not get spooked into going out on your own, taking risks. I don't want to frighten you, but... You should at least know what you're dealing with. In Cambodia, when people get mad or feel threatened, their first response is always physical—a grenade, a knife, acid. Did you know that torture is a daily event around here? Every day, innocent people are beaten black and blue with batons, iron bars, gun butts—whatever's handy. And not by bad guys, either. It's the police, the military, the security forces, men with legal power and authority. Electric shocks are routine, and whippings with wires, bamboo, rope, or belts. You name it, they've tried it. And—you're probably expecting this—torture almost always includes some kind of sexual abuse or humiliation."

Rex paused, while Lindsay tried to maintain her poise. "But Rex," she said slowly, "I'm just trying to learn, I haven't done anything. You don't really think anyone is going to feel threatened enough to really try to hurt me? I mean, wouldn't they understand that UNOIC can't offer its support to a project until we understand all its ramifications?"

"You'd think so, Lindsay. And you may be right. I just want you to be careful. You do what you need to do, but just remember that this isn't the Magic Kingdom. I'm hoping that you've started to realize that already, and are taking a few steps back."

"No, actually, I'm getting deeper. David's back, and he's given me the go-ahead to coordinate UNOIC's response to the government. I'm determined to find out what's behind their proposal before I recommend our support. That's why I'm here today, Rex, and I can't tell you how much I appreciate your candor.

"If it were just the nature reserve, without complications, there'd be no question. I mean, if Cambodia doesn't do something, and do it quickly, a major part of their rain forest will be razed in less than 20 years. But there are so many secrets! I've heard rumors of human rights abuses, like child trafficking—a nature reserve could provide a perfect cover for that sort of thing. And what about the drug running? and the gem mining? Hell, for all we know, someone could have discovered some ancient temples up there that they want to control for artifact dealing. I don't want to be responsible for putting UNOIC's name on something that turns out to be a farce at best. In the worst case, we could be supporting a contravention of international law. I know everyone thinks—or is hoping—that I'm stupid and naïve enough to just go along with whatever—but I'm not, Rex. I'm just not. And if I didn't believe in the United Nations, I wouldn't have taken this job. I won't sit back and sign my name to something just because it all sounds good on paper.

Rex sighed, smiled, and rearranged himself on his chair, placing his feet back on the ground. "Well, I figured that's what you'd say, Lindsay. You're a bit like me. We'll never make good bureaucrats because we care too much. Now, I'm here if you need to talk again, or if you need my help. And if I get wind of anything you should know, I'll give you fair warning. Us Americans have gotta' stick together."

"I can't thank you enough, Rex," Lindsay said, giving Rex a quick hug. Out in the street, she started to hail a *moto*, but changed her mind. The slow rhythm of a *cyclo* ride would be a good change of pace, and it was Friday afternoon. Her work for the week was done.

CHAPTER NINETEEN
SUNDAY, MAY 30, PART I

Bopha had scheduled Lindsay to meet with Nick Graham on Sunday afternoon at three at the Foreign Correspondent's Club, the FCC to its habituées. Although she'd ended the week feeling like she could sleep forever, it had taken only one day of rest to catch up, and now she was looking forward to her meeting with Nicky. She left home early, to allow for laborious movement through the clogged Sunday afternoon streets. On the way, the trip was further slowed by an afternoon rain squall, which forced smaller vehicles into the middle of the road to avoid the flooded gutters.

The *cyclo* driver dropped her off in front of the UNOIC office, grinning his thanks when she handed him *riel* amounting to three times the usual fare. She picked up a Land Cruiser from the UNOIC fleet and drove the short distance to the FCC. This could be a late night, and she didn't want to be on the back of a motorcycle after dark. At least there were some risks she could control.

After finding a place to park, Lindsay ran up the dark stairwell, emerging into the dark wood and airy spaciousness of the club. Along the bar sat an assortment of Phnom Penh's fourth estate, ranging from pressed khaki sobriety to falling-down-drunk inebriation. She dodged a bleary fume-laden kiss, peering around the thick wooden pillars in search of her date. While she waited, she studied the photographs along the wall, an exhibit from the early 1970s when the Khmer Rouge had overrun Phnom Penh.

Knowing how the country had spiraled downward since then made the images particularly eerie, and she jumped when Nick gripped her shoulder from behind. "A wee bit nervous, are we?" he queried, guiding her to a low table beside the railing that overlooked the river.

Their waitress, a young girl with a red satin ribbon tying her long hair into a glossy pony tail, approached promptly. "Gin and tonic, dear," Nicky said. "And for the lady..."

"Johnny Walker with ice, double," Lindsay said promptly.

Nick's eyebrows raised. "That bad, huh?"

"I don't even know, Nicky. I'm hoping you can tell me."

"I am utterly at your command," he declared, placing a hand on his heart. While they waited for their drinks they enjoyed the view of the river just outside. As usual on a Sunday evening, the riverside park was thronged with picnicking families, busy vendors, courting lovers, and skilled pickpockets, all looking for enough pleasure to see them through the coming week.

When the waitress approached, wielding a tray with their drinks, Lindsay grabbed for the glass, sipping it immediately, grimacing, and sipping again. Nick watched, his question unspoken.

"Yes, Nicky, I had quite a week," Lindsay explained. "By Friday, I was a bundle of nerves. I thought a slow Saturday at home had calmed me down, but I guess thinking about what's ahead is starting me worrying again."

Nick pulled a pack of Player's cigarettes from his pocket and offered it to her. She shook her head. "I still get a cheap thrill from that initial light up," she confessed, "but I'm not going down that road again, no matter how nervous I get."

Nick shook his head. "I've quit more times than I can count. Sometimes I think it's the delight of forbidden pleasures that makes me go through all that nonsense. So why are we here, Lindsay? Tell old Saint Nick your problems, darlin'."

Lindsay went right to the point. "Nicky, David has asked me to coordinate UNOIC's involvement with the king's proposal. And I want to do it, but I don't want to come out in favor of supporting a nature reserve that is not really a nature reserve. If you know what I mean."

"My, aren't we suspicious," Nick laughed, brushing the graying shock of red hair from his hazel eyes. "How could you possibly think any of Cambodia's finest could be motivated by something other than saving the poor animals of the northeast?"

Lindsay joined Nick's laughter, but her eyes were serious. "I knew you'd understand, Nicky. I need to find out the real reason why the military supports this, not to mention that Hoktha guy. That's why I'm here—so what can you tell me? For starters, what did you mean by that coy remark you made on the boat when you rescued me a couple of weeks ago. You know, about the Colombian connection?"

"That was probably just my intuition working overtime, darlin'." Nick said a little uncomfortably. "After all, Cambodia is the new drug frontier, and you couldn't find a better place to transit drugs than his royal highness's new pet project. But you know how I feel about royalty anyway."

"I thought that was just the British line," Lindsay said. "At any rate, I don't think you're suggesting that Sihanouk himself is the villain in this piece. So what have you heard about the man who's been named director of the nature reserve?"

"Som Hoktha? Even the King wouldn't be reckless enough to choose him if he could avoid it. If Som Hoktha's got the job, he got it from somewhere other than the King. And for some other reason than his phony forestry degree and his devotion to the seamier sides of Cambodian pleasures. Yes, darlin', I've heard some stories... You stay just as far away from Mr Hoktha as you can, and if you can't stay away, just be sure you don't cross him."

Lindsay shuddered, remembering the look in Hoktha's eyes as he'd watched her at the dock. "My sentiments exactly, Nicky. But unfortunately, I'm going to have to deal with him, if we decide to support the project."

"If he's the guy in charge, I wonder if UNOIC should be supporting this, darlin'?" Nick asked.

But Lindsay was distracted by the pack of cigarettes on the table between them. "What?"

Nick repeated his comment, his eyes amused at the look of pure longing on Lindsay's face as he lit another cigarette. "Let me explain, darlin', why Hoktha would be a very unsavory partner for you."

Keeping his voice matter of fact and his eyes focused somewhere behind her shoulder, Nicky spent the next half hour telling Lindsay the life story of Som Hoktha. He'd been raised by his uncle, the powerful General Som Sak, although his parents still lived in his native province of Kampong Cham. "The word on the street is that Hoktha brings young virgins from the countryside—no one's sure, really, whether he kidnaps them, buys them, or lures them with fantastic promises of some kind. Here in Phnom Penh, he's got a safe house where the girls are kept until they're ready for the use of the men who can afford to pay for them."

"What do you mean, 'ready'?"

"Hang on, darlin'. I'll get to that. The thing is, the girls' value drops once they've been used, and that's when their worst nightmares begin. Now, I don't know whether Hoktha was one of those kids who pulled the wings off flies, but he's that kind of grown-up. The violence started when he was still in high school and raped one of the family's maids. After that, it just got worse. Each time, the violence and brutality escalated, but because he is who he is, he was never arrested. Finally, though, the General couldn't protect him, and he sent him off to a boarding school in France.

"After he graduated, he came home—and it started again," Nicky said soberly. "It got worse and worse, until, again, Sak couldn't shield him. Last year, he shipped him off to Indonesia, for further studies, they said. Once he was gone, things quieted down."

Lindsay was staring blankly at Nick, finding what he was saying almost incomprehensible. She felt a need for a steaming hot shower, to wash the contamination of his words from her body. "So...there's the trafficking. And there's the brutality. I suppose...there must be some connection?"

"I'm afraid so, Lin. Once the girls have lost their virginity a few times, to the highest bidderd, their value drops, and Hoktha gets free rein with them. He's so rough that most of them don't live through the experience. And those are the girls that somebody finds, dumped in a gutter or trash heap, their bodies naked and mutilated. I'm afraid that his idea of a nature reserve will be having his own private supply of virgins from the hilltribes up there."

"He's the one who's killing the prostitutes?" Lindsay inquired, a horror of recognition shuddering through her. "Nicky, do you mean to tell me...Is there any evidence?"

"I don't think anyone who has followed these stories has a doubt, Lin. But to answer your question, I have to say no. No one's ever proved that Hoktha is responsible. But when you consider that the killings stopped when he left for France, started up when he came back, stopped again when he left for Indonesia—and started again two months ago, when he came back waving that phony diploma, well, what else can we think?"

"But this is horrible, Nicky! Why would the King honor him when he should be slapping him into irons? I just don't get it." She found herself staring again at Nick's pack of Players. "Give me one of those," she demanded roughly, before helping herself to a cigarette. Her fingers shook as she waited for Nick to light it, and she inhaled deeply before meeting his eyes again. "There's more, isn't there," she said flatly.

"There's more to it than sex, that's for sure," Nicky said. Sometimes Lindsay seemed so naïve, and he hated to shock her, but if she were going to get involved with Hoktha, she needed to know. "There's politics. I told you, Hoktha is the adopted son of General Som Sak. Do you think any Cambodian is going to risk Som Sak's wrath just to report the death of a golden flower? No way! Even if someone witnessed Hoktha in the act, they'd be too scared to do anything about it."

"Well, I guess there's no question then, Nicky. There's no way UNOIC is going to support Som Hoktha, even if it means that the nature reserve just doesn't happen. I've got to tell Max—I can't say I have a very high opinion of him, either, any more, but I know he wouldn't be involved in this—"

Lindsay stopped, studying the expression on Nick's freckled face. How could he be laughing? "Max probably doesn't know anything about Hoktha's real reason for wanting the park, or about his history," he said with a devilish smile, "but he's definitely part of it."

He leaned closer to the table, reaching for Lindsay's shoulder and whispering into her ear. "Listen to this, it's a real joke on the guy. He deserves it, too, he's so full of himself. Remember I said there's a place where the girls are kept until they're ready? Well, being 'ready' means they're trained to satisfy the dissolute desires of Phnom Penh's wealthiest men. They learn to be born-again virgins long after their hymens are broken, and they learn how to stimulate wild desire, even in the most dissipated of men."

"Come on, Nicky! You're telling me that Hoktha's operating some kind of prostitute academy? Right here in Phnom Penh? I don't believe it! And besides, what's it got to do with Max?"

"I'm getting to that, darlin'. It's not just right here in Phnom Penh—it's in the Royal Palace! They say General Som Sak's got something on Princess Juliette Sovannalok, and has blackmailed her into mentoring the girls. She teaches them what to do, then finds men for them to practice on."

Nicky held up his hands, forestalling Lindsay's next expression of disbelief. "I know, I know, it is beyond belief. But wait'll you hear the good part. Last week, I heard Maximiliano in a bar, bragging how he'd screwed the Princess the day she rescued him at the ramp when he got back from Ratanakiri. But the story from the palace— it's all over town—is that Juliette let Max think she was succumbing to his charms, enticed him into a darkened room, and inserted him into her lesson plan. Can you believe it? She just stood there by the bed while he pumped away on one of her students, all the time thinking it was her. 'Course the Colombian's not admitting it, but everyone knows."

Lindsay's response wasn't what Nicky expected. Her expression horrified, she drained her whisky. Slamming the glass down on the table, she stammered, "Nicky, I, I've got to go," and lurched away from Nick and down the stairs.

From his table at the railing, Nicky watched her stumbling her way toward the UNOIC Land Cruiser. *Why the hell am I such a damn gossip?* he muttered, pounding the table angrily. But his face was puzzled. *And how the fuck was I to know she'd fallen in love with the South American?*

CHAPTER TWENTY
SUNDAY, MAY 30, PART II

After the morning they'd spent with Lindsay, Sam and Olga began meeting at the end of each day, telling themselves that they needed to keep up to date on developments in their campaign to stop child trafficking. But although they said nothing, it crossed both of their minds that they were really just enjoying each other's company.

Six o'clock Sunday evening found them lingering over beers at the outdoor tables near Vimean Aikreak, Phnom Penh's infamous monument that changed its name and its history with the political winds. The conversation, desultory, had focused on the strangeness of their alliance, the way fate had brought them together.

Little rays of sun danced on the canopy of bougainvillea above their heads, occasionally breaking through to highlight the reddish gold of Olga's hair. A posse of small children ran out onto the pavement in front of them, competing fiercely for a carved wooden toy, their shrieks and laughter reaching the shady quiet of the corner where they sat. The smallest child, losing out on the race for the toy, stood sniffing sulkily near their table. Olga watched the child, while Sam studied Olga—the way her face changed as she looked at the little girl, her features younger and softer than he would have thought possible when they first met.

As Sam continued to watch the subtle play of emotions flicker across Olga's face, she stiffened. She turned back to her beer and drank deeply, draining the glass. Turning to catch Sam's eye, she said, "I am not that interesting, Sam. Why are you staring?"

Sam's fair skin flushed. Was he really so transparent? But he determined not to hide his feelings. "You are that interesting, Olga. To me, anyway."

She laughed, a dismissive snort rather than an intimate chuckle. "You do not know, Sam. You would not find me interesting at all if you did."

"I may not know your life story, Olga. But I judge people by what I see—and I like what I've seen so far. And...I'd like to know more." Watching Olga's eyes shift away, her hand rising to call for more beer, he reached out to place a finger beneath her chin and return her gaze to his. "And no, don't pretend to misunderstand me."

"I am not sure what you mean, Sam, so I do not need to pretend," Olga responded promptly, shifting away from his touch. "Believe me, I do want to understand you. You and I, we are two ordinary people with an extraordinary task, and if we cannot understand each other, we have no hope of succeeding. We must learn to know each other and trust each other completely."

Olga's words were innocent enough, but she was still avoiding his eyes. Understanding intuitively that Olga was not yet ready to admit her interest in him as a man, he tried a different approach.

Smiling, he said, "Okay, then. I'll go first—when you call for a third beer, I'll know you're bored and stop. How's that sound?"

For a moment, Olga's eyes met his, flashing a glimpse of her soul. And that moment filled Sam with joy, because what he saw there told him that if he played by Olga's rules, everything would work out. As he talked, he watched closely, but Olga's eyes never glazed, her attention never wavered as he told her about his early years in Australia, the torment of the Vietnam war, and his subsequent discovery of Buddhism and the contemplative life.

Olga interrupted the narrative only to ask questions that led him to reveal even more about himself than he had intended. He finished by describing his friendship with Annie, Mathak, and Peter and how their orphanage had come into being.

Olga laughed and looked around at the chaotic traffic whirling around the monument. "You must be finding Phnom Penh a bit of a shock after so long in the temple, then."

"You know, it's surprised me how easy it's been. I'm afraid I was starting to feel wasted, almost decadent. In the temple, there was no way to serve—and finally, at the ripe age of 48, I've come to the conclusion that service is what it's all about. And—I didn't tell the abbot this, but it was starting to get just plain boring. Boredom is a hell of a lot worse than adjusting to chaos, I've decided." Sam stopped, hesitating to further reveal himself. But he plunged ahead. If Olga couldn't deal with his honesty, better for him to find out now. He leaned forward, looking again deep into her eyes. "It's all true, Olga. But what makes me certain that leaving the temple was the right decision is that I've found you."

Olga looked away. "Do you always say exactly what you think?"

"Always. But never if I think it will cause pain."

Again, that derisive snort of laughter. "I guess it is not pain, but you are making me more uncomfortable than anyone has for a very long time."

"Olga, you're not really upset, are you?" Sam protested. But Olga's smile admitted that they were still friends, and he felt better. "Okay, it's your turn. I promise not to interrupt."

Olga shook her head, maintaining her smile and glancing around their table. "It is lovely here, isn't it?" Sam joined her in looking about, taking in the garbage heaped along the edge of the street, and they began to laugh.

Olga respected Sam's willingness to confide in her, and determined to be honest with him as well. But it wasn't easy. Because Olga knew about suffering. Born 54 years earlier to a

Swedish father and Lithuanian refugee mother, whose union had been far from happy, Olga had grown up watching her mother suffer. Then, when she reached her teen years, she learned about degradation firsthand. Her father's bouts of drinking became more frequent, accompanied by violence that sought to inflict pain. Olga's already unhappy childhood turned into a nightmare when, at age 14, her father began to direct more than just the occasional kick or cuff her way. The sexual abuse continued until, three months before her high school graduation, Olga packed a bag and boarded a ferry to Germany.

"That must have been a nightmare for you," Sam said gently, covering Olga's hand with his own. "You wouldn't have known anyone there—how did you manage?"

Olga squeezed Sam's hand, then gently released it. She had to face this and tell it on her own. "How else?" she said. "I ended up on the streets, on the Reeperbanh in Hamburg. It was not just that I had no friends. I also had no work permit, and no money. And, thanks to my father, there was only one thing I really knew how to do."

Responding to Sam's questioning look, she explained. "Not that. Anyone can do that. No, what I knew was the trick that makes prostitution endurable—being able to shut the mind, to move out of the body and into a fantasy world until...until it is safe to come back."

Remembering Sam's description of his university education, Olga became defensive. "And in case you are wondering, no, I never did finish high school. But I have gotten an education just the same. You would be amazed at the women on the streets. There were students working their way through university, bored housewives, and beautiful sad girls from poor countries whose foreign husbands forced them to work by taking their travel papers and threatening to report them to the immigration police."

Sam's voice was husky. "Olga, you're wiser than anyone I've ever known. Education is important, but it doesn't matter whether it's from school or from life. Keep going—I'm dying to know how you ended up here in Cambodia."

Olga studied the fronds of the palm trees, swaying above them in the evening breeze. She was puzzled. Where had this sudden urge to confide in Sam come from? Here he was, untidy, disarmingly naïve, impossibly young, expecting her to mentor him in a dangerous game. If he were really as innocent as he seemed, he could be more of a danger to their rescue operation than a help. And if he really meant what those warm eyes were saying to her, well, that was the most dangerous thought of all. He could threaten the work of years, the wall that she'd carefully built around her badly bruised heart. But she continued to describe her climb up from hell, because in spite of her reservations, and most disconcerting of all, Olga wanted to trust Sam.

"Well, Sam, those women I met taught me what it means to be practical, because they had learned to accept their business as a means to a better end. So that is what I did. They showed me how to take advantage of special programs, how to find my way into the educational system. Then I was working for a reason, and that made it easier. Two years later, I had a certificate in social work, through a Hamburg trade school."

This time it was Olga who reached for Sam's hand as she continued. "But the most important things I learned did not come from the course. I learned the awful ways that poverty debases people. And I realized that it is money—the evils of economics—that keeps the world spinning."

Sam studied Olga's face, wondering if he should ask the question that was filling his heart. He sipped his beer, reminding himself that there was no time like the present. "Olga, I won't say I understand—there's no way I possibly could. It sounds like pure hell. But look at you—you're vibrant, beautiful, intelligent. Somehow you survived. Why? Was there—is there—someone, someone who touched your heart?"

This time when Olga smiled back at Sam, her eyes were moist. Annoyed, she closed them, brushing the tears away. "It is almost funny, that these memories can still bring tears to my eyes," she said. "But yes. There was someone—and he did teach me to love, it is true. One of the professors seemed to take a personal interest in me, right from the start. The whole school experience was a high for me, and then, falling in love for the first time. It was beautiful..."

"But?" Sam said, hearing the sadness in Olga's voice.

"Yes, but. He also taught me that with love comes betrayal, and that it is better not to trust."

"What happened?"

"He said he wanted to know me, everything about me—just like you, Sam. He demanded more and more details. When I finally broke down and told him about my father, and about my years on the streets—and that it was the streets that were paying for my education—he threw me away."

"Why is it that it's our highest and best emotions that bring us the most pain?" Sam mused, his fingers rubbing the back of his neck and his eyes clouded with reflected pain. After a moment, he added, "So, how about now?"

Olga was shaking her head, even before he finished his question. "No, no, and no!" she said. "There has not been anyone else. Believe me, with the work I am doing, it is easy enough to remember the dangers of love. My poor girls, suffering just because they are weaker than the men who abuse them. It is a constant reminder to keep my distance."

Before Sam could reply, she added, "But you, Sam Jarrett. I wonder if there is a chance that you really are different?"

CHAPTER TWENTY-ONE
SUNDAY, MAY 30, PART III

L indsay was trembling. Anger. Frustration. Self-loathing. The emotions were overwhelming, and she was oblivious to her surroundings. Walking away from the FCC in the glow of the late afternoon light, she'd twice narrowly avoided death by motorcycle, and had sent a covey of orange-robed monks scurrying into the street to avoid her the contamination of her touch. *It's contaminating, all right*, she mumbled bitterly, ignoring the calls of *barang chkuat*—crazy foreigner—issuing from passing cars.

The last straw was when she failed to see, just outside Wat Ounalom, an open storm drain. She had tripped and crumpled painfully into it to the delight of the children playing with rusty cans by the roadside. Climbing to her feet, her twisted ankle throbbing, she redirected her steps, entering the relative silence of the temple grounds.

Outside the towering doors of the central pagoda, gaudy with red and gold carvings, she placed her shoes beside those of other worshipers and tiptoed inside. She took a seat against the wall at the back of the temple, folding her legs properly to one side beneath her. *Here I am, Lord Buddha*, she whispered, her eyes watering. *Everything I touch falls apart—what am I doing wrong?*

But the Lord Buddha, rather than whispering in Lindsay's ear, directed her attention outward, to the scenes around her. The soaring roof of the temple, its walls and ceiling bright with colored murals depicting both religious and local scenes, soothed Lindsay's tattered spirits. Focusing her attention on the outsized Sleeping Buddha at the front of the temple, she forced herself not to think of Max or Hoktha, David or André—forced herself to bring to the Buddha a mind empty of thought and desire.

And it worked. In moments, her heart rate had slowed and she was breathing deeply. At the front of the temple, through the blue haze of incense that spiraled from red sticks sprouting from pots of sand, she saw that school was in session. A wizened monk, probably nearing his tenth decade of life, sat cross-legged in front of five white-robed nuns, their shaven heads gray with stubble. The monk was leading the nuns in a chant of haunting beauty. Lindsay remained hidden in the back of the temple, listening until the chanting faded away. Rising to her feet, she slipped quietly away, her heart at peace, her determination renewed. She would do her best to understand the course of truth and justice—and would follow it, regardless.

When Lindsay stepped outside the doors of the temple, her head once again held high, night had fallen. The rain had stopped, and the streetlights were reflected in the inky puddles filling the potholes that mined Preah Sisowath Boulevard. Oblivious to the jarring bumps, Lindsay drove, unseeing, toward home. It was worse even than she'd thought. Max had not only made a fool of her—he was a total fool himself, and he was fast becoming the laughingstock of the city.

Still thinking about Nick's revelations, Lindsay almost failed to see the ancient Citroën at the side of the road, its wheels submerged. A man stood bent and half-hidden behind the car's raised hood.

Slowing the Land Cruiser to avoid splashing the stranded motorist, Lindsay recognized André Balfour's wiry figure. He was leaning on the radiator, shaking his head in disgust as he watched the smoke rising from his car's engine. She braked, creating minor havoc among the *motos* riding in her wake, and pulled to a stop in front of the broken-down vehicle.

She reached across the passenger seat and rolled down the window. "Anything I can do?" she said.

A look of amusement crossed André's face. "Why, you know something about French carburetors?" he inquired.

You'd think he'd at least be polite, Lindsay thought, and she let André wait in the rain a moment before answering. "No, I'm afraid I don't, and I doubt you'd want me to experiment. But I can offer you a lift. Even a tow."

He looked uncertainly at his car, then slammed down the hood, put an anti-theft lock on the steering wheel, and double-checked the doors. Climbing into the Land Cruiser, he said, resignation in his voice, "I'll probably never see it again. Goodbye, my beauty!" Turning to Lindsay, he said, "Could you take me to the Cambodiana? I can get a taxi from there."

"Why?" Lindsay asked, her tone insolent. "Do you have such an exciting life that your destination is confidential? Or is it the rendezvous rather than the destination that you're keeping secret?"

"Even worse," André grimaced. "I'm off to a Chinese wine bar of the lowest sort, I'm afraid." He looked thoughtful, and offered no further explanation.

"Is there a name to the bar, or maybe even an address? I'd be happy to drop you. I'm just on my way home, and I need to talk to you, anyway."

André glanced at her curiously. Without speaking, he pointed to the intersection they were approaching and said, "All right, then. Go on around Wat Phnom, then right on Street 47. We'll need to make a left turn there, on Norodom. I'll tell you when to stop."

As they splashed through the flooded road, they chatted inconsequentially about the horrors of the rainy season, Lindsay interjecting occasional muttered oaths as unlit *cyclos* darted across her path. Suddenly, André pointed to a garish pink neon sign, flashing "Special Snake Soup Restaurant."

"There," he said.

She braked and veered to the curb. "Are you sure?" she inquired, half serious. Why on earth would André brave the rain to come to a dive like this?

"*Oui, oui,*" he was saying, clearly distracted. "*Merci,* again." He turned to shut the door, then reconsidered. Why not let them wait? And find out more about Lindsay. He gestured to the blinking sign. "You said you wanted to talk. Would you join me for a drink?"

Lindsay's expression was dubious as she looked again at the open-air restaurant, its interior glowing cheerfully in the reflected light of the sign, but she nodded shortly. Better to get this over with. The proprietor followed them to a corner table near the street and took their order for hot tea. As they sat, André said, "I'm very curious. I got the impression at our last meeting that you had no interest in listening to anything I might have to say."

Lindsay bit her tongue. André had the knack of setting her on edge, but she needed information, and that meant she had to behave herself. "Major," she began, "David Bullford has returned to Cambodia and has assigned me to work on the park project. I'm trying to interview as many people as I can who might be able to give me background information. And yes, I'm interested in hearing both pros and cons. I planned to call you tomorrow, but if you have time to talk now..." she trailed off.

"Of course. I believe I gave you most of the background on human trafficking I could when we met last week. And although I didn't say so at the time, the reason I'm as familiar as I am with the issue is because I'm working on very real trafficking problems that are taking place right here, and right now."

Lindsay nodded. "In fact, André, I've just come from another eye-opening meeting, and I'm beginning to understand why you think there is a lot more to this project than pacifying the tree-huggers."

"I'm impressed that you're open to finding out you were wrong," André smiled. "The problem is that your Max is in over his head. That's a dangerous place to be—and I wouldn't like for you to find yourself in the same situation. And—"

Annoyed again, Lindsay interrupted. "For one thing, he's not 'my' Max," she said, her voice louder than she'd intended. "And for another, why do you think I'm demeaning myself by asking everyone I can think of for help? Precisely because I don't want to get sucked under by all of this."

André held up both hands, palms out. "Sorry! I understand that you can take care of yourself, but I...worry about you." Should he say more? He glanced at his watch, and realized that personal issues would have to wait. "Lindsay, I really am late. Could we meet again, perhaps for dinner, later this week?"

Lindsay waited while André settled the bill, wondering what he had been about to say. Dinner, even a business dinner, might be more of him than she could handle. She temporized. "I'm not sure of my schedule, André. Why don't you give me a call tomorrow, so we can set something up."

As André walked out of the restaurant, Lindsay breathed a sigh of relief. Perhaps the Frenchman was not as annoying as she had thought. He certainly had a way of intruding on her thoughts at the oddest moments. And he did have those compelling blue eyes. She smiled back when he turned to wave, climbed into the Land Cruiser, then watched as he crossed the street. But when he ducked into the narrow alley beside the Lily Hands Beauty Shop, just opposite the restaurant, her eyes widened.

It was Pink Alley. This is just too much, Lindsay thought to herself as she sat, staring into the alley. First Max proves his stupidity with Juliette—now André's off in search of ecstasy in Pink Alley. Could he possibly have some other reason for being here? She laughed softly, realizing that, at 28, she was still expecting to find a hero.

Although Lindsay had visited the Lily Hands for a shampoo once or twice, she'd never gotten any closer to Pink Alley than a sidewise glance. Even then, it had been during the day, when the small wooden shop fronts and pajama-clad girls had merely seemed dreary. With darkness, the alley had been transformed into a lurid world of flashing pink lights casting macabre shadows on the painted faces of the prostitutes that lined both sides of the alley like a gauntlet.

Lindsay considered as she watched André stepping heedlessly through the mud. Should she follow him? But then, what business was it of hers if he had so little respect for himself? Even so, when André suddenly turned and entered one of the few two-story buildings in the alley, she determined to confront him, to find out what kind of man he really was. Although the rain had dwindled to a fine mist, Lindsay grabbed her rain parka from the glove box and locked the Land Cruiser before dashing across the dark street and into Pink Alley.

Lindsay had underestimated the stir that her entrance into the alley would create—foreign females were apparently not among the regular clientele. Almost immediately, she felt the speculative glances of the drunken men who loitered in front of the first establishment, and she could hear the word *barang* sprinkled liberally in the river of female conversation that streamed through the alley.

Recognizing that discretion was her only option, Lindsay banked her burning curiosity and retreated. She would settle for the chance to observe André, unseen, when he returned. Glancing behind her, she realized that the snake restaurant would provide a perfect surveillance point, giving her a clear view down the alley without arousing the curiosity of the women and their clientele.

She crossed the street and re-entered the open façade of the restaurant, again taking the table nearest the sidewalk. The proprietor greeted her as if she were a regular, bringing her hot tea without asking. It was a delicious jasmine blend, and the hovering proprietor beamed with pleasure when she expressed her approval.

While she waited for André to reappear, she watched the comings and goings of commerce in the establishments nearest the alley entrance. With the easing of the rain, traffic had increased. Some of the girls were little more than children, like porcelain dolls, while others revealed a premature haggardness that disguised their real age. The clients, too, were interesting—some

196

moved surreptitiously, clearly ashamed of their purpose in the alley, but most were filled with alcohol-induced *bonhomie*, strolling hand-in-hand with friends as they inspected the girls before making a selection. From each house came the beat of cheap stereos, and the cacophony of loud music clashing with the shrieks and chattering of the girls made Lindsay wonder what would happen if someone were in trouble on this street. *No one would ever hear them scream*, she thought.

She continued to speculate on André's reason for coming to such a place, something wriggling inside her brain insisting that it must be something other than the obvious. She continued to wait, sipping her tea while warming her hands on the smudged glass.

Twenty minutes later, now nursing a glass of thick, sweet coffee, Lindsay saw André emerge from the building he'd entered halfway down the alleyway. When he turned left, heading away from her and deeper into the alley, she quickly slipped a handful of *riel* beneath her glass and dashed across the street and back into the alley.

Pulling her parka from her bag, she slipped it over her head, shielding her face with the hood and hoping it would keep her from being noticed. She was determined to find out what André was up to! Dodging through crowds of customers, her eyes riveted on André's rapidly disappearing back, she failed to notice a ferret-faced man watching her from the doorway of the building that André had just exited.

Nearing the end of the passage, where it emptied back into Preah Sisowath Boulevard, André turned to look back up the alley. Quelling an impulse to call after him, she ducked into a darkened doorway. Breathing heavily, she closed her eyes for a moment, then turned back to the alley.

But the doorway was blocked by the pinched features of a short man whose face was inches from her own. He was grinning insanely, and Lindsay shrank back against the rough wooden planks of the wall. One gold tooth glinted in the dimness, as did the blade of the knife with which the man was motioning her up the stairs that disappeared into the darkness behind her.

"*Laung!*" the gold-toothed man commanded in a harsh whisper. "*Leuang dtao!*"

Although his words were unintelligible to Lindsay, his meaning was clear. Keeping as far from the man as possible, she began to back slowly up the stairs. Gold Tooth had other ideas. With his free hand, he grabbed her arm, spinning her around, then pinned her against his chest, his hand cruel on her breasts. Although she squirmed away, the point of the knife on her right arm forced her into a docility that enabled the man to drive her up the stairs, taking every opportunity to enjoy the curves of her body on the way. Remembering her idle thoughts earlier, she didn't bother to scream, although she continued to struggle.

At the top of the stairs, the man showed his teeth again before shoving her through the curtained doorway of a small room.

"Well, Linseed," an oily voice said softly—and her heart began thudding within her chest, choking off her breathing as her eyes fell on the smug face of Som Hoktha.

"I'd been hoping to see you again, but I wasn't sure just how to arrange it. Now I won't need to. It seems you are more interested in Hoktha than you let on last week. At least, let's assume that's why you're here, shall we? It seems you found me so fascinating that you've been asking all sorts of people about me." He paused, and his smile broadened unpleasantly. "I bet you're going to wish you hadn't done that."

Lindsay was breathing quickly, and thinking faster. *Why, oh why, hadn't she listened to Rex?* Remembering André's final glance back into the alley, she prayed he'd seen her, and would come back. Because if he didn't—well, she would have to think her own way out of this. The little voice at the back of her brain gave her strength, urging her to act, to be the one setting the tone for what would happen next.

"I have been surprised not to hear from you, Hoktha," she said, striving for composure. "There are a lot of things we need to cover before UNOIC will be able to make a commitment to your project."

Hoktha laughed, caressing his chin with one hand. "I don't really think getting UNOIC support is going to be all that difficult, Linseed. In any case, you are not one of the things we need to cover," he said softly, rising from his seat on the floor and walking toward her. When she began to back away, she saw him nod and felt smooth hands grab her arms from behind.

The man with the knife stepped through the door and, following Hoktha's instructions, sliced through the vinyl of Lindsay's poncho, dropping it onto the floor. Hoktha nodded again, and the man returned to his post outside the door. "Warm in here, don't you think," Hoktha said, reaching for the front of her blouse. Lindsay squirmed away from him, but the hands on either side held her fast as, one by one, Hoktha unfastened each button of her blouse. He was breathing quickly, his nostrils flared.

"Hoktha, what are you thinking? Don't you care about the park? Because UNOIC cannot support you after this! Surely you don't want that to happen!"

Hoktha's hands moved to the waistband of her jeans. "You are a fool, Linseed," he said, smirking. "Your body will never be found— although I will certainly offer the full resources of the government in searching for it. And I will recommend," he added, his laugh a sharp bark in the quiet of the room, "that the park be opened as soon as possible—in your memory. In fact," he added slyly, "we might name some natural feature for you, not just an orchid. Perhaps...the waterfall?"

The man holding Lindsay dragged her arms roughly through the sleeves of her blouse and pulled her legs from her jeans, leaving her standing, shaking, in nothing but her French lace underwear, the unrelenting grasp of a pair of smooth hands, and the evil eyes of Som Hoktha.

"On second thought," Hoktha said, running his hands over her shoulders, "perhaps it would be best to keep you alive. That way I could bring you news of the park—perhaps you could watch the dedication on television." Lindsay watched Hoktha run his eyes down her body, and closed her own when his hands reached under her bra and lifted it above her breasts. But to her surprise, he pulled it back down, gently enough, and said, "You are a bit old— but not in bad shape, for a foreigner. I may find some further use for you."

"No!" Lindsay, horrified, could read Hoktha's thoughts only too well. "You don't want to do this. My—my friends know where I am. They'll find me here, like this, and you will be finished."

Hoktha looked at her, his small eyes shrewd and his voice amused. "I don't think so, Linseed. My friend with the knife has been watching you since you dropped Major Balfour off at the entrance to the alley. You are alone. However, perhaps I'll just give you a little lesson on the Cambodian economy."

At Hoktha's nod, her arms were freed, and she found herself pushed down onto a rough wooden folding chair. She started to rub the soreness from her bruised arms, but her hands were jerked backward and tied to the chair behind her back.

"My friends tell me that you have developed some interest in the business of prostitution?" Hoktha said.

When it became clear that he was waiting for her answer, Lindsay said. "I am concerned, yes, Hoktha," Lindsay said, "but I don't know very much about it."

"Oh, how very convenient, Linseed. You 'are concerned,' but you 'don't know very much' about it. I am so pleased, because I know just how I can help you. Don't look so frightened. You won't need to do anything you're not accustomed to—your friend Max told me about the services you provided him at the Linseed Waterfall."

Lindsay gasped and heard, again, that insidious laugh. "The girls of Pink Alley, Linseed, are not the only women who provide pleasure to men in Phnom Penh. There are many women who provide more...specialized, and more expensive services. But, sad to say, sometimes powerful men become, shall we say, bored. When they want something a little different, they come to me. I try to satisfy their whims by providing girls who are younger, or girls who are from one of our more exotic tribes—or girls who are...lighter-skinned, if you will.

"Some of these women are foreign tourists who have run out of money and found themselves unable to pay their hotel bills. Others get into difficulties with the authorities, for smoking marijuana or being on the street after curfew. And some, like you," he said, his voice sharpening, "got themselves involved in something that was none of their business."

How could she have been so stupid? First, Sam and Olga had come to her with their suspicions. Rex had warned her. Nicky had even named names just hours ago. Now she was sitting in her underwear at knifepoint, listening to Hoktha brag about his horrid business. Looking into his deranged eyes, she knew that everything she'd been told was true—and that it was too late for her to do anything about Hoktha now. But since there was no longer any reason to pretend her ignorance, she screamed, "I know you're the one who's killing the tribal girls! I won't stop until you're punished for all of the women you've hurt!"

Hoktha looked straight into Lindsay's eyes with such venom that she was forced to turn away. And then he laughed. "You? You will stop me from opening my park? You will not stop me—and you will pay for your interference. But don't worry—my girls are not abused until they are no longer of use to me. Nor will you be."

Hoktha turned to speak to the man behind her. She heard footsteps on the wooden floor as the man left the room, then looked back as Hoktha stepped behind her and began untying the rope that bound her wrists. "Don't get your hopes up, Linseed, they are waiting just outside. Yes, the man with the knife, too. You understand, I'm sure, that I must ensure that the services I am making available at such high prices are satisfactory in every way?" he said, as he reached to unfasten her bra.

Lindsay turned in the chair, looking for an opportunity to send Hoktha to the floor with a knee to his groin. Hoktha caught her eye, smiled, and stepped away. She rushed after him—and suddenly found herself flipped through the air to land flat on her back on the mat in the corner of the room.

Hoktha pinned her legs to the mat with his own, and called out to the man outside the door. "I suspect you may be more cooperative if you are able to keep your eye on the knife until we're finished," he said, almost pleasantly.

CHAPTER TWENTY-TWO
MONDAY, MAY 31

Although Hoktha yelled for Gold Tooth again, his voice becoming shrill, the man did not reappear. Angry voices were rising from the stairway, and Lindsay struggled more energetically as she heard a man's voice speaking in French. André! The voice grew louder, accompanied by the pounding of feet on the stairs. As Lindsay and Hoktha both turned toward the curtain, it was pushed roughly aside and André made his way into the room.

"Hoktha! Lindsay!" he said, managing to sound amused. "I'm so sorry. I didn't realize you'd formed a *liaison*. Lindsay, my apologies, I know this is a special moment, but I'm afraid I've left something of great importance in your Land Cruiser. Lindsay rescued me from my misbegotten vehicle earlier," he said, explaining gravely to Hoktha. "I'm sure you understand, Hoktha. It is that item which we were discussing earlier...? Damn silly of me to leave it behind, and unguarded."

Hoktha had by this time gotten to his feet and fastened his pants. "Your timing is most unfortunate, Major," he said coldly. "But you are right. You must bring the emerald before we can conclude our agreement."

André spotted Lindsay's clothing strewn beside the door and carried it over to her. "I don't know, Lindsay. You are becoming quite the adventuress. Please, if you could get dressed quickly. I am an old man and need my sleep. I'm sure Hoktha will be polite enough to wait until we have retrieved my possession from your vehicle."

Hoktha glanced at Lindsay dismissively as she struggled into her torn clothing, "Surely you are not concerned about Linseed, André? This is what she likes—she came here on her own, you know. And the South American has described to me in detail their romantic embraces in the jungle. She is no innocent, believe me."

But he did not try to stop them as André supported Lindsay, still shaking, down the stairs. "Walk normally," he instructed, his tone stiff, when she tried to break into a run as they crossed into the alley. In silence, they waded through the crowds of men toward the pink lights of the restaurant. André ignored the joking comments and ogling glances, maintaining a steady pace until they reached the Land Cruiser. Lindsay handed him the keys without speaking, and sat frozen as he drove away from Pink Alley.

When Lindsay started to laugh, a shrill, hysterical laughter, André stretched his arm behind her shoulders and pulled her across the seat to clasp her against him. "Iwatchedyoufromtherestaurant," she said, the words spilling out of her in a purging rush. "Iwantedtocatchyou. But, but, but..." Her laughter turned to great, heaving sobs, and André continued to hold her tightly, clenching his jaw tightly to control his anger.

What was Hoktha thinking? And Lindsay? Between the two of them, he realized, his own cover had probably been blown. He laughed inwardly, realizing that in spite of the damage that had been done, he was feeling a little flattered. After all, how many men had a woman intrigued enough to actually spy on their movements?

But how frighteningly large a role luck had played in Lindsay's rescue! Thank God Som Sak had selected a new low in meeting places tonight. Although he could barely stomach the sight of those young girls, grotesquely made up, pandering to the obscene fondling of Som Sak's henchmen.

Som Sak himself had seemed bored with the girls' attentions, but the meeting had certainly held his interest. At long last, André's patience was paying off. They'd reached an agreement on price, and a delivery date had been set. André had agreed to hand over the giant emerald, Evita's Teardrop, as earnest money. Although it had been—and still was—nestled securely in the inner pocket of his shirt, he'd not wanted to make it that easy, promising instead to return with it, wanting to give himself some moments of concentrated thought to consider whether he was handling things correctly. Then, as he'd headed down the alley for a stroll, he'd seen Lindsay disappear into the darkened doorway halfway down the alley.

As for Lindsay, somewhere inside the hysteria she knew that she was deeply ashamed. Ashamed that she had followed André in the first place and thus put both of their lives in danger. Ashamed that she had not been able to protect herself from Hoktha. But what bothered her most was that André now knew about her encounter with Max.

André pulled the Land Cruiser to a halt in the bougainvillea-sheltered drive of his small house on the riverside behind Wat Ras Chak. Lindsay stirred against him, sitting up with a dazed expression. "I've brought you to my place, Lindsay," André said, his tone neutral. "I don't want you to be alone tonight. And nothing will happen to you here."

The young man who opened the gate politely averted his eyes, asking André in French if he'd be needing anything. He looked relieved at André's quick shake of the head, and turned back to fasten the gate for the night. Inside, André settled Lindsay on a worn leather sofa, covered her with a heavy Korean blanket, and poured a large amount of brandy into a water glass.

"Drink this, *cheri*," he ordered, his concern evident in his eyes. When Lindsay didn't respond, he held the glass to her lips and waited while she took three tiny swallows. Setting the glass down beside her, he said, "Just keep working on it until it's gone." He inserted Kitaro's *Silk Road* into the CD player, and turned the volume low.

Suddenly feeling an urgent need for food, André rooted through his refrigerator, wondering if Lindsay had had a chance to eat during her vigil. His movements quick and practiced, he whipped eggs, cream, cheese, and *herbes de Provence* together, but when he carried the omelet into the living room ten minutes later, he found the brandy glass empty and Lindsay fast asleep, curled into a tight ball on the sofa.

***

Lindsay woke early to find André already gone. A note on the table beside the couch offered French bread and coffee, said he was off to see about his car, and requested that she lock the house when she left. The note also suggested that she would be interested in the videotape that lay beneath the note. *Thank God I don't have to face him this morning*, she thought, penning a heartfelt 'thank you' beneath the words of André's note.

Lindsay drove rapidly through the still quiet streets to her home. After showering, she dressed quickly, rushing to get to the office to report everything she'd learned to David. The trauma of the encounter was working like speed in her system, making her fierce.

Jumping back into the Land Cruiser, her eyes fell on the videotape André had left for her. Should she take time to watch the tape, in case it had some bearing on the nature reserve? More likely, she thought, it's something André's found to make fun of me for supporting it in the first place.

Nevertheless, she grabbed the tape and dashed back up the stairs into the house. With one eye on the clock—it was seven-thirty—she turned on the television and slipped the video into the VCR slot, tapping her front teeth impatiently as she waited.

It took less than a minute for Lindsay to realize that, in addition to being disgusting and embarrassing, this tape was exactly what she needed. Thank God she had taken the time to watch it before going to David. No need for further investigations now. It wasn't only her word—now she had evidence.

On the way to the office, she reviewed her strategy. She would go straight to David's office, tell him about her weekend, including the trip to Pink Alley, and show him the tape. It would be a relief to turn the whole thing over to him—he would know what to do, who to call, how to make sure that Hoktha's awful trafficking was stopped.

But when she reached the UNOIC compound, David was not available. Bunna looked at Lindsay coldly, saying she had no idea what time David would be in. "Thanks, Bunna," Lindsay said, wondering why the woman was always so crabby, "Could you please let me know when he gets here?"

Feeling dull with letdown, she forced herself to deal with the minutia that had filled her in-box over the weekend. An hour later, she looked up from the paperwork to study her purse sitting there on the chair. She could almost see the video, with its silent contents, explicit photographs, and almost professional performance, burning a hole in the black leather of the bag. If only she could broadcast the awful thing on national television right now. Instead, she forced herself to press on with the dozens of email requests forwarded to her from David on a hundred sundry issues.

It was just trivia David had invented for her, an avalanche of busy work, but in a way she was grateful to him. She put together a chart on salary ranges for government counterpart staff as part of a brief on appropriate supplements, and reviewed budget requests for mother-child health care workshops. They were like balm, numbing her outrage, but temporary in their effect—her mind soon turned back to the nature reserve conundrum. Where could David be?

She knew she would have to make the most of her one opportunity to convince David. But how? So many things were against her. David was sure to place his confidence in a royal advisor and the nephew of a four star general, especially if he knew who she'd been depending on—the French military attaché and a couple of eccentrics who were scorned by the international community. Lindsay debated telling David of Hoktha's assault, quickly quashing the idea. It would be beyond his competence to understand or deal with in any way.

She pictured Sam's straggly figure in rubber sandals and Olga the ice queen, and felt fiercely protective toward them. She'd made them a promise, and she wouldn't let them down. But more importantly, the people they were trying to protect needed her help.

Who else could she turn to who might have more influence with David? Her face flushed at the thought of André. She knew David disliked him simply because he was French, but in any case, André would have only disdain for her because she'd refused to listen to him. And he was right to be contemptuous.

She had just turned back to the computer when an email referenced "Dedication Ceremony" jumped out at her. Her eyes scanned the brief message. A dedication ceremony for Norodom Park was to be held Saturday, June 5, at the governor's mansion in Banlung. At the same time, UNOIC Country Coordinator David Bullford would pledge the full support of UNOIC to the Kingdom of Cambodia's efforts to preserve the forest and its endangered species.

Curious, Lindsay thought, *apparently I have been removed from the loop.* And David had evidently prepared the press release himself. Well, maybe he was right not to trust her. Where was he, anyway?

She looked up to see Bopha staring at her. God, she must have been muttering to herself. "Hi," Lindsay said with false brightness.

"You want some tea? I think you should have some," Bopha said, going to the water kettle. Bopha wasn't usually this assertive, but Lindsay thought tea sounded great.

As Bopha finished preparing the pot and cups, arranging everything on a napkin-covered tray, David strode into Lindsay's office. "Hello everybody!" he announced cheerfully. "Ah, Bopha, such good timing," he said, eyeing the tray. "I'll take it in my office. Perhaps you could join me, Lindsay?"

Bopha exchanged a sympathetic glance with Lindsay, then they both followed David into his office. He waited for Bopha to leave, then closed the door. *Uh-oh*, she thought. David quite vociferously prided himself on his open door policy.

"I have much to tell you." David began, before Lindsay could say a word. "I had a stupendous weekend. I met Vega y Ortega at La Paillote Friday night. We got to talking about Norodom Park—and Saturday he and Som Hoktha flew me up to Ratanakiri."

"And what did you think of it, David?" she asked calmly, although her head was spinning. Surely he had more to say—otherwise, why the closed door?

"Oh, I can see it now. This project is going to make a real difference for Cambodia." He laughed shortly. "It won't hurt my career, either, because its going to be one of the best things that UNOIC has accomplished in this country, and it will certainly have the most long-lasting impact." He paused and cleared his throat. "Now, Lindsay, I understand that you have a real personal interest in the park concept, and it's thanks to you that we've had the opportunity to offer our support. I appreciate that, and I'll make sure you get credit for it."

"Uh, David. I have something to tell you, too, about Som Hoktha. Because I can tell you, he is definitely *not* stupendous." Lindsay couldn't keep the bitterness out of her voice, and David picked up on it immediately.

Shaking his head, he said, "Look, I know you've had some difficulties with Hoktha. But Lindsay, these are great people, they're true visionaries! They know how to get things done, and they have the ears of the right people. Working together with them, this park could become a model for other developing countries. It's amazing what you can do when you get the right people involved."

Difficulties? Difficulties? She couldn't help it, the words boiled over. "David! Hoktha tried to rape me last night! And Vega y Ortega is playing sex tutor to the children Hoktha is abducting from the park! David, this proposal is not a career maker—it's certain death, and you should let go of it right now, before UNOIC—"

But David interrupted her, annoyed. "Lindsay, grabbing you by the shoulders is hardly rape." He held up a hand, forestalling her interruption. "I've spoken to Hoktha this morning. He apologized for his behavior last night, and it's in your interest to accept his apology. Even though he'd had too much to drink, he understands that he can't treat UNOIC people like that. And how could you possibly believe such a ridiculous thing about Vega y Ortega?"

Lindsay stared in disbelief as Bullford continued. "You must realize, Lindsay, that both of these men come from very different cultures than ours. They haven't even a basic understanding of women in the workplace, let alone gender equality and women's rights. And it'll be eons before either of them would even consider sexual harassment a legitimate problem. They're both used to getting their own way, and you should know better than to stir them up."

Lindsay started to respond, but David stopped her with a raised finger. "I know, it's not the ideal, but you have to accept these things if you're going to work in international development."

"David, you have to listen to me. Hoktha's lying. It's not just what he did last night..." she paused, swallowing away the acid taste that rose in her throat when she remembered the upstairs room. "That was bad enough. But there have been murders, David. No one has enough evidence to arrest Hoktha, especially since he's under the protection of General Som Sak, but people know that he has been brutalizing and killing prostitutes for over two years. One of the victims who lived even described the mole on Hoktha's lip!"

By this time David was looking frustrated, leaning his forehead on one hand, his elbow resting on his knee. "Lindsay. You have to stop this. You cannot—UNOIC cannot—go about making allegations of criminal behavior against government officials. Surely you know that?"

Oh dear Lord, she thought, her head bowed, too, under the weight of the crap she was hearing. How could David be so blind? He was a seasoned professional even if he was officious.

"At the same time," he went on, blithely ignoring her, "we all know that positive results can come from challenging circumstances. This park gives us just that opportunity. By allowing Hoktha his day in the sun, we can create something that will impact the long-term future of Cambodia."

How pathetic it was to hear her own misguided naiveté coming out of someone else's mouth. Unfortunately, David's words were all too true—Hoktha's evil activities would indeed affect the entire country, not to mention ruining the lives of any Cambodians unfortunate enough to cross his path.

"I see. The end justifies the means," she said, trying to keep the sarcasm out of her voice.

"Yes, exactly. Isn't it just great when the expeditious serves the greater good?" He actually laughed at his own cleverness. Lindsay badly needed to vomit. Then, she remembered her secret weapon.

"I have something you need to see," she said, standing to her feet.

"Sit down," David said shortly. "My point here, Lindsay, is that you are no longer assigned to this project. And by the way, protocol does not permit you to visit heads of agencies behind my back."

She looked at him, startled. She simply couldn't believe that Rex would have said anything to him. "I saw Rex last night at a reception for the Singapore ambassador," David told her. "He warned me off this project, as if I were some P-2 or something. Told me you'd discussed it with him! I simply will not tolerate that kind of insubordination. Branson may be a D-1, but it's only because of his emergency work."

The statement spoke worlds. Rex had headed emergency operations in Somalia, in Sierra Leone, and in Angola, operations that others wouldn't touch. His D-1 status was the third highest level attainable in the UN hierarchy, granted in recognition of the quality of his work. David, on the other hand, had entered the United Nations as an Oxford graduate, and had never worked an emergency station. But the snobbery of the development bureaucrats over the emergency cowboys permeated the entire organization. She wanted to kick him.

"I needed advice, David, and Rex offered it. If you'll remember, I told you, in advance, that I was going to do everything I could to find out the real story behind the king's proposal. Please, I have something that you have to see," she repeated.

"And I'm telling you that you are no longer involved. I don't usually get tough in this office, but you've already alienated our most important contacts, and I'm doing you a favor by not disciplining you more than this little talk. I don't want to hear any more about it. Please leave the door open when you leave."

He poured himself a second cup of tea, not looking at her. Lindsay stared at him in disbelief, the combination of shock, shame, and anger threatening to overwhelm her. Taking a deep breath, she stood and left the office, obediently leaving the door open behind her.

Back in her own office, Lindsay felt tears burning beneath her eyelids, and her hands were trembling. She swallowed hard, trying to breathe normally. The next thing she knew, Bopha had taken her by the hand and was leading her out the back door. In silence, they walked to a little tea stand in the alley. Bopha ordered coffee, gripping Lindsay's hand in both of her own.

The coffee came, and she sipped it automatically, the heavy acrid mixing with the strong sweetness. It gave her just the physical jolt she needed, and her tears began to flow. Within a few moments, she felt better, grabbing a napkin and noisily blowing her nose. She took another and wiped her face.

"Thanks," she said finally.

"You are my *bong srei*, Lindsay," Bopha said simply, acknowledging both duty and affection for her older sister.

Lindsay took her hand and squeezed it. "My little sister," she said, tears again filling her eyes.

"Tell me what is going on, Lindsay? Is it true that David went with those men to Ratanakiri?" Bopha asked.

"Yes. He thinks they're wonderful. Hoktha and Max are his best buddies now."

Bopha shook her head slowly. "David is not very clever, is he?"

Lindsay couldn't help it, the response was so sympathetic, so simple, and so true. She began giggling, then Bopha started smiling, and in moments they were doubled over, laughing so hard that the middle-aged proprietress behind the counter joined in, tears running down her chubby cheeks as well.

When their laughter had finally subsided, Bopha said, "What are you going to do, Lindsay?"

It took Bopha's question to make Lindsay realize that she most certainly was going to do something—that she would do almost anything to stop this fiasco from becoming a reality. That she was going to stop it because it was the right thing to do.

"Bopha, do you know about the dedication ceremony?"

"Yes, David already gave me to type the agenda. There is the ceremony for the monks, then the speech from the governor, and a dance with the Khmer dancers. Then the king will speak and show an old movie made by the French in the 1950s about the northeast. Then Hoktha will give a speech, and there will be a big lunch."

"I've got to be there, before then," Lindsay murmured.

Bopha paused in thought, not questioning Lindsay's need to go. "What about your friend, the one who rescued you with his fast boat?"

"Nicky. Yes, I'm sure he would help. Now all I need is to get someone else, someone with some influence. David, I'm sure, will never listen to me again."

"Maybe *Om* André?" Bopha asked timidly.

"Are you joking? He'd die laughing," Lindsay said. But he would have been perfect, she admitted to herself. If only he didn't despise her already for supporting Max and the park from the beginning. And for...but that didn't bear thinking about. But he had given her the incriminating tape...No, it was impossible.

Bopha didn't bother to argue. "I need to go back now," she said with some urgency.

"Of course you do. No need for you to catch the fallout from my troubles. I'll be fine. Bopha—I don't know what I would have done without you. You go ahead, I'll stay and have another coffee."

Bopha nodded, but as she was walking away, Lindsay called after her. "Wait, Bopha. I need you to contact someone for me, okay? Call Sam Jarrett at the Boun Thong Orphanage. Tell him about the reception, and that I'm going to Ratanakiri to try and stop it."

"Yes, Lindsay. Is Mr Sam's card in your file?"

"I'm pretty sure it is. There's a woman, too, Olga Herrin. I don't have her number, but Sam will know it. And Bopha—if anything else comes up while I'm gone, call Sam. You can count on the two of them."

As Lindsay sipped her second coffee the obstacles began crowding in her mind like little goblins. The instant she'd heard Bopha reciting the agenda, she'd known what her act of rebellion would be—and that such an action was sure to have serious repercussions. As those repercussions blossomed in her mind, she was reconsidering seeking André's support when a skinny little old man sat down at the rickety table next to her. A woman's straw hat bedecked with flowers adorned his head. He looked like a lot of Phnom Penh *moto* taxi drivers, although the hat was stunningly unique—white and pink plastic hibiscus woven in a thick ring around a beautiful kelly green crown. A gnome king, Lindsay automatically dubbed him.

As if he'd read her mind, the gnome turned and grinned straight into her face. Alarmed, she recognized the ugly puckish features of Kal, Hoktha's driver. They were following her! After what happened Sunday night, she should have known Hoktha wasn't finished with her. Agitated, she waved frantically to the owner of the shop for the check, now eager to escape back to the relative safety of her office.

Before she could move, the little man stood, took his hat off, and with it in his hands in front of him, came to her table. "I can sit?" he asked in English. Lindsay nodded, shaken. Could he have a gun hidden behind the hat? He nodded politely, and sat, carefully placing the hat in front of him on the table.

"I didn't know you spoke English," she said, the first words that came to her numbed brain spilling out into the lengthening silence.

"Yes, yes. Lots of English." He winked and nodded knowingly before adding, "Maybe better to say American." He seemed so pleased at her observation, as if she'd been terribly astute.

She studied him more closely. Although he was scrawny and appeared at first glance little different from all the other impoverished day laborers of the city, his ancient eyes were clear and his weathered face conveyed an innocent intelligence.

"Don't you live in Ratanakiri?" she asked.

Again the enthusiastic nod. "Yes, yes, now, yes."

She began to nod with him. They must look quite a sight, bobbing their heads up and down like fishing lures.

"So, uncle, what are you doing here?"

This made him positively delirious with amusement. He shook with laughter, covering his mouth with his hand. The wrinkles around his eyes crinkled up like well-cured leather.

Lindsay wondered if he might be mentally ill, not an uncommon thing among people of his generation who had been through a particularly horrific experience with the Khmer Rouge. Pity filled her. "Please, can I offer you coffee, or tea, something?"

This seemed to settle him down a bit, although he was still highly amused. "Tea, yes. Very good." She caught the attention of the proprietress, who seemed to be concerned over the little man, too, and brought the tea quickly. The Gnome King didn't touch it.

"I used to work with you. With Americans," he said cryptically, speaking out of the side of his mouth without moving his lips.

"Oh? When was that?" Lindsay asked, humoring him.

"1968," he said with no hesitation. "In the war. I am Kui. Sometimes I worked with *montagnards*. But then when the communists come, I never let them know I speak English. I never speak English again."

"Until now?" she asked, stunned.

"Yes. Now. Today. Thank you so much."

Lindsay was speechless. What could she say, hearing this bald assertion—and the story that lurked beneath it?

Her current crisis returned to her like hot water turning cold in the shower. Could this be a trap? "You are here with Hoktha then, visiting the city?"

The gnome's amusement vanished, replaced by a completely blank expression.

"No. He must not know. I am here for many days already. I am trying to find out where my nieces went."

"Your nieces?" Lindsay asked.

"One of my wives is Tamin. When we go to the villages, Mr Hoktha, he arranges for my nieces to get jobs. I know that maybe some of them get to be bad girls. That is what happens in the city. I know about those things. But I need to see that they are all right. And since you are the first American I see in 30 years, I think the spirits want you to help me. Can you help me?"

Lindsay put aside her doubts. "Yes. Of course I will help you. But uncle, I am afraid that your nieces, they may have been taken away."

He seemed to understand that 'taken away' could mean several bad things. He looked very sad, his face crumpling up for a moment in pain. Then he said, "Okay. But I must find out. I must do this for my wives."

Lindsay couldn't help herself. "Uncle, is it true you have eight wives?" she asked, her expression inviting his confidence.

He looked bashful. "I am a good provider. My first wife asked me to marry her cousin. Then there was another cousin. Then, when a man in the village died, his three wives had no one to take care of them. Now that they are all very old, they wanted to be taken care of, too. All our children have married to other villages, so my wives found two more wives, young wives to take care of all of us. But I keep very strict rules, so that they are good to each other."

"Oh. That's good. I guess." Lindsay figured she still had a lot to learn about the mountain cultures. She paused to sip the coffee, considering her next words. "You know that your boss, Mr Hoktha, is the one who is doing bad things," she said, hoping he was already aware of this.

"Yes. I must keep checking on him. I must know before he leaves Phnom Penh so that I can leave first. I must be ready to drive for him when he arrives in Ratanakiri. He is very bad man." He spat on the ground, a curiously appropriate gesture.

"If we want to stop him, we have to work as a team—" she began.

His enthusiasm returned. "Yes, yes! American team work. Each pulls his share." He must have really liked working with Americans.

"So, I'm not sure yet what you can do, but let's meet here every day to make sure we know where Hoktha is, and what he is up to. Can you do that?"

"I will come here every day, same time, okay!"

He got up then, put on his wonderful hat, and pulled a thin fold of hundred riel notes from the pocket of his tattered corduroy shirt.

"Please, uncle, put them away. Take care of yourself."

"You too, Mrs Lindsay American," he said, before scurrying away.

Suddenly, Lindsay felt bolstered by the motley group of supporters she had acquired. Maybe her plan would work—maybe purity of heart could win out over greed. *Yeah, right*, she said aloud as she walked back to the office, o*n the Disney Channel*. She patted the lump in her purse fondly as she walked through the reception area, prepared to bide her time to lull David into complacency.

CHAPTER TWENTY-THREE
SATURDAY, JUNE 5

S he what? Please, tell me this isn't so."
Bopha bit her lip, wondering suddenly if it had been a mistake to tell André that Lindsay had gone to Ratanakiri in Nicky's boat, planning to arrive in time for the dedication ceremony.

"Okay. Okay, when did she leave?" André said, forcing himself to speak gently, although his jaw was clenched.

"Around seven this morning, *Om.*"

He calculated roughly that in three more hours Lindsay would arrive in the town of Stung Treng. Then, it was another four hours to Ratanakiri by hired motorcycle. *Incroyable!* She might make it, too, before the day's festivities were completed—provided she wasn't waylaid by bandits, killed in a crash, trampled by wild buffalo, caught in a downpour, or abducted by the driver.

And of all days, it would have to be today. The generals, finally were ready to deliver a consignment of girls. Somehow, he'd manage to retain their trust in spite of Sunday night's little adventure with Hoktha. And now that he was finally going to net them—damn it, how could she? He thought quickly. How to manage everything and still get to Ratanakiri before Lindsay's arrival?

"Kmuey," he said, "you must go to the Hu Fang and warn Vanna that I cannot be there as planned. Tell her..." He hesitated. He wanted to tell Bopha to just go and get Vanna out, but realized that Vanna herself would have a better sense of the safest course of action. "Just tell her to be careful," he said finally.

Bopha agreed. "I will go now, *Om.* You must take care of Lindsay—I will take care here in Phnom Penh."

Next, André contacted the Russian pilots' charter helicopter company \. By the time he reached the military airport later that morning, a helicopter was standing by, its rotors revolving lazily. He jumped in and donned the head phones to reduce the deafening noise as the copter lifted into the air.

***

Lindsay stood next to Nicky almost the entire trip, her eyes fixed on the pregnant rain clouds massed to the north. She willed them to keep their distance, and so far they had obliged. Her face was numb from the pressure of the constant wind, and her hair had blown free of the plait she had braided before they left Phnom Penh.

"How much longer?" she asked every half hour. Nicky answered patiently, not even teasing her by suggesting that there were too many digits in her age for such nagging questions.

She was trying desperately to keep from thinking about her gamble. For she had met the Gnome King again at the little tea shop. He had seen Hoktha making arrangements for the flight north for the ceremony, and needed to leave immediately himself. On the spur of the moment, she had given him the videotape, explaining carefully what he was to do.

"This will help to stop those bad guys?" He asked, thrilled at the intrigue and the opportunity to play the hero. She loved how the words came out of his mouth, like he'd been possessed by a ghost from New Jersey.

"If you follow the instructions, it will," she said, with more confidence than she felt.

"You can count on me, Mrs Lindsay American," he promised, his face serious for once.

Had he made it to Banlung? Had he been successful? During the first couple of hours, Lindsay wished Nicky would flirt with her, just to keep her from going crazy with worry. But Nicky, too, was more serious than usual, looking like the dour Scot he loved pretending to be. Now, as they neared the town of Steung Treng, he finally spoke. "I suppose you know what you're doing?"

"No," she said, "Not in the least."

"Hmph. At least you know enough to be honest about it. Tell me this, then. Do you know what you want?"

"I want integrity. I want to live an honest life," she said without hesitation.

"Lindsay, there's no honesty in the grave. I'm fearing that what you are doing may be suicidal."

"That's a risk I'm willing to take."

He pulled a pistol out from under the dashboard of the boat. It seemed alarmingly large in his hand. *Was he going to try to stop her?* she wondered crazily.

"Do you want this?" he asked her.

"It's way too late, Nicky. And violence begets violence. But thanks. One thing you could do…"

"Anything."

"If I don't show up in Phnom Penh by tomorrow afternoon, pull out all the stops. Call the UNOIC Security Officer, call the US Embassy, everyone. Sam Jarrett at the Boun Thong Orphanage, too. Okay?"

He nodded, looking away. Moments later he pulled up neatly at a wooden dock jutting into the river from the huts and houses of Steung Treng. She jumped out, feeling a little wobbly from the movement of the boat. A small group of rasty looking men with worn out hats and equally worn out motorscooters waited at the top of the river bank, slouching against their machines. She waved in their direction and a couple of them started their engines, maneuvering their way down the slippery mud bank to haggle. Feeling like the outcome had been foreordained, she chose the man who looked a little more careworn, his face a dark wood carving. Before straddling the seat, she wrapped a *krema* over her head and around her neck and donned a pair of sunglasses. With her long sleeved shirt, she could have been just another villager traveling the back roads of Cambodia.

The first few kilometers were exhilarating, the wind cool in her face, the landscape green and calm. After a while, though, she began to feel the bumps, and by the second hour her backside was numb. Every few minutes, she used the *krema* to wipe the road grit from her lips. But the driver held steady, not stopping even for a cigarette. Just when she was beginning to nod off, they reached the first signs of cultivation, green fields of rice seedlings. Ten minutes later they entered the outskirts of Banlung, and she directed him toward the governor's mansion. On the way they passed school children in their blue and white uniforms running up the lane to join the ceremony.

At the governor's mansion, the villagers, all sporting bright blue *kremas,* huddled together on the ground around an elevated platform. Apparently she'd missed the king's distribution ceremony. At the far end, nearest the platform, sat a small group of men, all of them Tamin. They were also holding new *kremas*, but wore only their loincloths. There were no women with them.

Minor functionaries in Western dress filled perhaps 100 folding chairs beneath a blue plastic canopy. She noted wryly the white UNOIC emblem emblazoned on the plastic. *Nice to see it going to good use,* she thought. After moving into the shelter of a massive tamarind tree just inside the courtyard gate, Lindsay studied the faces of the VIPs seated on the raised platform. There were about twenty of them, resting placidly on huge easy chairs upholstered in shiny mauve vinyl. A child held a black umbrella over each VIP's head as they sipped soft drinks through neon colored straws. An ornately embroidered yellow silk umbrella shaded a taller, more ornate chair. In it sat King Sihanouk. He was chatting jovially with the guests seated nearest him. Chea Ros, the rubbery little governor, kept bouncing up and down in his seat like a child who's been neglecting to take his Ritalin. Lindsay spotted Hoktha, and Max, and then Juliette, looking like a jeweled doll in her dancing costume. Beside her sat David, dressed in an ivory safari suit, laughing attentively at something Juliette was saying.

The King stood and cleared his throat, bringing the crowd to an instantaneous silence. His speech was a mad mixture of English, French, and Khmer. Even so, Lindsay might possibly have followed it if she hadn't been so nervous. He was describing his own years living in the forest with the Khmer Rouge, and the French presence in the area before that. "You will see, nothing has changed. Everything, everthing here is natural, still the same as in the old days."

Sihanouk's high-pitched voice was always a surprise, even when you knew what to expect. She swallowed nervously at his next words. "Please enjoy with me these views of our beloved Ratanakiri, filmed during the peaceful years before the war."

Dear God! What if the Gnome King hadn't been able to get to the machine? She watched, mesmerized, as the governor knelt low and extended both hands to offer the King the remote control. The king swiveled and clicked the remote at a 50-inch television that had been mounted prominently on the platform. A whirring sounded, and then stopped. He clicked again. More whirring, then silence.

The governor hurried to the VCR and ejected the tape, giggling nervously, sweat marks dark against the light blue silk of his tunic. He flipped the tape over and put it back into the player. Sihanouk clicked the remote again, and this time something did happen. A deep distorted voice came through the speakers, and static seams buzzed across the screen. The king frowned with impatience, appealing to his Special Advisor for assistance.

Max stood and went to the machine, fiddled with a control, and there it was—a beautifully clear picture of Max himself, with Juliette. Young girls with tattoos twining their bare breasts surrounded him, caressing him awkwardly, their hands and arms

221

tiny against his tall form. Juliette's voice boomed out of the loudspeakers connected to the television. "You see Max, even in their innocence they are irresistible."

The crowd, including the king, seemed frozen, watching in silence as the girls undressed Max like actresses in a cheap porn flick. At the point when Max ceased to play a passive role, grabbing at first one girl and then another, the small group of hill tribe people went berserk. They stood, calling out at the screen, as if the images could hear them. Their anger was hot and dangerous, and two of the King's North Korean bodyguards pointed their guns menacingly.

The Kind took charge. He held up his arms and spoke a single word. The guards froze, then returned their weapons to their holsters. The king clicked the remote to mute the sounds now coming from the speakers, then handed it to the governor, who fumbled for it without taking his eyes from the screen.

As Sihanouk approached the irate tribesmen, one of their number began a monologue, pointing frequently at the figures still moving on the screen. The King listened in silence, nodding periodically. As he continued the conversation, the tape ended and static again filled the screen.

Lindsay watched the tableau unfold before her on the platform. Max was looking for all the world like nothing unexpected had happened, while beside him Juliette's face was a demon's mask under the glittering tower of her ornate headdress. Ah, and there was David, standing to join the King. She snickered, watching him desperately trying on different versions of concerned expressions as he knelt down, trying to be part of the discussion. Hoktha had disappeared.

The tribesman had finished his lengthy speech, and now the King was responding. His words must have satisfied their concerns, because the anger had been smoothed from their faces as they turned to face inward in a tight circle, each man bending forward to light his pipe.

She sensed someone behind her. Turning, she saw the Gnome King, his face wet with tears. "Two of them, they are my nieces," he whispered. "How can I find them?"

"We will find them, uncle," Lindsay promised. "And Uncle...you were a true hero today. Thank you."

"I thank you, too," he said, still whispering, before turning to rejoin his people.

Lindsay shook her head. She'd done what she'd set out to do. Time enough to catch the fall-out back in Phnom Penh. She glanced at the lowering clouds, then looked around for her driver, ready to start the return trip.

Spotting the motorcycle outside a soft drink stall about 200 meters away, she realized suddenly how horribly thirsty she was. About half way to the stall, the heavens opened with a roar of thunder that almost drowned the heavy hum of a vehicle bearing down on her at high speed. Before she could react, the Land Cruiser had braked to a stop in a spattering of dust and mud. The muzzle of a large handgun extended through the open window, pointed at her.

"Get in," Hoktha ordered, his nostrils flaring.

Lindsay looked behind her, but there was no one near by. *Should I make a run for it?* she thought. But the ache of her muscles from the morning's trip would barely let her move, much less run. Sighing, she opened the door. Would this never be over?

She climbed into the Land Cruiser's high front seat, and Hoktha was accelerating down the dusty road before she had closed the door. He swore violently for some long moments, a monotonous dirge that she barely heard through the torrential rain of the monsoon drumming on the roof of the Land Cruiser. He still had the gun trained on her with one hand as he steered erratically with the other. Having run out of suitable curses, he began to talk.

"You are an imbecile! You have no idea what you have done. You think you've destroyed me, but you are the one who will be destroyed. You will wish you were dead," he said with satisfaction. "I will personally see to you. And then my uncle will see to whatever's left of you when I'm done. There will be no Major Balfour to rescue you this time."

Adrenaline shot through Lindsay's blood, piercing through her dull exhaustion. She reached for the door handle, but Hoktha shoved the gun into her ribs. "Move and I will shoot you. I'd prefer to kill you slowly—but I have nothing to lose, either way."

She slowly moved her hand away from the door, trying to think. But the only thought that registered was that her demons had come home to roost. She sat, in shock, as Hoktha drove away from Banlung and up the road toward the park.

At the point where the forest began, Hoktha stopped the car. "My uncle insists that I bring you to him alive," he said, his voice a belligerent whine. "But first I will teach you some lessons of my own." He opened his door and dragged her toward him across the seat and onto the ground. She stood, waiting for what would come next. "Take off your shoes," he ordered. "I don't think you will try running away barefoot through this jungle."

Lindsay bent to unlace the sneakers, moving as slowly as she dared. There had to be something she could do. Thunder clapped again, now further off in the distance, and the afternoon downpour settled into a wet, heavy rhythm.

Finally, she placed her shoes carefully side by side, tucked the laces neatly inside, and slowly rose to face the inevitable. But Hoktha's angry glare had been replaced by a figure with a black sack over his head. Pinning its arms to its sides was Major André Balfour. Looking bland and businesslike, he took a length of rope in one hand and rapidly bound Hoktha's hands behind him, then stretched the rope down to tie his ankles. Within seconds, Hoktha lay on his stomach, trussed up and bawling like a rodeo calf.

Lindsay laughed out loud, hysterically. Adrenaline had done its work. As it left her dehydrated body, she passed out.

She woke to the sensation of a cool cloth over her eyes and forehead. She reached up to lift a corner, and found herself looking into the brilliantly blue black-fringed depths she'd first seen at the palace reception. It seemed so long ago. Her first attempt to speak came out in a croak. André held a water bottle to her lips and gently tilted it so the liquid trickled down her throat.

"How? Why?"

"What, where, when, and who! That is a long story. You, on the other hand, are a brave little fool. And what is this strange attraction you have formed with Hoktha, anyway?"

She felt the tears seeping down her cheeks. "What a mess I've made of things."

"Oh, not really. It could have been worse."

She lifted an eyebrow skeptically. "This I've got to hear."

"They could have had the park. They could have kept on stealing the children. Hoktha—" this was accompanied by a well-timed kick, followed by a burst of Khmer curses "—could have become Cambodia's environmental poster child. Honestly, I could not imagine doing this myself. You were perfect."

"Yes. A perfect fool. And you got everything you wanted, didn't you? No park now, thanks to Lindsay March, ex-UNOIC Public Information Officer."

"Not quite everything I wanted," he said softly. He leaned down and kissed her firmly on the lips. Then he sat up and looked down at her gravely. "Since I first saw you at the king's reception, I've been trying to deny my feelings in every way I could. I don't like Americans, and I can't stand UNOIC bureaucrats. And then you go off with the Colombian, which really made me wonder what the hell I was thinking. You have been absolutely infuriating."

He was about to go on when a musical tinkle interrupted. He held up one finger, then pulled the tiniest phone she had ever seen out of his back pocket. "*Oui.* Oh, Vanna. What? Are you all right? And Bopha? Are any of them left? Who? I see... Yes, soon."

He looked dumbfounded. "I should never have left her to those animals," he began. Lindsay started up with alarm, but the slightest movement felt like shards of glass behind her eyes. She relaxed, collapsing back to the ground. "What about Bopha?" she demanded faintly. "Tell me."

"Bopha and Vanna, another girl I know, went to find Madame Nhu, shipped the girls off to my house, then waited for Som Sak—he's the one behind all of this—to show up."

"What does 'a girl I know' mean, exactly?" Through her pain was an urgent need to confirm that André was not just one more guy who considered that relationships with Asian women didn't count.

"Vanna is a little sister, like Bopha," André said soberly. "When Som Sak and the other generals showed up, the girls were waiting

225

behind the door and hit them over the heads with the statues from Madame Nhu's ancestor shrine. Although—here is the part I don't understand—a Lithuanian behemoth and an Australian hippie were with them. But it was Bopha's idea to take the generals' clothes, their guns, their mobile phones, everything."

"Oh dear."

"Yes. You haven't seen those fellows. I'm surprised the girls survived the sight of such horror." André reached over and jerked the rope that connected Hoktha's wrists and ankles behind his back, dragging his face in the dirt. "Did you hear that, Hoktha?" he said. "I would hate to be you when your uncle finds out this was all your fault."

Lindsay giggled as André continued. "Anyway, when the generals came to, I'm afraid they were quite desperate. The only clothes they could find were some nylon lingerie items hanging out to dry in the yard of the brothel next door. Once they were dressed, they went out and tried to steal a couple of motor scooters to make their escape." André paused, stroking his moustache before saying, "Do you know what Phnom Penhois do when they catch motorcycle thieves? Over 30 of them were beaten to death by mobs, just in the past year. It is a miracle those pigs of generals didn't suffer the same fate, especially since they were dressed in sleazy neon orange nylon and pink lace! Solange fortunately showed up with Interpol back-up just in time to save them from the fury of the crowd."

"Is that what you do?" Lindsay asked.

"What, you thought I was a crook? Sorry, I'm one of the good guys—and thanks to us, those bad guys won't have the opportunity to be bad again for a long, long time."

Lindsay didn't answer, helping herself to more water.

He sighed. "So. The only possible explanation for this whole fiasco is that I'm in love with you. Why else would I be such an idiot?"

"Don't I have anything to say about it?" she asked. She realized that he had cradled her head in his arms, and that it felt extremely comfortable. She almost didn't want to argue with him. Almost, but not quite.

"I have absolutely no doubt whatsoever that you will momentarily jump up and tell me to go to hell," André said expectantly.

"Ha. Fooled you," she chuckled, and closed her eyes, promptly falling asleep.

CHAPTER TWENTY-FOUR

FRIDAY, JUNE 11

L indsay stared at her computer screen, struggling to word her report on the success of the Cambodian Red Cross Bazaar in a way that wouldn't put everyone to sleep. *No one will read it anyhow,* she told herself, *but still...* She tapped her front teeth impatiently with one fingernail, trying to keep her attention on the task at hand.

Glancing at the door, she watched it swing silently open, followed by the bristles of André's moustache. He was carrying a black cardboard box.

"No, not again," she moaned. "Please tell me it's not another jungle cat!"

Bopha followed André into the room, her smile sunny as always when André was nearby. "It's not a jungle cat, Lindsay." she said obediently.

André centered the box on the table in front of Lindsay's rattan chairs and eased the lid open. Before he could reach inside, a tiny, solid black face peeped out, followed by a madly wriggling rear end and a stub of a tail. *"Voila, cheri,"* André said. "No more cats for you. It's clear you will not protect yourself, so I have brought you *un petit chien* to do the job!"

Lindsay held the puppy in the air, letting it nuzzle her face. "But André," she said innocently, "you did such a great job of rescuing me that I was hoping to hire you on as my personal bodyguard."

"You must be reading my mind," André said. "I am here to bring you the puppy, but I am also here officially. Have you heard the news?"

Lindsay looked at him suspiciously. When he didn't speak, she shook her head in resignation. "All right, I give. What's the news?"

"I'm surprised at you, Lindsay," André said, still teasing. "I thought you kept your finger on the pulse of Phnom Penh. Well anyway, here it is. Because of our victory in Ratanakiri, the King has invited us to organize an exploratory trip to newly discovered Angkorian ruins in Preah Vihear province. He would like to proclaim the entire province a national monument, and he would like me to coordinate the process to be sure there is no human trafficking or other criminal activity involved. I have invited your friends Sam and Olga from the orphanage to assist us. Of course, the King would also like to have the support of UNOIC. Are you free for a reconnaissance trip tomorrow?"

ABOUT THE AUTHORS

The adventure of writing *Taming the Savage Monsoon* began in Phnom Penh, Cambodia in 1995, where the four authors were all working for different UN organizations. We began meeting over beer and pizza once a week—and found ourselves joined by Lindsay, Andre, Max, and all the evil generals! Over the years since then, we scattered to work in different countries, but we continued to develop the novel by email until August of 2003, when our friend, colleague, and co-author Martha Teas was killed in the bombing of the UN Headquarters in Baghdad. This story is our memorial to Martha, and all royalties from *Taming the Savage Monsoon* will be donated to the Martha Teas Memorial Fund, which supports child amputees in Banteay Meanchey Province, Cambodia. Please contact us at *kkhopper@adelphia.net* if you would like more information about the Martha Teas Memorial Fund or the Child Amputee Project.

Printed in the United States
35179LVS00004B/154-177

9 781591 137863